The Game

NIKKI JEWELL

This one is for all my hockey smut loving reader friends.
I like my men with big sticks too.

CW & TW

Content Warning

Thanks for choosing The Game. Here's a few things you should know going in. There may be some spoilers, so feel free to skip if you've got no triggers.

This is a steamy romance novel and contains explicit open door sexual situations, as well as alcohol consumption. The hockey boys are a little crude and use a fair bit of adult language, so if this offends you, this isn't the book for you. This is intended for a mature over eighteen audience.

Some events or situations may be triggering for some including talk of past cheating and a controlling ex boyfriend. There are some scenes which contain aggression, verbal abuse, and threats by this ex. Although there is nothing too graphic on page, I would read with caution if this is a trigger of yours.

I care about my readers well being and mental health.

1. COFFEE GIRL – THE TRAGICALLY HIP
2. GIRL – JUKEBOX THE GHOST
3. CHAMPION – BARNS COURTNEY
4. ALONE SOMETIMES – THE MOWGLI'S
5. ALASKA – LITTLE HURT
6. MIRROR – SIGRID
7. I'M NOT MAD – HALSEY
8. 2/14 – THE BAND CAMINO
9. GOOD AS IT GETS – LITTLE HURT
10. BURNT SUGAR – FELICITY
11. JEALOUS – INGRID MICHAELSON
12. LOST IN THE JUNGLE – KID POLITICS
13. DOESN'T REMIND ME – AUDIOSLAVE
14. CLOSING TIME – SEMISONIC
15. FIRE AND THE FLOOD – VANCE JOY
16. LIKE LIKE – VICTORIA IX
17. DAYDREAM – LILY MEOLA
18. ELECTRIC LOVE – BORNS
19. BRICK BY BRICK – AMERICAN AUTHORS
20. TEMPORARY – DREAM WIFE
21. UNTIL I FOUND YOU (WITH EM BEIHOLD) – STEPHEN SANCHEZ, EM BEIHOLD
22. SAD (CLAP YOUR HANDS) – YOUNG RISING SONS
23. DON'T WORRY, YOU WILL - LOVELYTHEBAND

Chapter One

Cinnamon Apple Fail

Jazz

The insistent trill of the store phone sends my already pounding heart into overdrive, but the pasted-on smile is still plastered to my face. I can't even imagine what I look like to the blonde woman staring at the menu behind my head. My eyes flick from her to the phone on repeat until I finally give in and reach for the damn thing. No one else is going to answer it. A sick flutter twists my stomach when I see the name on the call display. Sam.

Please let him be running a few minutes late. I've already fielded one sick call that was impossible to fill the first week of school. Everyone is reconnecting with their friends and spending too many late nights drinking and partying. Work is not a top priority if you've got a lot of parental help in the money department.

"Hello."

The customer gives me a dirty look as I answer the store phone. Even though she's the one who just spent five minutes staring at the menu while the line built up behind her. My eyes are wide, heart racing at the sight.

"Hey, Jazz. I've come down with some flu thing and I can't come in for my shift this afternoon."

"Ok, Sam. Let me know if you'll be able to make it in tomorrow."

"I will."

The edges of the phone dig into my palm as I give it a squeeze after punching the button to end the call.

I shut my eyes, dragging a deep breath into my lungs before I can look back up at the customer in front of me. I'm doing my very best to ignore the fact that the line is now spilling out the glass door into the university center.

The girl doesn't look so pretty now with her face scrunched up in a sour pout, disdain clear in her expression.

"That was rude. Taking a call when there's a customer in front of you."

"I'm sorry. It was a work-related call."

She scoffs. "I'd like a Cinnamon Apple Latte made with oat milk, and no cinnamon powder on top. Oh, and only one shot of expresso and double syrup. And extra whipped topping."

My fingers dance across the computer on autopilot, typing in her order, as I inwardly cringe at her mispronunciation of the word espresso. "Would you like anything else to go with that? A cinnamon scone perhaps?"

The look of disgust she gives me twists her bright coral lips. "I don't eat dessert."

It's so hard to squeeze my lips together and keep the biting retort back, but I do. It's one of my specialties after all. Eight pumps of syrup, sweetened oat milk, and whipped cream. How dare I assume she might want a treat to go with it?

"Of course. And your name?" I've got the pink marker poised over the side of the cup to catch her name when she taps her card and walks away without a reply.

So, I guess I get to pick her name? Spicy Bitch, Slow-poke, and Cinnamon Apple Fail all come to mind, but I settle for a smiley face. Kill them with kindness, right?

The rest of the day goes by in a blur. That's one benefit of busy shifts. The minutes disappear faster than a bag of buttered popcorn at the movies. Sure my heart is pounding, my legs are aching, and my messy bun has escalated from minor incident to catastrophic disaster levels of chaos. But I'm still standing and still smiling as I pump out drinks. My entire body lightened when I got to hand the keys over to Joe, the evening supervisor, but I stayed on to help cover some of Sam's shift. Am I a chronic people pleaser who struggles to say no? Yes. But more important, I have rent to pay and new textbooks to buy. My accounting professor this year just had to pick a brand-new edition that costs the equivalent of a semester's worth of groceries, but who's counting? Oh right, him. Accounting professor and all.

My eyes keep straying to the clock on the wall opposite the cold drink station, where I'm blending and shaking until my right arm is wobbly. Five minutes left and I'm out of here. Thank goodness. It's been a brutal day. Most of the time, I love being here. I love the energy of the students. The buzz of conversation and getting to know my customers. But some days, like today, take their toll.

As the whir of the blender stops, an angry voice catches my attention. "You screwed up my drink."

I snap the lid closed on the mocha shake, and spin around to spot a guy leaning over the counter, getting up in Val's face as she works the espresso machine. There's an ugly sneer twisting his lips, and her eyes are wide as she leans away from him.

"I'm sorry about that." She smiles, picking up the drink, and glancing at the writing on the side of the cup. "What exactly was wrong?"

"I don't fucking know. Isn't that your job? It tastes like shit."

Her bright smile is wobbling as he leans farther over the counter. "I just want to make it right for you. It says here it's a mocha with three shots of espresso. Is that right?"

He mutters something incoherent before speaking up. "Yes, but it tastes like water. You must have forgotten to put the coffee in it or something. Can't you do anything right?"

I place the shake down on the smooth surface of the pickup counter, calling out the drink and using my body to shield Val. Technically, I'm not the supervisor on duty anymore, but I can spot the telltale glisten of tears at the corner of Val's eyes, and I don't let anyone talk to my employees like that. Unacceptable.

"Val, can you go make those cold drinks? I'll handle this." Her blonde ponytail bobs as she nods at me, turning away from the hostile customer.

"How about I remake this for you?" My lips are curved up in a customer service smile the man doesn't deserve as I steam the milk and re pull the shots.

The brown liquid flowing out in a smooth stream settles my mind a little, and I watch it like a hawk to make sure the shots are pulling correctly. Dark heart at the bottom, rich brown middle, and perfect light beige crema to top it off, sliding out rich and thick like honey. Looks good to me. I swirl the chocolate sauce into the espresso and top it with milk and perfectly swirled fluffy whipped cream. The real stuff, not that oily fake crap that comes in a can.

"There you go."

His dark eyes don't leave my face as he takes a sip before slamming it back down. "Still wrong. It's supposed to have peppermint in it. What are you? Some kind of moron?"

"I'm sorry. It doesn't say anything about peppermint on there, but I can fix that right up for you." I'm not sure where the miscommunication came in, but Joe is working the register, so I have my doubts that he was the one that messed it up. Not to mention the guy said nothing about peppermint when Val read his order back to him.

My hands are getting a little shaky as I remake his drink a second time, making sure to add the peppermint.

He snatches the drink out of my hand before I can place it on the counter,

swearing as it spills over, burning his thick fingers.

"What the fuck. You stupid bitch. No one here can do anything right." He takes another sip before tossing the cup at me. I duck out of the way to avoid the hot liquid, but tears start to blur my vision and his face morphs into Darryl's. He's got the same look of disdain on his face as my ex during my brief encounter with him my first week back at school. And it makes me feel small and incompetent, just like Darryl used to.

"You should be fired. Your entire job is to make drinks and you can't even do that right." Other customers are staring as his voice gets louder. I'm again reminded of Darryl shouting at me in the middle of the quad while students gathered around to watch our blow out.

I take a shaky step back as my vision goes fuzzy around the edges. Angry responses that I know I'm not going to say are tumbling through my head too fast to grasp hold of.

"I think you should leave." A deep voice cuts through the fog that's blanketed my mind. It's smooth and calm, flowing over my skin like a soothing river.

"Who the fuck do you think you are? This isn't your business."

The angry customer turns his attention to the dark-haired guy that dared to confront his assholery. A new tension is gripping me now, fear for the guy who stepped in to defend me. Then I take a good look at him. Maybe the guy looked bigger, looming over me with his threats, but now that he's standing next to my white knight, he looks almost small. My rescuer is four or five inches taller with muscles straining his black t-shirt that speak of a level of dedication to the gym that I will never have.

"Bitch messed up my drink." The futile rage churns my stomach to the point I'm now worried I'm going to hurl on both of them.

There's a flash of fury behind his dark eyes. "How dare you speak to her like that. Get out of here before I call the campus police to drag your worthless ass out."

"Hiding behind the campus mall cops? Too afraid to fight me?"

Dark-haired guy snorts, his lips twisted in disdain. "I have absolutely zero desire to fight you. If I fought you, you wouldn't be walking for the next week. So, if you know what's good for you, get the fuck out of here. Clock's ticking. Wait too long and I might decide it's worth the week off the ice if they give me a temporary suspension."

The Good Samaritan backs up his words by stepping forward until his thick chest is inches away from his opponent's. Their proximity only emphasizes the glaring differences in their heights and builds. The asshole's bulk is mostly of the soft beer-drinking variety.

Asshole's skin pales the slightest bit and realization dawns in his eyes. He doesn't have the physical advantage, and he knows it. Not like when he was towering over Val and me.

"Fine," he says, turning to walk away.

"And don't come back here again. If you do, I'm not so sure I'll be able to resist messing up that ugly face even more than it already is."

I can't help following the brown leather back of his jacket as he makes his way through the cafe and out the front door, so when I turn back to thank the guy that rescued me, he's gone. I scan the cafe to see if he sat back down at a table. Nope.

There's a figure heading toward the door that might be him. Black track jacket with three white stripes up the sleeves, dark hair trimmed into a fade at the back and sides and longer on top. I think that's him. I was so hopped up on adrenaline I didn't really process the details.

My head spins as the overwhelming scent of sweet chocolate and peppermint surrounds me when I reach down to grab the cup he tossed at me. I throw out a hand to brace myself on the counter as I stand back up. That was a terrible idea. I should have left it there in the pool of dark brown liquid and sad, melted whipped cream.

Right, adrenaline. The whereabouts of mystery guy suddenly doesn't seem so important as the adrenaline seeps away. My heart is still pounding, and my hands are still shaky, but now my head is throbbing, and my mouth is dry as Las Vegas in July.

Val slides in next to me, closing her fingers around the paper cup I've got gripped so tight in my hand that it's no longer remotely cup shaped.

"I got this, Jazz." She passes me a glass of cold water. "Go sit down in the back for a minute before you leave for the day." At least some of my coworkers are looking out for me.

"Thanks, Val."

I take her advice, pushing through the gray swinging door and collapsing into the old office chair that sits behind the battered wooden desk. The chair creaks under my weight, and icy water hits my thigh, shaky hands causing it to tip over the rim of the glass.

Placing it on the desk, I drop my head onto my arms, taking some deep breaths and trying to remember the meditation exercises I learned in that yoga class I've been taking with Jordan. It's fairy yoga. The instructor wears pointed ears and a crown, and there's an enchanted mural that stretches around the walls.

That helps. I close my eyes, taking deep breaths, and trying to clear my mind until the trembling eases. Usually, I don't let asshole customers get to me this hard. I can't if this is going to be my own business one day. Well, not All Capps, but a coffee shop. One day maybe I'll even get to open my dream coffee shop and bookstore combo with my bestie. I wish I could go see her, but she graduated last year, and with her man in the NHL, she's dividing her time between here and Chicago until she can officially move there.

A long sigh hisses out through my lips. I have no idea how I'll survive my senior year without her in the area full time. I've got a few other friends, but no one close enough to tell all my deepest, darkest secrets to. Especially after I let Darryl consume my life and push them away. It's going to be a long year.

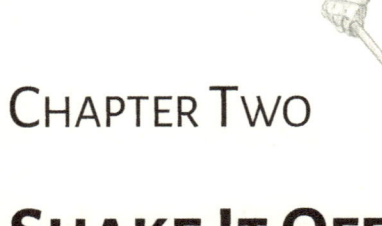

Chapter Two

Shake It Off

Cole

As Mabel's engine rumbles up the driveway of the hockey house, I'm still a little on edge. My knuckles are white against the faded black of the steering wheel, and I'm not sure if I should have driven home in this state. I couldn't stay there though. If I hadn't forced myself to leave the cafe, I might have stalked that asshole back to his car and embedded his teeth into the back of his skull. Few things piss me off more than people treating other humans like shit. Especially women, service workers or anyone their limited brains consider inferior. Guy was an absolute ape. I shake my head. If this is the state of humanity, I don't even wanna.

The buzzing of my phone pulls my attention. I frown at the unknown number, tapping it to delete what I'm sure is a spam text. A tingly feeling crawls up the back of my neck as I scan the message. You have got to be fucking kidding me.

> **Hi, Cole. It's Char. I got a new number and I really need to talk to you.**

My ringtone breaks the silence before I've finished reading the brief message. What the fuck? I blocked her old number, and she hasn't tried to contact me in several months. My guts are roiling again at the unwelcome contact from my ex. I thought I was long rid of her. I silence the call and block the number, tossing my phone into my bag with more force than necessary.

When I've gathered myself enough to keep it together, I think, I slide out my car door, boots slamming into the pavement, and stomp up the path. The red front door appears to have gotten an unnecessary paint refresh while we were off over the summer. Place still looks the same. Porch swing swaying slightly in the breeze as if someone just stood up and abandoned it. Neat green hedges lining the front of the house. Good thing those are low maintenance because I have never seen a soul here touch them. Beau's parents must pay to get them trimmed.

My key clicks in the lock and I swing the door open quietly, hoping to avoid detection. Last year, I became an expert at slipping in and out of this house unnoticed until Jackson decided to insert himself into my life. I was kinda hoping I'd be able to ease back into my previous state of blending in with the furniture now that he's graduated.

No such luck. Beau and Dev are horsing around in the living room with JJ and Grant watching from the sidelines. Those goofballs moved in to replace Seb and Jacks after they graduated last year. Grant is ok, if a bit pushy sometimes, but JJ our goalie is... let's just say he's a goalie. He's loud, and opinionated and thinks he's god's gift to hockey. Suddenly I kind of miss the days of Seb brooding over his girl and trying to start shit with me on the ice over it. At least he was a little quieter around the house.

"Coco!" JJ calls out. "What's happening, dude?"

"Nothing." The new nickname he christened me with is already driving me up the wall. Nicknames are the norm when you play on a hockey team, but no one bothered to give me one last year. Probably due to the way I avoided all unnecessary social interactions. But Jenson just couldn't seem to help himself from coming up with one the day he moved in. And he outdid himself. It sounds like he's calling for his pet poodle with a fancy pants haircut any time he shouts it out.

I keep walking, hoping my determined strides toward the stairs will discourage him from questioning me. Nope. He bounces over.

"Come on. We're going out tonight. Join us."

My first thought is to bite out a no, but they are my team members, and I might not want to become besties with them, but I also shouldn't piss them off. They're the ones who might be able to make me look good on the ice. I've got the talent, but if no one will pass the puck to me, I'm sunk.

"Maybe."

"Maybe! I got a maybe!" His high-pitched excitement makes me wince as I look over to find the others staring at me with gaping mouths.

"It was a maybe, not a lifelong commitment," I mutter, as I make it to the stairs, taking them two at a time to escape to the relative peace of my room.

Sanctuary. As soon as the door clicks shut and I flip the lock, a weight lifts off my shoulders. Trying to keep the guys at arm's length while they try to draw me in to their group has become an uncomfortable burden. Moving into this house last year after the nightmarish mess I escaped from at my old school might have been a mistake from that point of view. But it is a fucking nice place. The cool blue walls of my room are a soothing escape, and the only thing missing is my own bathroom. Dev claimed Seb's old room before he'd even moved all his stuff out to head off for his new life in LA, so I'm still stuck sharing with the other two.

The stacks of thick books on my utilitarian black desk are calling my name. I've got a heavy workload looming over my head for senior year. Heavier than I should have given the hectic hockey schedule, and my need to make an outstanding impression. If I'm going to catch any team's eye this year, I've got to step up my game. If my world hadn't blown up in my sophomore year, things would be different, but there's no use dwelling on the past. On things you can't change.

After dumping my backpack on top of my dark blue comforter, I rifle through it to find the reading assignments for my Evil in The Contemporary World course.

The slightly used but still overpriced textbook is smooth and comforting under my hands when I pick it up and flip to the correct page.

I'm lost in Kant's words when the chirp of my phone startles me out of the trance I fall into while deep in my studies.

A warm feeling settles in my chest at my youngest sister's name on the screen.

"Hey, Liss."

"Big brother! How are you? You haven't called yet."

"I've got nothing new to share."

"Come on. It's the first week of your senior year. There's got to be something to share. Girls? Parties? I want to live vicariously through you until I get to go away next year."

"I don't have time for parties. There was a girl at the coffee shop today. She was making drinks and this asshole, I mean jerk, was treating her like shit, umm dirt, so I stepped in."

Her laugh has approached full on cackle zone by the time I reach the end of the story.

"Cole, I'm in my senior year of high school. You don't need to censor the swearing around me. Trust me. I know assholes, and I'm glad you stood up for this girl. Did you get her number?"

I shake my head. Sometimes it's hard to remember my sisters are growing up. Liss is in her senior year of high school. Bella's already in her second year of college. Sometimes I wish I could have convinced her to come to Lakeview with me, but it was New York or bust for my fashion forward middle sister.

"No, I didn't get the number of the traumatized girl at the coffee shop." Or any girl, for that matter. Ever since…yeah, dating is not on the table.

"Well, you need to go out and have some fun. Hang out with your team. Don't waste your entire senior year sulking in your room like you did last year. You need this. You'll work better with your teammates if you're, I dunno, nice to them."

"Aren't you suddenly all wise and knowing with your high school senior status? What would you know about being on a hockey team?"

"Nothing, but I know lots about being on a soccer team. The worst team I was on had a couple of the best players on it, but since they refused to work together, we didn't even make the playoffs. Remember Melinda Jameson? She was a nightmare."

My body relaxes once the heat is off me, and I listen to her babble on about her new team and some new girl in her class she has a crush on. But her words settle into my bones while we're chatting. Somehow, I find myself taking her advice and joining my roommates at Wright's Wingers for dinner.

I've only been to Wright's a few times since I started at Lakeview. It's the closest sports bar to campus with a heavy focus on hockey. The jerseys hung on the wall are the first things that catch my eye as we jostle our way through the crowded tables and people wandering around. There's an unspoken rule that the two huge booths at the back are reserved for the hockey team, so we settle into the furthest one.

"Glad you came out, Schaeffer. I hope we see more of you out of that room of yours this year." Beau's smile is all charm and polish. He's the only one wearing a crisp black button-up shirt to the casual bar, but he doesn't look out of place. He looks effortless, as if he could fit in anywhere he showed up.

I nod. "Maybe I will."

"So, Grant. Do you think you have any shot at living up to Woodsy's legacy?" Dev cuts straight to the point. Aspen Ellory was the star center, captain and backbone of the team. He kept everyone on track, and he had more talent and dedication than almost any other guy. Except me. I'm determined to live up to his work ethic without taking on the leadership role he excelled at. That's for Beau.

Grant shoots the question back at him with an arched eyebrow. "I don't know. Are you?"

Beau laughs, but there's a slight tightening of the skin around his eyes as if he's not as at ease with his new captain role as he's pretending to be. "I think I can handle it."

I haven't contributed too much to the conversation by the time the waitress drops off a couple heaping platters of wings and fries, but I'm here. That's gotta earn me some points, right?

I grab a wet wipe to clean off the mess of sticky wing sauce that's coating my fingers and face before hitting the restroom. We were making fun of Beau for using a knife and fork, but maybe he's got the right idea.

"Gotta take a leak."

"Good for you. Don't fall in the toilet," Jenson chirps.

I'm already up and walking away with a shake of my head.

As I'm leaving the men's room, a hint of blonde hair catches my eye, and a queasy feeling twists my guts up in knots. What is wrong with me? There isn't a chance in hell that's her. Except. She's caught sight of me and, with a single-minded intensity, she's heading in a straight line toward me. My fingers are numb, knees shaky and threatening to give out on me when she stops inches away from my chest. She has no right to be wearing that huge fake smile in front of me.

"What the fuck are you doing here, Charlene?" All traces of the quiet, polite version of my self fled the area at the sight of the crime scene that she represents.

Her shiny pink lips push out into a fake-ass pout. "Surprise. I'm here for you."

"Go back to Tampa. Go back to fuckface." He used to be one of my closest friends. Now the thought of saying his name rips at the tattered shreds of my heart. The fragile glue and threads that were finally knitting me back together tear open at the sight of her here. In my new home. The one she drove me to. "You don't belong here."

"But I do, baby. I know I screwed everything up, and I'm so sorry. I was all messed up, and it was a huge mistake. But you and me. We're end game. We were always end game. It was a stupid mistake, but you've always been the one for me. Always." The quiver of her lip and the shine in her eyes are as much of a lie as her words. Once upon a time, I thought they were true. I thought she was my forever, but she threw that all out the window like it was trash.

The laugh that rips from my mouth is bitter. "You and me." I point to her and back to myself. "We are nothing. We will never be anything, and I don't want to see your face ever again. Go back to Tampa."

Having said everything I've got to say about the matter, I spin around, eager to get out of the heat and claustrophobia of the bar. Why did I think this was a good idea? Although this is a scenario I never would have predicted in a million years.

Her fingers close around my biceps, and they feel like claws digging in to my flesh.

"I'm not going back to Tampa, Cole. I transferred to Lakeview."

What.

The.

Fuck.

My head is spinning, and every single sound in the bar is amplified, echoing off my skull in a ricochet of clinking glasses, overly loud laughter, and wailing guitars. She's lying. She has to be. There is no way.

"Maybe you're not ready to forgive me yet, but I'm not going anywhere. I'll be at every game, every party. I'll be there cheering you on until you're ready."

Terror gnaws at me. Her words ring true. She will. Her persistence was one of the things I used to love about her, but now. There's no way she'll let go of this if she wants to get me back. Not unless. Unless. I rack my brain, searching for a solution. Nothing, nothing. Maybe?

"I've moved on. Stay away from me."

I stalk off without waiting to see her reaction. How am I ever going to make it through this year with her haunting me from the shadows? It's like she's one of those ghosts who attach themselves to a person rather than a place.

The bar was hot and packed full of bodies when I got here, but now I can barely breathe. The mass of people is closing in around me. All the voices and laughter are chafing my raw nerves, and I need to escape immediately. I can't even take the time to stop and talk to the team, weaving through the crowd to get out the front door.

"Hey!"

I leave the indignant voice behind after slamming into someone in my rush, then lean on the squeaky metal bar to shove open the heavy front door. Fresh air washes over me and I can breathe a little easier.

I'm still leaning on the brick wall, gulping in the crisp air, when a heavy hand lands on my shoulder. My eyes fly open to find Beau staring at me. His eyebrows are pinched together, and he's standing a little too close for comfort. The scratchy brick at my back prevents me from escaping his scrutiny.

"You okay, man?"

"I'm fine."

He clears his throat, glancing above my head and back down to meet my gaze as if he can catch me in a lie. "Are you sure?"

"Yeah. Just ran into someone I wasn't expecting. I'm going home. I'll be fine."

"Let me give you a ride. You look a little shook."

"Nah. I'm fine. I got this. You go back to the team. It was fun." At least until my world got tossed upside down.

His nod is tight, and I can tell he still doesn't believe me, but he's going to let it go. Thank fuck. I can't get into this right now. I need to get home and hide out in my room. Figure out what the fuck I'm going to do about this completely unexpected complication.

"Okay. Text me when you get home, though."

"Will do."

I'd agree to anything to get him off my back so I can get the hell out of here. After he leaves, I head straight for Mabel, sinking into the worn velour seat, but I don't start the ignition. I just sit in the car until the chilly air leaves my fingers stiff on the steering wheel, and my mind is calm enough to make the drive home.

CHAPTER THREE

EXES AND COLES

JAZZ

I'm weaving through the scattered round tables with a cloth, wiping the rings of coffee and a handful of crumbs away on my last pass of the night, when Kate walks up to me.

"We good?" she asks, blue eyes darting between mine and the front door on repeat. Her boyfriend's probably waiting for us to lock up, so he can take her home.

"We're good. I'll just grab my bag and we can get out of here." I race to the back, tossing the dirty cloth into the laundry bin on my way, but I'm moving too fast and catch my foot on the pair of shoes someone left under the coat rack. My hand flies out, palm slamming into the wall to catch myself before I hit the floor. After grabbing my stuff, I slow myself down. Don't want to take an embarrassing tumble. Not that Kate would care, or probably even notice she's so anxious to get out of here.

When I make my way out front a little more cautiously, the back of Kate's dark bob is silhouetted against the light of the door. She's bouncing on her toes, peering out the window, so I pick up the pace.

I can't help one last look around as I'm heading for her. I'm going to miss this place next year. Hopefully, I'll have my own place. I've been saving up every cent I can, which isn't much. I've got a couple of scholarships that cover tuition, but there's still rent, and food, and all those other pesky bills that come before saving for my dream café. But there are always small business loans and grants. If I have to, I can get a job at another café while I save up to start my own place, but working for someone else is not it for me. I want the freedom and independence of being my own boss. After blending into the background as the youngest girl of six in my family, all I really want is something that is truly mine.

Kate's already in her boyfriend's arms as I turn my key, sliding the heavy deadbolt into place. "Have a good night," I call to her back, but her lips are far too busy to answer, so I head off toward the bus stop.

It's not too far from the university center on the well-lit campus, but I've still got my keys clutched in my palm. My eyes dart back and forth, searching the path for potential threats. Wouldn't it be nice to be able to walk across your own campus at 9:30 at night without fear? It's the only time I kind of wish I was a guy. Other than that. No way.

They can keep their precious dangly bits and repressed emotions. I'll pass.

A small huddle of giggling girls totters by on heels that are too high and narrow for the cobbled walkway. Another couple is off the path, sheltered by a cluster of bushes, taking advantage of the small amount of privacy afforded by the shadows. The closer I get to my bus stop, the fewer people I pass.

I pull my light jacket tighter, listening to my footsteps click on the path.

"Hey, Jazmin. Wait up."

I freeze mid step, and my skin ripples as icy fingers trail down my spine. I swivel my head around slowly, hoping that I'm mistaken. But I know I'm not. That deep voice is both very familiar and very unwelcome. The possessive way he uses my full name grates on me. He always refused to use my preferred nickname.

"Darryl, I have to catch my bus. I don't have time to chat right now. Text me tomorrow." My brain is as frozen as my feet, and I can't decide whether I should flee or face him.

"You haven't answered my texts, so I thought I'd catch you in person."

"Were you following me?" There's a tingle of warning at the back of my neck.

"I saw you at work, but you looked really busy, so I figured I'd just catch up to you after."

He was. He was waiting for me, like a cat stalking a mouse. I don't want to be the mouse.

A shaky sigh slips from my trembling lips as I turn around. We're doing this now, so I'd rather be facing him head on rather than give him my vulnerable back. Ok, then. "Darryl. We have nothing to talk about. We broke up at the end of last year and had zero contact all summer. Then you come strolling back in and act like we're still together. But we're not. It's over. We've already been over this." My voice comes out barely above a whisper. Everything I ate today is crashing around in my stomach at the memory of our confrontation a few days ago.

"Jazmin, I love you. Love like that doesn't just stop. I figured maybe we both just needed some space and then you'd realize how much you missed me. How perfect we are for each other."

Yeah, perfectly controlling. Perfectly in charge of every part of my life. No, thank you. "That's not the way it works. I'm not interested in getting back together. I'm sorry, but it's over." The sorry slips out. Why do I have to be so polite? I need to be firm. Unapologetic. That's the only thing that might get through the dense wall of overconfidence that's wrapped around his brain.

He steps in closer until he's all up in my personal space, eyes narrowed. The desire to step back has my leg muscles tense, ready to flee, but I ignore it. Be firm. Don't show weakness.

"Jazmin, don't you understand? You belong with me. You're mine." His tone is rough and demanding. Insistent. Not the velvety smooth tones he used on me when we were first dating. That was a façade.

I cross my arms over my middle, trying to hide my trembling hands. "No, Darryl. You need to leave. I don't want to talk, and I don't want to get back together."

His eyes have gone from pleading to wild. He's agitated, raking a hand through the sandy brown hair that's grown out past his ears as if he hasn't gotten a haircut all summer.

Then he reaches out, hands closing over my biceps too tight, bruising, and I struggle to get away. He jerks me in closer to him. "Please, Jazmin, just listen to me. I need you. I can't live without you. You can't do this to me." His lip twists in the telltale snarl, letting me know he's about to get nasty.

"Let go of me." I push on his chest, but I've got no traction, and he's stronger than me, controlling my upper arms.

"Not until you listen to me. Come on. You know your shitty life was better with me in it. Working at that coffee shop. I can give you so much more. I'll look after you. Don't be such a bitch."

There's a red haze behind my eyes, and a fiery ball of rage churning my guts. I've been called a bitch one too many times today.

I'm about to open my mouth to lash out when someone steps in behind Darryl, looming over his shoulder. My heart is pounding so hard I can hear it echoing in my ears at the new potential threat. But then I catch sight of the neon orange safety vest the guy is wearing.

There's a girl behind him in a matching outfit. My jaw unclenches the slightest bit. It's the Campus Walk Safe program stepping in. The ones I should have called in the first place to walk me to the bus stop.

"You need to take your hands off the lady." The calming voicing seeps under my skin, reassuring.

"This is private business between me and my girlfriend. It's fine. Leave us alone."

The guy's dark eyes meet mine over Darryl's shoulders and I shake my head the tiniest bit.

"She doesn't want you touching her, so you need to back off."

"Fuck off. What are you going to do about it?" My asshole ex rolls his shoulders as if he's gearing up for a fight but doesn't loosen the painful grip that's pinching my arms.

"I will call the police if I have to, but I'm sure you don't want that. Let go of the lady and go on with your night."

The threat finally has Darryl turning around to check out his adversary. When he catches sight of the tall guy with a bulky build, he finally comes to his senses.

I gasp as pain shoots through my muscles with his last squeeze before he lets go, taking a step back and holding his hands up.

"Fine. But this isn't over, Jazmin." My fingers are shaky, rubbing up and down my arms to ease the throb while I pull in a shuddering breath. His eyes are bright and intense with promise.

As he steps away, the streetlamp illuminates my rescuer clearly enough to see him for the first time. The shadows cut his face in sharp lines, but the menace in his dark eyes has softened to kindness and concern. A flare of recognition flashes in my brain. It's him. The guy who told off my asshole customer last week. Well, that's two rescues. He really is my knight in shining armor. Or orange iridescent vest, I guess.

His partner steps up beside him, holding her hands up, palms open as she moves closer to me. She smiles. "Hi, I'm Jenna. This is Cole. We're with the Campus Walk Safe program." She holds up the badge hanging on a yellow lanyard around her neck, so I can see the ID and matching picture. She nods at the guy who holds up his badge for my inspection. "We'd be happy to walk you wherever you're headed. Did you need anything else?"

I shake my head, studying his name above the picture on his tag. Cole Schaeffer. Why does that sound familiar? "No. I'm good." At least I will be when I reach the safety of my house. "I'm headed for the bus stop."

Cole's scratching away in a small notebook with a pen while we chat, waiting for the number five bus to arrive. He looks up when he's finished. "Was that guy really your boyfriend?"

"Yes. No. He used to be. We broke up at the end of last school year."

"Did you want me to write a report about this?" His tone is gruff, and his pen stills, hovering over the pad.

"No. It's fine. He didn't really do anything."

But that's the problem, isn't it? He never really did anything. He made me feel small. He hurt my feelings. He separated me from my friends. But it's not like he ever hit me or anything. Just that one time, he shoved me. The reason I finally came to my senses and broke up with him last year. I rub at my arms where I'm sure he left bruises. Plus that. How did I let it get to that point?

And now what am I going to do? I'm sure he won't just leave things be, and I won't always have someone around to protect me.

I'll just be more careful not to go places alone. Especially at night. And I'm blocking his number immediately. Something I should have done months ago.

I'm idly twirling a lock of hair around my fingers. It's a little greasy from another day at work. That's a situation I need to fix as soon as I get home. That'll be nice. A long, hot shower. The image pops into my head of steamy water streaming over my body, and it soothes my anxious brain until I wonder what he would look like there with me. Um, what? No. Did I not just get an unwelcome visit from the reason dating is a bad life choice for me? Sure, he's good looking, but my red flag radar is clearly nonexistent. I need to figure that out before I jump into anything new. Maybe I'll be ready in a decade or two.

Twin bright lights cut through the darkness accompanied by the roaring swoosh of my bus pulling up. Thank goodness.

"Here. Take this."

Cole holds out a card to me and I reach for it, fingers brushing mine in a brief touch that grounds me, helps calm my nerves.

"It's the number for the Walk Safe program, plus a QR code to download the app. You can request an escort right from there."

"Thanks. I will. And thanks... for everything." My eyes are locked on his dark ones, but I'm not sure if he remembers the help he gave me the other day. They give nothing away.

"You're welcome. Ride safe," Jenna pipes in.

The bus doors open with a swish and I hurry to clamber up the steps, scanning my pass before sliding into a cracked plastic seat near the front. Nothing more glamorous than the city bus.

Chapter Four

Smash Or Pass

Cole

"Where were you last night, Coco?" Grant whizzes by, spinning around to skate backward.

My knuckles whiten as I squeeze the stick I'm holding high above my head. The stretch pulls at the tight muscles of my upper back and shoulders. If I could get away with killing Grant and burying his body in the ice pile out back, I would. Unfortunately, he's a solid scorer, so we can't exactly afford to lose him.

"None of your business."

"I'd say he was out partying, but that might hurt my feelings if he chose to party without us. Probably at the library reading one of those philosophy books that's thicker than my dick," Beau chimes in.

"Maybe thicker than yours, but not mine." Jenson can't help but chime in.

"You wish," Dev says with a snort, dropping to the ice to do some frog stretches.

The entire conversation is beyond ridiculous, so I scoop a puck off the sidelines and send it down the ice to practice shots on the empty net.

I let one fly at each corner of the net, retrieving it after each shot. The last one flies wildly off my stick, ricocheting off the bar with a metallic clang after something catches my eye. Golden hair hanging over the purple shoulders of a long-sleeved shirt with the distinctive gold Lightning logo on the front.

She waves at me as if there's any chance in hell I'm going to be happy to see her.

"You've got to be fucking kidding me," I mutter under my breath.

Everything inside me is screaming to just ignore her, but I can't do it. She's got me all shaken up already and practice hasn't even started.

The normally relaxing feeling of smooth ice under my skates does nothing to soothe my agitation as I speed over to the glass, yanking my helmet off my head. "What are you doing here, Charlene?"

Her smile doesn't dim a single watt under my glare. Seeing that smile used to brighten my mood after a crappy day at school or a losing game. Now it has my stomach pitching and bile burning the back of my throat.

"I came to watch you play." She keeps on smiling, waggling her fingers over my shoulder at the rest of the team.

"You're not welcome here. Please leave."

"I was told Lightning practices are open to students. I'm a student, so here I am, and look." She spins around, tossing her hair over her shoulder to reveal the back of her shirt. Fuck that.

"Take it off."

She turns back around, head tilted to the side, cunning eyes gleaming. "Sure. Wanna come back to my place?"

Unfuckingbelievable. "No thanks. But I don't want the rest of my practice fucked up by thinking of you with my name on your back. I want you to leave, and I never want to see you in this arena again. Ever."

That smile finally dims a bit, slipping into a pout. "Fine. I'll leave today, but I won't promise not to come back to the arena. That's crazy. I'm going to be here to watch your games. I've missed seeing you play so much, baby. You don't understand. You haven't given me a chance to explain what happened. I was messed up, Cole. I didn't mean for any of that to happen."

My eyes travel up to the high ceiling, and I have to drag in a deep breath to keep myself under control. The urge to punch the glass is trembling down my arm. She can't do this to me. She can't mess up my second chance. I've been doing fine here. Away from her and him. My old team that I used to love. No way. I can't be thinking about her at every game when I need to be proving myself.

"Get out." All the rage comes roaring out of my mouth, since I would never use my fists on her.

She jumps as the words echo across the ice, and every-thing goes silent. The swish of skates, and crack of sticks comes to an abrupt halt.

"Fine." I lift a single eyebrow at her when her mouth falls open, as if she thinks any words are going to get her out of this situation.

There's not even any satisfaction at the sight of her retreat since I have to see my name on her back when she turns around.

I lift a shaky hand to brush a lock of hair off my fore-head, sighing and turning around, trying to salvage this practice. Everyone is staring at me, eyes wide, mouths open. Great. I can see them all reassessing their opinion of me. Apparently, I'm now the guy the neighbors "Never would have believed was capable of that."

I throw up a hand to ward off the comments that are about to come flying at me. "Can we please just get this practice going?"

The way they all hurry back into action is alarming. They really think I'm a psychopath now. Great.

My skates are practically vibrating when we hit the ice, so I push myself past my usual speed, blasting by my team-mates. I'm a sweaty, shaking mess after we're finished with our warmup laps. Coach divides us into small groups to run some drills as I rip my helmet off, running a hand through the dripping strands of my hair.

Great, of course I'm paired with Grant and Hail. The freshman was clearly the star of his junior team, but he let it go to his head, and is unbearably cocky. Didn't even bother to show up for practice on time. At least he missed my blowout with Charlene, but Coach is going to hand him his ass after practice. Probably won't do anything to shrink that ego of his. Doesn't seem to matter how many times he gets taken down by one of the senior members of the team, he always bounces back with a heap of sass. My mind is in way too much turmoil to deal with the rookie's attitude right now.

We're doing a one touch passing drill facing off against Dev and two of the younger D-men. Assistant Coach Bauer drops the puck, blasting his whistle as soon as we're in place on the face-off dot. I push off, snagging the puck and driving forward to take a shot before defense descends on us. Our second line goalie isn't prepared for my immediate assault, and it slides in right under his stick.

The piercing whistle from Hail slices right through my eardrum.

"Fuck, dude! Too loud."

He just laughs at me, chasing the puck that's back on the ice. The play is fast and furious and gets rougher with each reset.

Hail seems to have made it his personal mission to get the most goals, even though this is supposed to be a teamwork exercise. Not that I was setting the right tone when I took off with the puck as soon as we started. Any semblance of calm and control that I got from skating myself into the ground during laps is decimated by his obnoxious comments every time he scores a goal.

"I bet you wish you handled your stick as well as I handle mine, Schaeffer." He skates backward, shaking his stick at me, and the little voice on my shoulder is telling me to snap it in half.

"Fuck off, rookie."

I turn away, focusing on the puck. Dev snatched it from Grant, and he's playing keep-away with the rest of his side, while we're distracted. At least they seem to have gotten the point of the exercise.

I skate a tight circle, coming up behind Dev, while he's focused on Grant and snatch it from between his legs.

I'm about to pass it to the rookie because he's in the clear, when he skates toward me.

"That's not quite what your sister said last night." He laughs, and I can see it in his narrowed eyes. Idiot is going to try to steal the puck from me even though we're on the same team. I catch sight of Charlene over his shoulder, and rage consumes me. I shoot it off wildly toward the goal and lean down shoulder first, slamming into him.

He was moving too fast and not expecting the hit, so we both end up flying. My head snaps back, slamming into the ice, and I land on hard on my arm, pain wrenching my wrist.

Bauer blows the whistle, and chaos erupts in our immediate vicinity. We're surrounded. The team medic is in my face. Bauer and Coach are yelling, and Beau is just standing there looking disappointed as I push myself up, wincing as I head off the ice.

Can't believe I let that jerk-off get to me. This is not the way I was supposed to start this year off.

After getting checked for a concussion, I slink off to the dressing room, hoping I'll be able to avoid a second scolding by our team captain. Coach laid into me hard enough for one day. No such luck. Beau is sprawled out on the bench when I push through the locker room door. When did he even slip off the ice? Crafty bastard.

"We need to chat."

"I don't want to." The words sound like those of a petulant child, but that's kind of what I feel like in this situation. Getting called into the office by the team captain. Especially after I've already been reamed out by our coaches.

"You're not getting out that way." He crosses his arms over his chest, having caught me glancing over my shoulder.

"It's nothing."

He snorts out a laugh. "That was not nothing. Listen Cole. This year. There's a lot riding on it. We've lost some of our best players, but that means this is our chance to prove ourselves. Or more specifically, you. I've done plenty to prove myself." He looks smug and concerned at the same time. I don't even know how he can manage both of those emotions at the same time.

"It's fine. I'll handle it."

"Handle what, Cole?" He leans toward me as I hover by the door, still half in and half out of this conversation. "We've given you space. I know some shit went down on your old team, but I don't know what it was. And since you keep all the details hoarded away in that head of yours, I can only assume the worst at this point. Especially after that show out there. Where I'm sitting, it looks like you're a loose cannon. You got kicked off your last team for beating up a teammate. That's some scary shit. That's not what we're about here. Now I've let it slide because you've done nothing like that since you joined the Lightning." He leans back again, pausing. "Until now. So now you owe me an explanation. Who is that girl? And what was that all about? You're a fantastic player, but that means shit all if you're a terrible person. Prove me wrong. I don't want to recommend Coach take you off the first line."

Panic grips me, squeezing the air out of my lungs. He can't. He wouldn't. If she causes me to lose my spot, my chance. Fuck no. Not after everything she's already stolen from me.

He gives me a little space after he drops that bomb. I'm shifting from one skate to the other, staring at the blue line on the wall above his head.

"She was my girlfriend." I have to force the words through my teeth at first, but then they start to flow a little easier. "For a long time. I thought she was the one. You know. Like, forever. Stupid. And then I found out she'd..." I swallow hard to compose myself. I haven't said these words in a long time, "been cheating on me. With my best friend on the team. Fucking asshole. I fucking caught them." Acid is burning my throat again at the unwanted picture that pops into my head, seared into my brain for all of eternity. Maybe beyond.

His eyes soften, but his brows are pinched together in confusion. "And then you got into a fight. Understandable. What I don't get is why you were kicked off the team? And what is she doing here?"

The padding softens the blow as I slam my fist into my thigh. "I have no clue why she's suddenly appeared back in my life. Maybe he dumped her. I don't know and I don't care. She transferred to Lakeview. And now she's threatening to come to games and practices. And I don't think I can handle that. Seeing her face everywhere."

"Wow. That's big. Ok. Well, you need a game plan. Some way to keep her at arm's length. I'm sure we can arrange for her to be persona non grata at practices, but there's not much I can do or Coach can do to keep her away from you at games or the rest of campus. What else can we do for you?"

There's a shift in my shoulders. A tiny one. I've been keeping these guys at arm's length since I got here. Maybe more like the length of a giant's arm, but who's counting? And even after that, Beau believes me and is all in for helping with my problem. My shoulders tense up again. Of course he's trying to help you. He doesn't want you screwing up at games. That would look bad on him and on the entire rest of the team. I can't let myself rely on him or anyone else. There are lots of people I've trusted over the years and in the end, the only ones I can really count on are myself, my dad, and my sisters. I'll accept his help, but I think I've reached my limit for sharing for the day, or year.

"Thanks." I give him a curt nod. "I don't need anything else from you."

His smile is as smooth as one of his game day suits. "Listen. I'm not going to spill your secrets to the rest of the team, but I think it might help if you talked to someone else. At least to our roommates." He winces. "Or just Dev. I'm not sure why I let those other two clowns move in with us. Even if you just let the rest of the team know that she's not someone you have any interest in seeing around. You don't have to share all the details."

My back stiffens again. "I'll think about it."

His blue eyes drill into me as if can spot the lie lurking under mine. "You do that. Also, I think you need to work through your issues with the rookie. Yes, he's a loud-mouth, but he's still your teammate. It's not your job to take him down. You need to learn to work with your team, not against them. This isn't a solo project."

I sigh, running a hand through my still damp hair. All I want is to take a shower and disappear into my reading. This day is sucking the life out of me.

"You're going to work with him."

My soul leaves my body at those words. "What?" He can't have meant that. That's like lighting a grenade, toss-ing it on the ice and hoping for the best. I really don't want to be responsible for blowing up the team, much less my own career.

"You're going to work one on one with Hail. We've all been cocky stars of one team or another. It'll be good for both of you to work together."

"You can't make me do that. I can't handle it. Neither of us will make it through the year."

"I can and I'm going to. I'm your captain. You're going to put in some one-on-one practice time with Hail, and I'm going to consider him your personal responsibility. Help him get his head on straight and hopefully yours as well. Neither of you will be any use to a pro team in the shape you're in now. You're nothing without your team."

Fuck. I nod. Looks like I'm not getting a choice in this at all. "Yes, captain."

"Good. I'll arrange some extra ice time for you, and maybe you can hang out a bit off the ice with him, too. I know you're a good guy despite today's display. You got this."

Not sure I believe a word of what he's saying, but I guess I've brought this on myself. I shake the hand he's holding out for me, wincing at the stab of pain in my wrist. Definitely going to need to ice that when I get home.

"We done here?" I'm glancing over his shoulder, eager to take my shower and get the hell out of here. I've had more than enough of this session.

He sighs. "Yes. We're done."

I've got my gear off and am padding across the cool, tiled floor when he calls after my back. "What you really need is a girlfriend. That would keep her off your back."

I shake my head, stepping into the shower. Yeah, right. That's all I need. One more complication.

CHAPTER FIVE

TOP SHELF FRIENDSHIP

JAZZ

"I brought coffee." I can't help singing the words as I step through the swinging back door into one of my favorite places. Nothing compares to the gorgeous smell of ink on pages paired with rich roasted coffee. The touch of sweetness from the hazelnut puts it over the top, and my shoulders loosen when I spot my best friend.

"You are perfection." Jordan greets me with a smile. Mounds of curly red hair are swept on top of her head in a wobbly bun, and there's a set of cute gold glasses perched on the tip of her nose.

My eyes narrow in confusion. "You don't wear glasses."

Her lips twitch, and she sweeps them off her face. "Oops. Aspen swept into town for a very brief visit, and I was playing the sexy librarian."

"TMI, Jordan. I really don't need to hear about your sex life. Especially not with how mine is going." Still, I'm not going to deny her caffeine. That would be cruel and unusual punishment.

"Pass me that box by the window."

I scan the room, stepping around the maze of brown boxes to reach the only window in the overflowing stock room. There are way too many tripping hazards for my precarious balance. She's been absolutely killing it selling these special editions online. I aspire to success like she's been achieving this year.

"This one?"

Her emerald eyes flick up under light lashes. "No, no. The one on the left."

Got it. My fingers slide under the bottom of the box. It protests as hard as my back when I sink into my knees to lift the freaking thing.

"I hope this box isn't full of severed body parts. I'm too young to be an accessory."

"No way. What a waste of precious space." She tears the top flaps of the box open with a flourish. "Books!" She picks up a gorgeous hardcover with a rose gold dust cover and glittery gold writing on it. The edges are sprayed a deeper pink color with a delicate floral pattern. It's a work of art.

She passes me a stack of shipping labels, some bubble wrap, and cute turquoise mailers with the new Top Shelf logo imprinted on them.

"Those are all single copies. If you can get them packed up, I'll forever be in your debt."

"I'm sure you could just pay me the fifty bucks you promised, and we'll be good." I wink at her. "But if you want to declare a life debt to me as well, I won't say no."

I'm working on my third package, wrapping the bubble wrap around the precious cargo when she breaks our companionable silence.

"About that love life of yours."

"Nope." I pop the p. A tendril of hair sticks to my lip gloss as I shake my head, and I blow out a breath to clear it away. "Don't you dare try to set me up."

Her hands fly up in protest. "I wasn't going to set you up, but I think you should start shopping around. That asshole you were with last year wasn't worthy of the ground you walk on."

"I know. That's why I've got no plans for dating this year. I'm far too busy to waste my time on another useless college guy."

Her lips pull down at the corners. She may be sporting a more business-like look than usual in fitted black pin-striped pants and a crisp white blouse, but she's still rocking some glorious crimson lipstick. "Hey. They're not all useless."

"I'm sorry. Aspen is a keeper, but he's the exception that proves the rule. It can't be statistically possible for there to be more than a handful of guys of his caliber at Lakeview. Trust me. I know."

My eye roll morphs into a grimace when I think of the edgy nervousness that's been consuming me since Darryl tracked me down the other day. I will not let him ruin this year for me. He's taken up way too much of my precious time here at college.

She heaves another box of books off a towering shelf with a grunt.

"Careful, you'll throw your back out. Need some help?"

The box lands on the floor with a dusty thud. "Nope. I'm good. I think you should read this." A bright blue paperback lands in my lap.

"What?" I pick up the book, studying the cartoon characters on the front, wondering how this particular book is going to change my life. Because with Jordan there's always a reason. Every book has a life lesson in it. Even if I never needed to think about what it would be like if some guy accidentally opened my box of vibrators when he was helping me move. Don't be ashamed. Embrace your pleasure. I'm pretty sure that was the life lesson from that one, according to her.

"You need to learn to trust again and find the right guy. Not just any old guy. You've been burned before, and you're not willing to open your heart, right?"

I shake my head, knowing she's never going to listen to my protests. I may as well read the book and get some fictional man action even though I have zero intention of getting any real man action this year. Plus, it's probably got some top shelf smut in it. Jordan is the queen of smut. Book recommendations from her guarantee a good time.

"Ok, Jordan. I'll read it."

Her topknot bobs, eyes closing as she tips her coffee cup up to take a long sip.

"You must miss him."

She looks at me over the white paper cup. "Yeah, I do. But don't underestimate the power of some primo sextiming."

"Sextiming?"

"FaceTiming, only naked. You know."

I reach for another book to pack up, avoiding eye contact. "What? No. I really don't know."

"You are missing out. The other day he told me to sit on the bathroom counter and..."

"No, no, no. I'm good. Love you, but that's a hard limit for me. I do not need to know what you and Aspen are getting up to on your phones." If anything is going to cause me permanent emotional damage, that would be it.

"Sorry." The smirk on her lips says otherwise. "I miss him. I'm getting close to nailing down a home for Top Shelf, the Chicago edition. Things have been going so well with the online store. I've started putting plans together for decor and get this. You are the very first to hear this. Other than Aspen, of course. And Mom, because I need to keep her in the loop until I can buy her out. But this store is going to be dedicated exclusively to romance books. Top Shelf Romance. There's going to be a cozy little corner with a red couch and a selfie wall. I've got these stunning glass shelves on order. It's going to be amazing. And of course, I'll need to move down there to get it going, so I'll finally be able to move in with Aspen on a full-time basis."

I wrap my arms around in her in a hug. "I'm so happy for you. You are absolutely killing it, and I love that for you."

"Thanks, bestie. How about you? You said you had some information on small business grants you wanted to go over. Hand 'em over."

There's a stack of neatly packed books surrounding me, and I realize I've reached the end of the shipping labels she handed me when I got here. Time soars when you're with awesome women.

"Hey, Sadie." I smile and nod at the girl behind the counter when I grab my backpack.

She gives me the briefest of glances over the top of the book she's devouring. "Hey, Jazz." And back she goes. Perfect job for a bookworm. The store has its busy moments, but the bulk of the sales now are coming from online, which Jordan is mostly handling, so it leaves plenty of time for reading.

Laptop, pencil case, mouse, granola bar. I'm digging around the mysterious innards of my bag until my fingers touch the folder with all the business grant pamphlets.

The red file folder holds all the goods, and Jordan snatches them up right away to inhale the words.

"Oh, this one looks good. New graduates." She scans the paper. "Business degree, business plan. Have you made one of those yet? If not, I can help."

"I have. But I'd love for you to look it over. An extra set of eyes is always helpful."

She nods. "Of course." She flips through the pages. "Oh, this one is interesting. It's a little different. The Stephanie

Lorne Award for Outstanding Women in Business. It's perfect for you. It's exclusively for upcoming college graduates in Michigan. They're looking for community involvement as well as the other usual requirements. How's your community service game?"

I wince. Having focused so much of my attention on my studies, plus my part-time job at the coffee shop, I haven't had too much time to devote to volunteer work. "That's a weak spot right now."

She tucks her lower lip between her teeth, crinkling her eyes together in thought. "That's not a problem. You've got the rest of the school year. We can find something for you on campus, easy. There are tons of volunteer opportunities. What do you want to do? Hug puppies? Read to seniors? Hug seniors while reading to puppies?"

I laugh. "None of the above?"

"What? You don't like puppies? Old people are delightful, you know. Aspen and I might never have yanked our heads out of our asses if we hadn't gotten stranded at that B&B last year. Did I tell you about Norma? I still keep in touch with her."

I laugh. She has definitely told me about the spicy old lady who ran the Knotty Pine. "You sure have. But I'd like to do something that, I don't know, would make a difference for someone like me. The other day I ran into Darryl." Not entirely accurate, but if I talk about that right now, I'll lose my focus.

"Eww. Did you slap him?"

"No. That would be assault."

"Shame."

"Anyway. I was walking home from the coffee shop and ran into him. He was getting in my face again, and then these Campus Walk Safe people came up and intercepted. They walked me to the bus stop. I think I'd like to do something like that. Help other women on campus feel safe."

"That sounds like a fantastic cause, and I bet they're always looking for help. Especially at the beginning of the year." Jordan springs up from her cross-legged spot on the floor. She's halfway across the room before she finishes the sentence, leaving me with a mild case of whiplash.

"What are you doing, Jordan?"

Her fingers fly over the keyboard of the backroom computer. The huge gray box looks like the child of the very first home computer. How that thing is still running is way beyond my tech skills. I sigh when I don't get an answer, sliding my Spotify app open to find the perfect playlist. Dance vibes. This is what we need to stretch out our cramped legs after all the sitting.

As the first notes ring out, I'm pushing off the floor, leaning up to the sky to stretch my back out and Jordan's ass is already bouncing to the beat. She twirls her finger with a flourish, smacking it down on the keyboard. Her hands drop to the desk, then she swivels around, leaning back. "Done."

"Great." The tiniest bit of further explanation would be fantastic. I hold out my hands.

"I've got you signed up for the orientation session on Tuesday. You're welcome."

I roll my eyes. "What if I was working?"

"You're not. You gave me your schedule for next week. I've got you covered."

If that isn't Jordan to a T, I don't know what is. She's a one-woman whirlwind who gets shit done, and I'm not even mad about it. I probably would have looked it up tomorrow or the next day, thought too hard about it and missed the deadline. A laugh slips out as I shake my head. "Thanks."

"You're welcome." She drops in a deep curtsy before grabbing my hands to pull me into a full-on dance party.

By the time I walk out of the store, my arms are aching, but I've got a smile on my face, and a tingle of excitement about this new volunteer gig. I wonder if I'll see my rescuer again. Not the point, Jazmin.

Chapter Six

Dirty Hit

Cole

I'm pacing between the short rows of chairs lined up in the small meeting room we booked for the orientation. Freaking Kenneth, bailing out last minute and sticking me with the orientation session. I grab the sheaf of pamphlets he left, studying them one more time, hoping to gain some sort of inspiration from the pile of papers. Still no.

I hate doing things like this. Talking in front of people. You think I'd be used to being the center of attention as a hockey player, but it's different out there. I'm in my element. All my focus is on the ice, the puck, my teammates, and rivals. Not to mention the thick layers of gear that add that extra bit of security and separation from the fans. But every time I open my mouth to speak in public, my fear comes racing back, threatening to steal my breath and slam me into the boards. I can usually get through it if there's even one friendly face in the crowd, but none of the other Walk Safe crew could make it tonight. To be fair, if they could have, then I might not have gotten stuck doing the one thing I loathe most in the world.

The smile I flash at the first couple of students that trail into the room is weak, so I turn my back on them, wiping my sweaty palms off on my track pants. I snatch a red dry erase marker off the ledge and start making a few random notes on the whiteboard. Hopefully, they'll assume I'm actually busy, and not a complete asshole for ignoring them as they come in. The shuffling noises ease, and I glance at my phone to check the time. Seven on the dot. I guess I can't stall any longer.

My shoulders twitch, and I pull away from the hand that lands on my back. Sharp nails rasp along the knit fabric of my sweater when I spin around, backing up until my shoulders hit the smooth surface of the wall. Surprise turns to displeasure when I spot her. Popping up into my life yet again.

"Charlene, what are you doing here?" Her appearances are starting to feel like a broken record, or like I'm caught in some alternate universe living the same day over and over again.

"I'm here to learn about Walk Safe. What else would I be here for?" She steps in a little closer and the stubborn set to her jaw tells me exactly why she's here. Her eyes dragging down my skin might have turned me on once, but now they leave an uncomfortable trail behind that leaves me itching in my skin.

I cross my arms over my chest, keeping her from getting right up in my face. "Fine. Go take a seat." She pushes her lower lip out in a pout as I toss a chin at the seating area. "Go on. I have to start the meeting." I'm not going to convince her to leave, so I may as well ignore her and get this thing going.

A Charlene-induced tremble has me clasping my hands together to still them. There are too many feelings swirling around in my mind, and I've lost all of my hard-won composure. The carefully planned words are gone, vanished in the cloud of anger, sadness, and frustration that's fighting to engulf me.

Unfamiliar eyes are fixed on me, and everyone is murmuring and looking at each other while I stand at the front trying to get a grip on myself. I skip from face to face, avoiding only one as I search for something, anything, to help me through this, and then. A jolt of warmth hits me in a much more pleasant surprise when I meet a pair of liquid chocolate eyes staring at me with expectation and concern in their depths. She's wearing her hair down tonight. The shiny black curtain of it falls over her shoulders, complementing her smooth, light brown skin. The smile does it for me. Her lips are painted a bronze gold color and when they curve up at the corners, it reaches all the way up, crinkling the corners of her eyes. It's my coffee girl. The coffee girl. I've no idea where that came from. Her name is spelled out in loopy hot pink letters on her nametag. Jazz.

It's hard to tear my gaze away from hers, but I give her a nod, glancing back down at the bulleted list of notes I made for myself. The familiar face is enough to ground me.

"Welcome, everyone, to the Walk Safe orientation. Some of you may walk out of here deciding this isn't the volunteer opportunity for you." I give Charlene a long look as I say those words. But she misses the point, basking in the attention. She leans forward to give me a view of her cleavage peeking out from the low V-neck of her tight shirt. My eyes seek Jazz's again. Better. Much better. "And some of you may sign up right away. I'm going to tell you about how it works, and the required commitment and answer any questions you might have. After that, it's up to you whether this is something you're interested in."

I make it through my entire list of prepared points with only the occasional tremor in my voice, but it's all thanks to the girl that my eyes keeping returning to. It's good to have a touch point in the crowd to keep myself from getting flustered and losing track of my words.

"That's it. Anyone have any questions?"

A few students raise their hands, including Charlene, who I ignore until she shouts out her question without waiting for me to acknowledge her.

"Do we get to choose our own partners for our shifts?"

I'm frozen for a minute, not sure how to answer. The answer, in fact, is yes. You can choose specific partners if you want and if it works with the overall schedule. Since there's no chance in hell I'm ever going to put myself in a position to roam the campus after dark with her for a three-hour shift, I don't know what to say.

"Yes. If both parties agree. It is a possibility, but as a new volunteer, you'll get paired with a more experienced member of the team. You'll work consistently with them for the first couple of months until you're comfortable with the process."

My eyes stray to the barista I've now crossed paths with a few times. She drops her lashes down, fidgeting with the bright purple pen in her hands. I know who I want as my new recruit this semester.

"Great." Charlene's voice slices through my thoughts, bringing me back to my new dilemma. I need to find some way to get her to leave me alone.

"Ok, everyone. If you're interested in committing, come on up to the front at the end and we'll get you signed up. If you need some time to think about it, that's fine too. We'll be taking applications until the end of the week, or you can always sign up next semester if you're not ready now. Training sessions start next week. Thanks for coming out."

Bags drag across desks, feet shuffle on the carpet and the students either file out the back door or join the line down the middle of the row. I'm shifting from one foot to the other behind the table with the sign-up tablet on it. Occasionally, I dip my head or give a strained smile to the handful of new recruits.

Charlene shot to her feet before I finished talking, but she still ended up at the back of the line. She's tapping her foot and peering around the tall girl in front of her.

Jazz gives me a shy smile when she gets to the front of the line. "Hi. I wanted to say thank you."

"You don't need to thank me. That's what I'm here for." She winces at the loud pop of my knuckles, and I immediately stop cracking them. "Sorry."

"No worries. And I didn't just mean for the other night with Walk Safe. You stepped in with that customer at the coffee shop. I really appreciated it. Not many people would... you know, help like that."

My chest tightens. People suck. It's disgusting how anyone can stand by and watch someone else get verbally abused by some asshole who thinks he has the right to act like that. "Nobody should ever be allowed to talk to you like that. But I know you're not allowed to tell customers off, no matter what bullshit they say."

The murmurs behind her are increasing as she reaches out a hand to grab the tablet I've got clutched to my chest. I pass it over, getting a little tingle when her fingers brush mine. They're a little dry, rasping across my hand, and I glance down to see that her long fingers are red and chapped. She needs some lotion. I'm sure the constant hand washing leaves them dry. Reminds me of my dad's hardworking hands.

"You know I can stand up for myself." She's not looking at me as her fingers tap away, filling out her information on the screen. "Well, maybe not so much myself, but for my employees. If I hear anyone talking to one of the other baristas like that, I will ask them not to return. They're not going to fire me for defending someone. And if they do, I guess the job isn't the one I want. When I have my own place…" Her voice trails off and she glances down at her hands.

I want to delve deeper. Ask her to tell me more. There's something so soft and vulnerable about her, but she showed strength too. Stepping in so the other barista didn't have to deal with the customer's assholery. It's a bonus that she clearly has no interest in my hockey status. I'm finding myself wanting to connect with another person for the first time in over a year, but the loud clearing of a throat lets me know this isn't the time.

I drop a hand over hers before she can release the tablet. My eyes flick up to catch Charlene staring me down, and the words spill out. "Hey, do you wanna grab a coffee after?" I laugh. "Or maybe something else. You probably don't want to go to a coffee shop on your day off."

Her mouth falls open, and a tendril of disappointment unfurls at the apology in her eyes. I can spot a no when I see it. "I'm not really doing that right now." Her voice pitches up at the end as if it's a question.

My brow stretches to my hairline. "Drinking coffee? Or going places?"

She laughs. "Going places like…" she gestures a hand between us, "with guys. Like dates." She winces, throwing her hands over her face. "Oh god. You didn't even ask me on a date, and I just assumed. I'm sorry." She's pretty cute when she's flustered.

"I didn't mean as a date, not that I wouldn't want to… but I'm not dating right now. Listen." I look up at Charlene again. "You'd be doing me a favor. Remember the other night when that guy was bothering you? Your ex?" She nods. "I've kind of got a similar situation going on and I could use a rescue right now. If you could help me out, I'll buy you a drink and we can chat for a bit and move on. No pressure. Just friends."

Her weight shifts from one foot to the other, and she's staring over my shoulder at my messy notes on the whiteboard. It's not fair expecting other people to piece together the sad hieroglyphics that pass for handwriting in my world. Freaking Kenneth.

"Please. You'd really be helping me out."

"Ok. Friends. I can do that." Decision made, she smiles at me and there's genuine pleasure there, as if she's excited to do this thing with me and she only needed me to provide her with an excuse. A reason to say yes.

"Awesome. If you don't mind hanging around here until I'm finished with the rest of these sign-ups, we can head out from here." Now that I know I've got something to look forward to, I don't even mind facing my ex. Even though she seems determined to ruin my senior year of college like she ruined the last two.

Charlene steps up, running long fingers through her blonde hair. Her nails are filed in perfect ovals and painted a shiny pale pink color as if she just came from a manicure. I hand her the tablet and take a step back, folding my arms.

"Listen, Cole. I need to talk to you." She makes no move to enter her information on the tablet, but there's nobody behind her now. Not that making people wait would stop her.

"I told you I don't want to talk to you. Now, are you signing up or not?" I nod at the tablet in her hands.

"I will but listen. You need to give me another chance. You have to understand why I did what I did."

"And by that, you mean my best friend?" I drop my voice to a whisper, glancing up to spot Jazz waiting by the open door. She doesn't need to overhear this conversation.

Her lower lip quivers. "Yes, but you don't understand. It wasn't all on me. You were pushing me away. You were barely talking to me, but Jeremy. He listened to me. He talked to me, so it kind of happened. You were halfway out the door, and he was there for me."

Is that how she saw it? I rub the back of my neck. "You can't put that on me. I was busy. So much pressure with hockey. That doesn't excuse what you did. I would never have done anything like that to you."

"I know, but you know how things went down with my dad. He walked away from all of us. As if we didn't matter. It felt like you were doing the same thing."

I shake my head. "I'm sorry your dad left. You know that, but I was always there for you, and you betrayed me. You did the exact thing you were expecting me to do. Why are you really here, Charlene? Why aren't you back in Tampa with him?"

Her shiny teeth close on her lower lip, eyes darting down to stare at her feet. "Jeremy left. He signed with Colorado."

It hits me like a dirty elbow to the jaw, rocking me onto my heels. He got signed. That could have been me. I could have snagged my spot if it weren't for her and him. How did I not hear about this?

"He's in the NHL?"

She shakes her head. "He signed a two-way contract, and they assigned him to the Golden Bears, but he's convinced he'll move up before the season is over."

The AHL team. Well, at least he hasn't beaten me to the pros, but the knowledge still leaves a burning ache in my throat. But it only leaves me more determined to prove myself this year to earn my own spot. Then next year I can face him on the ice.

At least it explains why she's back in my life. He must have tossed her aside when he moved on. I don't feel sorry for her. Not this current version of her, but she wasn't always like this. Things were different when we were younger. I don't know how I missed the gradual changes that turned her into the person she is now, but it's not a good look on her.

I hold out my hand for the tablet that she's still clutching, as if it can tie us together somehow as long as she has it in her hands.

"Good for him." There's not a single ounce of sincerity in the sentiment. "Look, I've got somewhere to be, and I've got to lock this place up."

I turn my back on her.

"Please, Cole. Don't do this to us."

"I didn't do anything to us. That was all on you. We've got to get out of here. This room is booked for some other club."

She's still lingering by the door after I lock up the tablet. But I brush past her, holding out my hand for Jazz, hoping she gets the hint. She does, slipping her small warm hand into my palm. Charlene's big blue eyes widen, darting down to our joined hands, but she hustles out the door, sending a caustic glare at the other girl after I lock up.

I lean in close to Jazz's ear. "Thanks."

CHAPTER SEVEN

SPILLING THE BEANS

JAZZ

The fern overhanging our table in the university center food court casts an interesting shadow of stripes over the sharp lines of Cole's face. I've almost convinced myself this wasn't a terrible idea. Yeah right. A quiver of doubt has been fluttering around my stomach since we left the little conference room upstairs.

The gorgeous blond girl hung around until the rest of the students had filed out, and her glare was almost enough to send me scurrying from the room. Which was probably her goal. I didn't, and the relief on his face was palpable when he told her he had plans. She sent me eye daggers designed to carve my heart right out of my chest as she brushed past me while she was leaving.

Cole bought me a hot chocolate with marshmallows and crunchy peppermint sprinkles, and it smells glorious when I sink my nose into the warmth. I take a sip, rolling the smooth chocolate around in my mouth, letting it coat my tongue in comfort before I swallow it down, chewing on the marshmallow. There's a surprising burst of mint when I bite down on the soft pillow.

I groan. "That's amazing. We don't have peppermint marshmallows at All Capps. I'm going to double down on flavored marshmallows when I've got my own place." Did I just say that? The sugar must have gone to my head.

He takes a sip of his own, eyes rolling back in his head. "Fuck yeah. That is delicious. Good choice."

"Well, I am a bit of an expert. You might say." He laughs at my exaggerated wink.

"You mentioned before that you want your own place. So, you want to run your own coffee shop. Is that your plan after graduation?"

My guard flies up. It always makes me nervous talking about my business dreams. People are so quick to shit on them and tell me how hard it is to start your own business and how many restaurants fail in their first year.

I study his face, searching for the doubt, the skepticism that I always see when I talk about this, but there's nothing but interest. Eagerness even, in those eyes that match the rich chocolate color of my drink.

"That's the dream. To own my own coffee shop. I know it might not be feasible right away. I'm going to have to work and save, but that's my end goal for sure. And not just a coffee shop, you know. I want it to be a neighborhood spot where everyone is welcome. I'd love to host local musicians for performances, and local authors for readings. My friend Jordan owns a bookstore and we've even talked about opening up a combo bookstore/coffee shop. One day. She's a little further on than I am right now. Her mother owns Top Shelf here in town. Not sure if you know it."

His head tilts to the side, eyes widening as he studies me. "I know it. That's Aspen Ellory's girlfriend."

"Oh. You know Aspen?" I do a double take, narrowing my eyes. Those muscles stretching his thin black sweater look like they belong on an athlete. But I know a lot of the hockey guys through Jordan, and I've never seen him around. Maybe he knows him from somewhere else.

A shadow passes across his face, deepening the grooves. His features would be almost harsh if it weren't for those full lips that might be even considered kissable if I was looking for that kind of thing.

"Uh, yeah. I'm on the hockey team with him."

"Really? What's your last name? I know some of the guys through Jordan, but I haven't seen you around." Heat creeps up my neck. Is he going to think I'm prying or that I'm some weird fan girl?

"It's Schaeffer. Yeah. I don't hang out with the team that much." He presses his lips together, leaning back in his chair.

Schaeffer. There it is. I've seen his name on the back of a jersey and there's something else lurking at the back of my brain. Some gossip about him, but I can't quite place what it is. I'm dying to probe. There's a story there. But I can tell this isn't a question I'm going to get answers for right now, so I try for a little something else. This one I need answers to. I can't see him again unless I know what's going on with that girl. More drama is not something I need in my life. "Tell me why you invited me here tonight."

"I wanted some coffee."

"Uh huh, and..." I lean in closer, letting him see that his evasion won't cut it.

His chest rises and falls, the moon shining down through the window to highlight his features. Sometimes not saying a word is the best way to get people talking. Something I've learned from my years in customer service. I don't always have a conversation at my fingertips, but if you let people talk, especially about themselves, they're usually happy to fill in the blanks.

He sighs. "Her name is Charlene. She's my ex. From my old school."

Their interaction makes more sense in that context. The way she was touching him was familiar with an edge of possessiveness, while he had a kind of trapped look on his face. Now I need to hear the story.

"I spent my freshman and sophomore years in Miami. We'd been dating for a while, but she did some things, and I broke up with her right before I left to move here."

Miami? Wow. That's a long way to run from someone. His gaze falls to the cup he's holding, pausing to take a sip. There's a vulnerability to the gesture that I understand, like he's back in that moment. Whatever it was that broke him. "What did she do?"

"She cheated on me. She's not the same person she was when we first started dating."

A pang hits me in the gut. "That is shitty. I'm so sorry. Is that why you left your team?" I reach over, but he pulls away when I drop a hand on top of his. My shoulders slump as I shrink away from him. I'm sure my entire face must be on fire now after the rejection.

He tilts his head up to stare at the high ceiling, Adam's apple bobbing. "Part of it."

There's more to it, but we don't know each other, so I don't have the right to pry, especially not after he pulled away from me. He's giving me an incomplete picture. I wonder why.

"How long did you date for?"

"Almost four years." His gaze tracks over to the food court where they're sliding metal gates down over the kiosks. When did it get so late?

"Four years. So before college even? Wow."

"Yeah. She was my first serious girlfriend." He snorts. "Probably last."

"Feel that. Relationships suck."

"Sure do. What's up with you and the guy from the other night?"

I can feel my soul curling back into my body as he turns his attention on me, dark eyes intense and searching.

"Come on. You've got to share. At least a little. Lay it on me, otherwise this friendship thing will start out all unbalanced and we can't have that."

"Unbalanced?" I ask.

"Yeah, you've got my dark secret, and I know nothing about you. You're just this beautiful mystery."

A shiver runs down my spine, leaving a trail of warmth, and my words flow.

"I'm in my last year, too. I met Darryl in the fall of junior year. At first, I wasn't sure. I said no when he asked me out. Some unconscious part of me was a little uneasy. He was a little too forward. A little too insistent. Should have trusted that feeling. But I didn't. He kept coming back. He pulled out at all the tricks. Roses, meals out, and he'd pick me up, drive me to campus. I don't even like roses, but it all seemed so romantic."

I'm waiting for him to offer his opinion, but he doesn't. Just sits there quietly listening. It's refreshing. Hanging out with a guy who doesn't need to inject his voice into every spare bit of air.

"So, I gave in. We started dating, and it was consuming. Have you ever been so swept up in someone that you spend all your time with them? Have zero desire to be apart?"

He nods.

"Right. And then I realized I was seeing less of my friends. I've got a little study group of business majors I met in first year. They're great. We've all got entrepreneurial aspirations, so we study together and brainstorm, but I realized I'd missed all their get-togethers for a month. When I told Darryl I was going to go to the next one, he flipped out. That was the first sign, but then he covered it up, said he'd bought us tickets for this movie I wanted to go see, so I let it slide."

I look up to see if he's still even paying attention, and he is. He's looking at me like every word I say has value to him.

"Anyway, by the time I realized things weren't so good, I'd lost a bunch of friends, and he'd kind of become the center of my universe. Stupid me. Getting my grades at the end of the year was a huge wake up call. My eighties had slipped to seventies, and when I told him I needed to spend more time studying for exams, he lost it again. He..." I break off, shaking my head. I've shared way more with this stranger than even my closest friend. There's no way I can tell him what happened. I don't even want to think about it. No matter how many times I tell myself it wasn't my fault, I'm still ashamed that I let it get that far. That I didn't see the aggression lurking behind his eyes. The potential for violence and destruction.

I can't even meet the searching look in his eyes. "But it was the end of the school year, so after exams, I cut and run. I told him I didn't want to see him anymore. He lives far enough away that I could avoid him all summer, even though he texted and emailed me until I blocked him. Maybe I should have called him, been firmer. Not hid away with my family, hoping the problem would go away." There was a shadow over my summer knowing he'd be waiting for me when I got back to school, but I was hoping he'd found someone else. Clearly, that was a desperate delusion. We're more likely to see a UFO land in the middle of campus.

Cole weighs his words for a moment. "You did what you had to do for yourself. Sounds like. What do you think now, though? Do you think he's going to keep arranging these little meet ups and trying to get you back?"

A soft sigh slips out. Unfortunately, I do think that. I remember how very persistent he was when he first wanted to get together with me. There's no reason to think he won't do that again if he's decided he's not finished with me yet. "Yes."

He nods. "Ok. Well, call me if you need someone to run interference. That's one of my special skills as a hockey player, you know. A little body check to get him to lay off can't hurt. Metaphorically speaking, of course."

"Of course. Thanks. I'm glad I came with you." Spilling some of my secrets provided a little relief from the burden I've been lugging around. I don't want my family or friends to know how bad it got. That I let it happen. Maybe it's him, and the fact that he was also betrayed by someone he cared for, or maybe there's less shame and fear of judgement talking to a stranger. But my story flowed easier than I expected. Even if I held back some of the worst things. The picture of my trashed room flashes in my mind, and a lump forms in my throat, making it hard to swallow.

The smile on his face softens all his hard lines, and it eases the tightness in my chest with the warmth of its glow.

"Me too. I guess we'll just have to be sharing buddies."

"Sounds good. Like we're bus or line buddies in grade school?"

"Sure. Something like that." I can't help but notice how large his hands are when he splays them on the smooth beige surface of the cafeteria table to push himself up. I bet he's really good with those hands. Nope. Bad. Tuck that thought away.

"Can I give you a ride home?"

"Sure, that would be nice, thanks." The weight of my confessions, piled on top of a long day of lectures, is dragging me down, so even the thought of taking the bus has my shoulders drooping. I'd probably fall asleep and end up at the wrong stop.

He holds out a hand to help me up from the table. But as tired as I am, I ignore the offer. He's stepped in to rescue me twice now, and I'm not interested in making a habit of playing the damsel in distress.

CHAPTER EIGHT

NOT HERE FOR THE FRESH AIR

COLE

Our first game is creeping up on us, and a restless itch pulls me out of bed earlier than usual. Tired of tossing and turning, I yank on a loose pair of jogging shorts and a compression shirt, grabbing my ear buds off the scratched dresser as I head out.

A dense fog settled over the neighborhood overnight, so I can barely see a foot in front of myself as I push off into an easy jog at my warmup pace. My battered sneakers hit the pavement in a steady rhythm, calming all the thoughts that popped up during our non-date last night. Seems like we both have similar dilemmas. I feel like there's a solution somewhere in there.

I don't even look back as another set of footsteps sounds out behind me. They're traveling at a much faster rhythm that almost pushes me to increase my pace. Damn competitive nature serves me well when I'm playing hockey but is not always necessary in everyday life.

I finally tilt my head when the person attached to the footsteps pulls up beside me, slowing to match my pace. Beau. I've never run into him before while I was out jogging. He's more of a treadmill at the gym kind of guy.

After the pace he was pushing himself at, I'm expecting him to pull ahead, but he doesn't, and suddenly my solitary run is not so solitary anymore.

"How's it going?" he finally asks between rapid breaths.

"Good."

"Come on, man. Gotta give me a little more than that. I dragged my sorry ass out of the house on a Sunday morning to come running with you out here." He waves a hand in front of him as if the fresh air and sunshine are extremely distasteful.

"Nobody asked you to."

"I know, but the team is my responsibility now, and you're part of the team, so guess what?"

My breath puffs out in a cloud as I sigh. "You're not going to leave me the fuck alone?"

"Ding ding ding. You got it."

"Awesome." Now I've got a shadow I didn't ask for, and I sure as shit don't want.

"To keep you posted. Your ex has been sniffing around the team, trying to get invited to outings. She's been at

Wright's a few times, and she's been hanging around a few of the usual bunnies."

"Too bad for her." I guess my antisocial tendencies have served their purpose. Funny thing is, I never used to be antisocial. I've always been a one-woman guy, but I still went out with the team. Went to parties. I had friends. Last year was kind of lonely until Jackson finally forced his way into my life, but I still didn't make a habit of hanging out with the team off the ice. After he graduated, I figured I'd be back on my own, but it seems like Beau has decided to worm his way in through the crack left open by Jacks. Must be a captain thing. Not sure he would put this much effort into it if Charlene hadn't showed up, but here we are.

"Yup. She hasn't found out much. I told the guys not to give her the time of day," he huffs out between breaths. "But some of the younger guys are particularly bad at using their higher brains sometimes, so they might do something stupid."

There's a satisfying crack when I roll my neck. "Why are you here, Beau?" I know it's not just to give me an update on my pushy ex.

"It's a beautiful fall day for a run. Look at all those colors."

You can't even see the oranges, reds, and yellows past the ominous layer of fog that surrounds us. "Sure."

"Fine. I was thinking you should come out with us tonight. We're going bowling. It'll be fun. No way your ex will know to follow us there."

"Bowling?" I look at him. I haven't been bowling since I was in high school.

"Yeah. Sounds lame, but it's fun. They serve beer there too. Last time your captain will condone drinking for the rest of the season. Don't miss out."

Not that I need a drink to have a good time, but it might make bowling a little more fun. I really should hang out with my team more this year. I'd already resolved to when she showed up and blew all my plans out of the water, turning me back into the hockey hermit.

"Fine."

He pitches forward, catching himself before he can hit the pavement. "Really?"

"Yeah. I'll come."

"Fantastic. Now about the girl thing, there's this really nice girl in my psych class. You might like her. It might get your ex off your back if you were seen dating."

Now he's going too far. The last thing I want is a girlfriend. The seed of an idea that's been germinating in my brain bursts into a fully grown thought. I don't want a girlfriend, but it really would be the best solution to my big problem. Keep Charlene's advances at bay. Stop Beau's matchmaking schemes in their tracks. I need a girlfriend. Just not a real one. "I'm seeing someone." I blurt out, my mouth committing me to the plan before my brain can overthink it.

"Really? That's great, man. Can't wait to meet her."

Shit. Shit, shit, shit. Why did I say that? Jazz's face popped into my head, but who knows if she'll agree to this? She's the perfect candidate. I'm pretty sure she's as uninterested in a real relationship as I am, given her history. And it'll help keep her asshole of an ex off her back. Solve both of our problems. But it's a wild idea that she might not agree to. And then where does that leave me?

"It's late notice. She's probably busy, but I'll ask."

Instead of turning off to do my longer loop around the middle school, I cut back toward the house, and Beau shadows my steps.

I pick up the pace, sprinting the last stretch to avoid any further conversation. Beau keeps up and we end up racing back to the house. I'm completely winded with an ache in my side when I catch sight of the house, but I push myself until I'm a couple of strides in front of him.

He glowers at me as I slam a palm on the front door, looking back at him. "I win."

Surprisingly, instead of challenging me to another battle or some other stupid thing to prove his superiority, he slaps me on the back.

"Good hustle."

The camaraderie feels good and sets me on edge at the same time. The people you let closest are the ones who have the power to shatter you, and I'm really not up for that. What happened to keeping everyone at a distance? I race into the house to do my stretches in my room, putting a more comfortable distance between us.

CHAPTER NINE

CHAOS AND COOKIES

JAZZ

The ugly screech of my apartment buzzer startles me away from the oven. Who could that be? My heart stutters in my chest, and then takes off at a gallop. What if it's Darryl? Should I answer it? I hate the way an everyday noise can send me spiraling. Especially here in my apartment. This should be my safe place.

It sounds out again, but I straighten my back, refusing to be afraid in my own house. If it's Darryl, I just won't let him up. Problem solved.

Sharp pain shoots through my knee, snatching my breath as I slam it into the little table by the front door in my rush to answer the call. "Shit!" I call out through the speaker.

"Umm. Hey. It's Cole. Can I come up?"

"Cole?" I'm not sure I heard him properly through the fuzzy old speaker, and I can't quite wrap my mind around why he'd be here. "Sorry, hit my knee."

It's hard to identify the sound through the box, but it sounds like he's laughing around his words. "Yes. Cole. From Walk Safe." His need to clarify is kind of cute. As if I could forget him after the double rescue.

"Come on up." A shrill beep sounds out as I let him up.

My tiny apartment is not ideal for pacing, so I'm taking three steps across the living room and back while I wait for him to make it up the stairs. What is he doing here? We exchanged numbers but didn't make any plans to meet up or anything.

The oven timer buzzer cuts through my apartment at the same time as the knock on the door. I wobble one way then the other, ending up going for the oven first. Grabbing a dish towel to pull the cookie tray out of the oven turns out to be a poor decision. It slips, sending searing pain through my thumb. I drop the tray on top of the oven with a clatter and kick the door shut as I head back to answer. This is not my day.

Surprise and confusion are all over his gorgeous face. His eyes track my thumb as I pull it out of my mouth, realizing what I must look like. Hair all over the place, pink leopard print leggings, probably covered in flour. Glancing down, my fears are confirmed. Oh, and sucking on my poor baked thumb.

I hold it out to him. "Burnt my thumb."

He stretches his neck, checking out the small space behind my shoulders. Right, let him in. I back up, swinging the door wide to let him pass, but he's too big. I can still feel the heat of his body as it passes barely an inch from mine.

"Did you run it under cold water?"

"What? No. Not yet. You got here at the same time as the cookies were done. I had to make a choice."

"And you chose cookies over me? I'm hurt." Those full lips turn down in a frown.

"No, no. It wasn't that. It was just that the cookies would have burned...." The frown twitches into a smile. "You were joking."

"Of course. Cookies always come first. What kind are they? Smells delicious."

I take in a deep breath and all I get is a sharp spicy aroma that's all male. His scent overpowers the sweet vanilla and sugar of the fresh-baked cookies.

"Oh, they're snickerdoodles. You can have one if you'd like."

"Let's look after that thumb first." He follows me the five steps through the opening into my tiny yellow kitchen.

He turns on the sink, checking the temperature until it meets his standards, and holds out a hand. I look down at my reddened thumb again, and he gently grabs it. His much larger hand swallows mine up, and he tugs me over to the sink, flipping my hand around to hold it under the cool water. I close my eyes, dragging in a deep breath at the soothing relief of the cool water numbing the pain.

We stand there in silence for a few minutes, but it's comfortable. Feels natural even though we barely know each other.

"Better?"

I nod. "Better."

"Have you got a clean dish towel somewhere?" He scans the handful of cupboards and drawers.

I nod toward the drawer on the left and he pulls out a dish towel, laughing when he sees the unicorn farting rainbows on it. He runs the towel under cold water, then carefully wraps it around my thumb.

"Keep that on there and run it under cold water if it starts hurting again."

"Are you secretly a doctor? Like, who was that kid from the old TV show that was a teenage doctor?"

He snorts. "Doogie Howser?"

"Yeah. That one. From the memes."

"No, I am most decidedly not a doctor. Just have some experience looking after my siblings."

Interesting. Now that we're standing, the awkwardness of a stranger in my space is setting in, so I move away from him over to the offending oven. I scoop a perfectly golden cookie off the tray, sliding it onto a small plate.

"Cookie? As thanks for the medical attention?"

His smile spreads, and he reaches out to accept my offering. "Only cause they look delicious. You don't owe me anything."

I jerk it away. "Wait. You're not allergic to nuts, are you?"

"Nope." He chases the plate, snatching the cookie. After stuffing three quarters of it in his mouth, chocolate oozes out, dripping onto his chin. "Mmm, that's fantastic."

The compliment fills me up with a warm glow. I love experimenting with different recipes, looking forward to the day when I can serve the favorites in my own cafe. Darryl wouldn't even try my baked goods. Said it wasn't part of his healthy eating plan. Didn't have a problem with pizza once a week though.

"The secret is the combination of milk and semisweet chocolate chips, and a hint of cinnamon. With the walnuts..." I kiss my fingers, flicking them away. "Chef's kiss. Did you want some coffee as well?"

"No. I'm fine. I came over to ask you something. Can we maybe go sit down somewhere?"

"Yeah. Let me just..." I reach out with my good hand, swiping the glob of chocolate off his chin and holding it in front of his face. "You got a little something here."

I watch his eyes settle on my thumb inches away from his mouth. I blush, realizing how weird that was, and stick it in my own mouth, sucking off the chocolate and ducking my head.

When I look back up, there's a shine of laughter in his rich chocolate eyes as he tucks his lower lip between his teeth.

"Come on. We can sit on the couch. Or if you're feeling really spicy, there's the couch."

I lead to him to the daisy covered two-seater that is in fact the only place to sit in here. Other than my bed, of course. My eyes stray to the corner of my bachelor, where the bed is tucked away. I've never minded how tiny my place is. It is only me after all, but he takes up so much space it's starting to feel a little crowded.

"Have a seat." He sinks into the overstuffed cushion, and I almost plop down next to him. As my ass is hovering over the seat, I rethink my choice, standing up and sinking to the floor across from him. I pull my knees up to my chin.

"You don't have to sit on the floor in your own place, you know? I don't bite."

My face scrunches up. "I'm good. It's good for the back. Sitting on the floor." No idea if that's true, but he lets the bullshit slide.

He hunches forward, propping his elbows on his knees and dropping his chin onto his fisted hands. His eyes roam the tiny space, refusing to land on my face. Fine by me. I've embarrassed myself enough for a week or maybe a month.

"I rushed over here with this amazing idea, and now that I'm here, I'm regretting every life decision I've ever made," he says, shifting in his seat.

"Fantastic. That's promising. Did you need a kidney perhaps? I've got two. I might be able to spare one."

He laughs. "No. I'm good on that front. Thanks. I guess my question doesn't seem nearly as intense now, so thanks for that."

"At your service." He gets an awkward salute to match my awkward words. "I'm here for you." I don't want to owe him, or anyone anything, so if I can help him out somehow, that'll even us up.

"Ok, so you know how we both seem to have problems with our exes right now?"

"Yes." Where is he going with this?

"I was thinking of something one of my teammates said, about how I need a girlfriend."

He had me leaning in, hanging on his words, but this, this has me pulling back, wary. I shake my head. "I'm not looking to date. We talked about that."

He's shaking his head, leaning back. "No. I'm fucking this up. Sorry. That's what makes this so perfect. You aren't looking to date, I'm not looking to date, but we both need an excuse to keep our exes away, right?"

The words dangle in the air on the verge of forming a coherent thought, but remain elusive.

He leans forward again. "What if we pretended to be dating? It would keep our ex's off our backs, hopefully, and we could still hang out. Try out this friend thing."

The silence must have stretched on for longer than I thought, because he's shaking his head again. "Now that I say that out loud, it sounds crazy. I have no idea what I was thinking. I'm sorry. I'll let myself out."

He stands up, swiping his hands down the front of his pants, but the words finally sink in, so I hold up my hands to prevent him from taking off. "No. It's not. Fake dating. That's totally a thing."

"Really?"

I shrug, smiling. "In books and movies."

"What? Really? Is that common?"

"Yeah. Fake dating, fake engagements, fake marriages. Totally the stuff of romance tropes, and with Jordan as my friend, I know all about those. Of course, in books the fake dating always turns to real dating, but I guess that's the fictional part."

He still looks a little sheepish, but the shine of eagerness is back in his eyes. "So, do you think it might work? Are you interested?"

I tilt my head up to stare at the ceiling. Can we do this for real? It would be helpful to keep Darryl away. Not that I need an excuse to say no to him. But if he sees me with another guy, it might deter him from the relentless pursuit he's already started only a couple weeks into the school year. And I did want to hang out with Cole some more. He seems like a cool guy. And yes, he's attractive. I can look at him and see the objective handsomeness of that face, but I barely know him. If we're hanging out, I can quickly move him into the friend zone. Keep him at a distance.

"Yes."

"Really?"

"Yes. I think it's a great idea."

"Cool. Awesome. Then should we shake on it or something?" He still looks a bit like he's in shock. Like he's surprised I agreed to his impulsive plan.

I stick out my hand, and we shake on it. "Should we make some sort of a plan? Like, how is this going to work?"

"I don't know. You signed up for Walk Safe. I'll make sure I'm your trainer. We'll have a few hours together, so why don't we make a plan then? In the meantime. Some of the team made plans to go bowling. Would you maybe be interested in coming with us? That would be a good way to introduce you to them. Get the ball rolling, so to speak. Sorry, that was terrible."

"When?"

"Oh. Tonight. Sorry. I wasn't thinking. You probably already have plans. Don't worry about it."

Oh, just let me check my packed social schedule. Nope. I'm free and clear, but should I admit that? Kind of makes me look a little pathetic. At least it's a weeknight, and I do love bowling. "Actually, I'm free."

"Good. Cool. I'll pick you up at seven?"

"I can meet you there."

"No. Remember, I'm your boyfriend now. I can pick you up."

"Sure."

I let him get up for real this time, springing up after him. "Wait."

I fly off to the kitchen and dump most of the cookies into a plastic takeout container. "Here. Take these back to the house. Share them with your friends."

He takes them from me, moving a little stiffly and taking care to avoid touching my hands. "I don't know. Should I be sharing my girlfriend's cookies with other guys?" His eyebrow stretches toward his hairline.

This time he's got me laughing instead of groaning, even though that one was just as bad as the other. "Yes. Please share my cookies. But if anyone says anything bad about them, you'll be forced to defend my honor. Pistols at twenty paces. Or maybe you're better with a sword."

There's another tiny smirk tugging up the corners of his lips.

"I didn't mean..." What is wrong with me?

"I know what you meant." His smirk deepens. "But to be honest, no one could ever say anything bad about these. They're fucking amazing. See you tonight?"

"See you."

My mind is whirling as the door clicks shut behind him. What did I just agree to? I spin back to the kitchen to grab a cookie to nibble on. The spicy cinnamon explodes on my tongue, reminding me of the scent clinging to him. Warm, delicious, and comforting, just like these cookies. A new friend, and a way to keep Darryl at least a few feet away. My lonely year is looking up.

Chapter Ten

Easy Access

Cole

I'm out of the car and crunching up the walkway over the blanket of fall leaves when Jazz walks out the glass front doors of her apartment building.

"Hey, girlfriend."

She smiles. "Hey, boyfriend. You could have stayed in the car. No need for the chivalry."

The passenger door groans in protest as I force it open for her, waving my hand with a flourish. "Now that wouldn't be very boyfriendy of me and I can't have your neighbors getting suspicious. Not to mention the door is a little stiff." I run a hand through my hair, wincing as I look at the rusty heap of junk.

"Since I don't actually know a single one of them, that shouldn't be a problem."

"Well then. I'll just wait out here and honk impatiently next time I pick you up for a fake date. Better?"

"For sure. Sounds good. I'll wear my grungiest old sweats. The ones with the hole in the crotch."

I tilt my head to the side. "Easy access?"

She smacks my arm with a giggle. "Who's getting the easy access? There's zero access for fake boyfriends."

"Oh. Shit. Clearly, I had no idea what I was getting myself into. Fake relationship off."

Her laugh dies down, and her hair swooshes over her shoulder as she whips around to look at me. The dim light of the streetlamp casts a soft glow over her. "What?"

My lips are twitching as I try to keep the laugh inside.

"Oh. You think you're funny, do you?"

"I do actually."

The engine sputters to life, and I fall silent, patting the dashboard as I steer Mabel onto the street. It's fantastic to have the freedom of my own ride this year, but the old car is not always the most reliable vehicle. I'm glad she's feeling agreeable tonight.

As we're getting closer to our destination, she breaks the silence in a deliberate way, as if she's been gathering her thoughts on our drive.

"Guess we really haven't gone over the ground rules. I think we're supposed to make some sort of list of rules or something."

"Rules? Lists?"

"That's what they do in all the books."

"Well, this isn't a book. How about if we just wing it? Make the rules up as we go. Or not. We don't have to be or do anything we don't want to. Maybe for tonight we'll pretend it's real in front of the guys, and then next time we see each other, we can lay down some rules if you really want to."

Her glossy copper lip is tucked in between her teeth as she nibbles away on it. I flick my eyes back to the road, focusing on the turn into the bowling alley. Those lips are way too distracting. I may not be looking for a relationship, but that doesn't stop my lesser brain from admiring a pretty girl.

My fingers are flexing on the steering wheel. Now that we're here, my stomach is roiling with nerves. Get a grip. This isn't a date. But as much as I've avoided spending too much time off the ice with the guys, I am around them enough to realize they can be a bit much.

"Jazz." She's staring at me with a curious look when I turn to face her.

"Yes."

"The guys. They can be a bit much. Maybe I should have thought of that before I invited you out. If you want, we can turn around and find something else to do."

She tilts her head to the side, and I can almost feel those dark eyes reading my thoughts. "Are you nervous?"

"No. What are you talking about?"

"You are. You're nervous. These are your teammates. What are you nervous about?"

I swipe a hand down my face. It's a little unsettling to be read that easily. I thought I had some pretty impenetrable shields up. "I told you. The guys. They're, you know, jocks. They don't always know when to use their inside voices. I don't want you to get scared off. This is, after all, our very first fake date. It would be a shame if it was our last."

"Don't worry about me. You know I've hung out with some of these guys before, right? I told you I knew them through Jordan. I can handle a little machismo and posturing. From what I've seen, they seem like pretty decent guys underneath the loud mouths." Her silky hair looks so soft and touchable as it slides over her shoulder. It's very distracting when she wears it down. "Not to mention I grew up in a big family. Lots of siblings, cousins, nieces, and nephews. Herrera family celebrations can get pretty boisterous. If you don't want to do this, though, you're going to have to let me know now, otherwise I'm getting out of the car." Her hand hovers over the door handle.

Ok then. Time to do this. I pull my shoulders back, nodding at her. "I'm good. Let's go."

Her smile widens, and she's out the door before I can walk around to open it for her. I'm entranced by the sight of the round curves of her ass highlighted by the leggings clinging to them. It takes the slamming of her car door to break me out of my trance. Fuck. Not a great start there, Schaeffer.

We make it through the front doors of Lakeland Bowling without running into the rest of our group. We leave behind the cool calm of the parking lot, entering what can only be described as chaotic chaos. If that's even a thing. There are buzzers and bells ringing and flashing from the arcade to our right. Loud top forty music blares over the speakers, and a thundering roar of multiple bowling balls rolling down the alleys echoes through the place.

It's a lot.

"Coco! You made it. Didn't think you were coming. And you brought a date! And it's Jazz? What the hell, man. You've been holding out on us. What does Jordan have to say about this?" Grant says, eyes all lit up as reaches over to pull her in for a hug.

Coco. Jazz's lips are twitching as she mouths the stupid name at me over Grant's shoulders. I roll my eyes with a quick headshake.

"I said I was coming. I'm here. Apparently, you already know this asshole." I point at the asshole in question who's currently shaking the brown waves on top of his head after he steps back from drooling all over her. "Do you know the rest of the guys?" I turn to her, not wanting to look at the mangy group surrounding us like a pack of wolves that's discovered a piece of meat after a lean winter.

She smiles at Beau. "Hi, Beau." He's wearing a pale blue polo shirt, and khaki pants with his hair gelled smoothly to the side. But at least he holds out a smooth hand for a shake rather than wrapping his arms around her like Grant did. My jaw is still clenched from seeing that.

"Dev." Her smile is just as bright for him as she approaches our other D-man, Lucy.

He nods, crossing his arms over his chest.

She tilts her head, eyes narrowing when she spots JJ bouncing up and down on his toes behind Lucy.

"Do you know Jenson?"

Jazz shakes her head. "I don't believe we've met before."

"Oh, you'd remember if you'd met me before. I'm un-forgettable," he says, eyes twinkling.

If I was more comfortable with the team, I'd punch him for that. Luckily, Beau takes care of it for me. "Don't be a dick in front of the lady."

Apparently, she isn't bothered by his cockiness, shoulders shaking with laughter. "He's our goalie. Watch out for him. Goalies are a special sort of crazy town."

"Hey. I resent that. Nice to meet you." Our very tall goalie gives a surprised Jazz a hug that has me grinding my teeth again.

"Mackenzie and his girlfriend." One of the younger guys is here with his girlfriend. A twinge of guilt has me rubbing the back of my neck, searching my brain. I don't know her name. Luckily, she steps up, blonde ponytail bobbing, cheerleader smile on her face.

"Hi, I'm Serena. Nice to have another girlfriend here."

"Nice to meet you, too. Love your nails." Jazz's compliment draws my eyes to Serena's long pink claws. That's the only way I can describe them. They're about two inches long. The strobing lights send sparkling rainbows off the crystals embedded in the tips.

"Summer is coming with her friends in a bit. They had some sorority thing after class, so she told us to start playing and they'll join in when they get here."

"Just you and me then to balance out all this testosterone. At least for now." Serena loops her arm through Jazz's, dragging her off to the shoe rental counter.

I glance around the bowling alley, checking out the rusty orange carpet edging the room, and the big screens showing a football game in the sports bar area. This shouldn't feel weird. Hanging out with my team, but it does.

"Come on, Coco. We need to get shoes, and more important, beers. Pitchers?" Grant sounds confident, but his eyes give him away, darting over to Beau to make sure the captain is okay with his idea. He's all bluster, that one. Maybe I can intimidate him into letting go of the nickname. Probably not. There are benefits to that leadership role, that's for sure. Had I stayed with the Scorchers I probably would have been captain by now, but that was a different team and a different me. It's better if I just play my best game, not worry about all that other stuff. Sometimes I wish things were different, but what good does wishing do?

Jazz is long gone with Serena. At least they seem to get along. You never can tell with girls. They have more complicated relationships with each other than most guys do. At least that's what I used to think.

We reconvene in our lane, sliding the ugly shoes on our feet. Unfortunately, JJ takes control of the lane and labels us all by our nicknames. Except the girls, of course. Jazz and I are paired up with Mack and Serena, as well as Beau and Lucy. A now familiar hollow crash rings out as Jazz's purple ball mows down all the pins for her third strike in a row. I keep my eyes locked on her and sure enough, she throws her hands up in the air and wiggles her ass in a victory dance that's more than a little distracting.

Mack groans. "Schaeffer, you brought a ringer in on us."

"If I'd known she was this good, don't you think I would have insisted on being on the same team as her?"

Beau decided we should play three on three, but he insisted on splitting the guys up from their girls for this round.

I move over to Jazz as she dances over to the table, almost reaching out to grab those full hips of hers to pull her in for a hug. But I have to remind myself this isn't real, swerving last minute to throw my hand up for a high five. She pulls back confused, and then taps my palm in the most awkward high five known to humankind. I take a step back, shoving my hands in my pocket.

As if to drive the point home, a big slash flashes on the screen and Mack celebrates his spare by leaning down to pull his girlfriend into a borderline NSFW kiss. Lucy's eyes flick over to us, and my skin no longer feels like it fits. He might not say as much as some of the others, but I get the impression he sees everything. If I can't even convince my teammates of the truth of this relationship, it's never going to work on Charlene.

I lean in close to Jazz's ear, spotting the sparkly pink cat earrings as I brush her hair back behind her ear. It's as soft as I've been imagining, and an image pops into my head of what it would look like wrapped around my fist. "Hey, I feel like we're not doing this quite right. I think I was supposed to kiss you or something after your strike. Maybe I should pretend to be pissed off that you're beating me, and we can get into a big fight about it. That'll throw them off."

She shoves at me, then leans in. "I think that might have the opposite effect. Besides, I can't have a boyfriend who's intimidated by my bowling skills. Even a fake one."

"Oh, I'm not intimidated. In fact. It's kind of hot." Shit. Reverse. Why did you say that, dumbass?

"Coco. Peel yourself away from your girl. It's your turn."

Saved by the asshole, I walk away, hands a little shaky as I grab the neon green 16-pound ball I've been using. But I can't help glancing over my shoulder. Jazz is standing right where I left her, delicious mouth slightly parted. I let my last ball fly down the lane, but it swerves off into the gutter.

We're well into our second game when a loud giggle pulls my attention to the next lane over. After Grant's girlfriend showed up, the girls all split off into the next lane over, and my score plummeted into the double digits.

Dev corners me, groaning. "I enjoyed having your girlfriend on my team more than you."

I can't disagree with him. "Sorry. Bit distracted."

"I can see that. How'd you land her? She's always seemed cool when we've run into her at Top Shelf, but you've never come there with us."

Now I'm sweating. The web of secrets I've been keeping from the team are all tangled up. Reveal one truth and the rest all come spilling out. I could make something up, but starting off my team bonding experiment with a lie doesn't seem like a great idea. "She signed up for the Walk Safe program I volunteer with."

A light bulb clicks behind his eyes. "Walk Safe? Where you escort people around campus. Is that where you disappear to in the evenings?"

"Got me. Sorry, no dungeon orgies." With how closed off I've been, the guys have started all kinds of rumors about where I go in the evenings. The stories got wilder and wilder as the year went on.

He snorts. "You knew about that?"

"Yes, I did. You guys are not exactly known for using your quiet voices."

He rubs a hand across the number two shave of his dark hair. "True. I think my personal favorite was the one where you're a green alien observing earth from inside a human skin suit."

"Who's to say that one isn't true?" I flick out my tongue in a lizard move.

He slaps me on the back with a laugh. "Glad you came out tonight. It's about fucking time you joined the team for real, and if she's the one who got you to do it, then she's ok with me."

High-pitched cheers ring out from the next lane and I see Serena and another girl with blonde hair hugging Jazz. Summer, I think. They're jumping up and down. She takes a deep bow, and then they make their way back over to us.

I grab her hand, because there's an irresistible urge to touch her gripping me, but a hug feels like it might be a bit too much.

"Fantastic job. Where'd you learn to bowl like that?"

Her eyes are sparkling under the multi-colored lights sweeping the alley. "I was on a bowling league growing up." She smacks her hands over her face, sliding her fingers open a crack to look at me. "Does that sound as incredibly dorky to you as it does to me?"

I nod. "Yes, but I love it. I've got my share of dorky hobbies, so I'd never judge."

"Good. I mean, it's a chore being seen with a hockey player, but I'm willing to push through if you are."

"Uh huh. Is that so?"

Her soft hand squeezes mine, feeling just about perfect against my fingers.

"Yup. But I guess I'll just have to bear with it."

"Good to hear. You ready to head home?"

"Yeah. I think so."

"We're out guys. Thanks for the fun time." I wave the ugly shoes at them with my free hand.

"You don't want to keep the party going? We're heading over to Wright's," Grant says.

"Nah. Not tonight. Unless you want to?" I turn to Jazz.

"I'm good. This was great, but I've got an early shift tomorrow. I should get home."

While the thought of more socializing is exhausting, the last time I went to Wright's, I ran into Charlene. "Are you sure? It might be a good idea to at least make a brief appearance as a couple in a public place. Especially one where the hockey team is known to hang out."

She pauses, nibbling on her lip, and I can see the conflict on her face. She's thinking of saying yes, but if she does, I feel like she'll be just caving to the pressure.

"Umm. I guess I could go for one drink."

It's written all over her face now, lips pressed together in a thin line, shoulders tense. She's saying yes because she feels obligated, not because she really wants to.

"Don't worry about it. We can do it another time." I feign a yawn that turns into a real one. "I'm pretty tired myself." It's not a lie.

There's gratitude shining in her eyes that I don't deserve.

We don't say too much on the way home, but I get out to walk her to the front entrance of her apartment building.

I throw an arm over her shoulder when she shivers. The temperature dropped while we were at the bowling place, and a slight sprinkling of rain has us hustling up the walkway.

I follow her through the unlocked glass door, waiting while she fumbles in her big bag for her keys.

"Need some help? I think Grant is taking some archeology classes."

She looks up from her scrabbling, blowing a bit of hair off her face. "What?"

I shake my head at her, pressing my lips together to control the laugh. "You look like you might need some specialty tools to find anything in that bag. What are you keeping in there? A guitar?"

The look she gives me could probably freeze my balls off if she really meant it, but then her lips twitch up too, and the frosty glare melts into mirth.

"You never know what you're going to need. Always be prepared and all. Isn't that what the boy scouts say? Ha." She pulls her keys out of her bag with a jingle, shaking them at me triumphantly.

My attention is pulled from the keys back to her face. That killer smile of hers is crinkling the corners. It knocks the breath right out of my chest.

I lean in a little closer, drawn to her warmth, lifting a hand to sweep that one errant strand of black hair behind her ear. "I was never a boy scout. I wouldn't know."

Her smile falters, lower lip falling open, shining eyes lifting to meet mine, and she leans in a fraction of an inch. Just enough to give me the encouragement I need to follow suit. I'm drawn to her. The curves of her cheeks, the full lips, long lashes dropped half closed over her beautiful eyes. This wasn't part of the plan. This attraction tugging me closer to her. I'm mesmerized by her molten chocolate eyes, and her easy camaraderie with the team. Even her awkwardness and unexpected bowling skills are adorable.

Our lips are so close I can feel the heat of her breath brushing mine when a gust of wind sends a shiver up my back. Jazz's keys hit the floor with a clatter that breaks the spell. That was close. What just happened? This is not how this is supposed to go.

My head bumps hers as we both bend down to pick up her keys.

"Sorry." Our words ring out at the same time.

I shoot a dirty look at the back of the man that's opening the inner doors to the building. It felt like a chance we might not get again. Probably for the best, though. This whole thing between us is fake. I don't want to get wrapped up in a real relationship with real feelings. That's what I've been trying to avoid here. When we agreed to this, I thought it would be fine. But maybe I've been celibate for too long. An innocent conversation is getting me all worked up. It's just lust though. I'm not some horny sixteen-year-old. I can keep that shit under wraps.

CHAPTER ELEVEN

PRACTICE RUN

JAZZ

M y eyes scan the room when I get to entrepreneur-ial business class, seeking a familiar face. When they land on Amira, I make a beeline to grab the seat next to her. I've got some damage to repair. Might as well start now. It's only September. The perfect time to make up for the mistakes I made last year. Otherwise, it's going to be a really lonely one with a fake boyfriend and only occasional time with Jordan.

"Hey. Can I sit here?" I don't want to make any pre-sumptions. This girl used to be my friend, but that doesn't mean she wants anything to do with me anymore.

Her deep blue eyes flick up from the sparkly silver notebook in front of her. She's always got the best acces-sories. "Jazz?" Guilt twists my guts at the surprise in her eyes. We used to be close.

"Yeah. Look. I'm sorry..."

"It's fine, Jazz. How are you doing?" She glances over my shoulder as if she's expecting the shadow of my ex to be lurking there. And I guess I've been feeling like that too.

"Yes. I'm good."

Other students are hustling in, filling up the seats in the smaller classroom. If she says no, I'm going to have to traipse around looking for an empty spot.

She seems to realize my dilemma. "Sit. Yes, please. I'd love for you to sit with me."

Relief rushes over me. My hand is a little shaky as I drop my bag onto the desk, pulling out all of my supplies. Pencil case, notebook, textbook.

By the time I've finished shuffling everything around on my desk, I can feel eyes on the side of my head. I swivel around to see Amira staring at me, curiously. Her hand falls on top of mine, stilling the constant motion.

"How are you really doing?" There's a soft unspoken question behind her words. One that I can identify but makes me a little uncomfortable. It's hard to face people I care about knowing let myself get into a such a bad situation. Let a guy control me.

"I'm doing well. I had a good summer, worked at this new cafe near my house. It was good. Just what I needed."

"And..." She nibbles on her lower lip as if she's debating her next words. "Darryl? Are you still with him?"

"Nope. I broke up with him before I went home for the summer." My hands are busy again, shifting things around the smooth surface of the desktop. I may have dreaded talking about him, but my shoulders feel just a little lighter saying them out loud.

Her smile widens. "Good to hear."

Chapman rushes down the aisle at that moment. His cell phone is pressed to his ear as he makes rapid progress to the front of the room. As he steps behind the podium, he slides the phone into his pocket and swipes a hand through his close-cropped dark hair.

"My apologies. Just a minor emergency." He's flipping his laptop open and clicking some buttons to share his screen on the board as he's talking. "The calls never stop when you're running your own business. Sure you all still want to be here?"

Polite laughter ripples through the student body and I turn to Amira one more time. She's focused on the board, listening to the professor as he launches into his lesson.

My next class is at the other end of campus, so I don't get another chance to connect with my former, hopefully current, friend again. Gotta hustle to make it to Redman Hall, but as I'm rushing through the heavy wooden doors, a text notification pops up.

> **Having a little informal get together with the gang next week before we dive into our game plans for the year. Wanna come?**

I'm almost floating after reading the message from Amira. Maybe this year is salvageable after all. I'm so preoccupied staring at my phone my shoulder is colliding with a person before I spot them. I glance up.

"Sor..." The apology dies on my tongue and my limbs feel like they've been filled with lead weights.

Darryl's turned all of his charm on, and he's got a lot of it when he wants to, but he can't fool me anymore. I can see the darkness underneath the thousand-watt smile.

"Jazmin, I brought you these." The sweet smell of the red roses is enough to turn my stomach sour. Roses were never my favorite flowers, but he never listened when I told him that, and now the sight of them sends a chill up my spine.

I glance over his shoulder, searching for an escape route, or someone to help me out, but everyone is in a hurry, rushing to their next class. Everybody probably thinks this is some romantic gesture from a sweet boyfriend, anyway.

Other students are milling around, heading off down the path I need to follow as I try to duck around him. "I've got to get to class."

He shadows my movement, blocking my path. "I just want to talk to you, Jazmin."

His heavy hand lands on my shoulder as I flinch away. This is what I get for avoiding conflict. Now it's haunting my every step this year. I can't have him showing up every single place I go.

"I'm going to be late, Darryl. Please get out of my way so I can get to class."

"Take the flowers and promise you'll talk to me later and I'll let you go."

Flames rip through me. "You'll let me go? You don't get to let me do anything. I've got to go. I'm not making you any promises. My boyfriend wouldn't like it if he knew you were threatening me." My mind was so clouded with fear, I didn't think to drop that oh so important fact before. The whole point of our fake relationship.

He jerks back, so many emotions crossing his face. Shock, then doubt, then the smug satisfaction I hate. As if he still thinks he can control me. His fingers clench in a painful squeeze then relax, giving me my chance.

I pull away, darting around him to hit the path. I can feel him behind me, but I don't turn around. He won't do anything out in the open like this. I don't love that he's following me to my next class, but he clearly knew where to find me. He probably knows where all my classes are. I clutch my bag to my chest, pushing myself into a walking speed that verges on running.

"Who is it? Who are you dating?"

Who do I need to threaten is what I'm hearing. The tiniest of smiles cracks my lips at the thought of him trying to take on Cole. That would be a fight he would lose.

"None of your business."

"I don't need you to tell me. It's got to be that hockey player. I've seen you hanging out with him."

That almost stops me in my tracks, and my blood turns to ice in my veins. "What?"

"I've seen you around with that Schaeffer. I looked into him. He's bad news. Got kicked off his last team for fighting."

It would be hilarious if it wasn't so creepy. Cole is bad news? Compared to him. I leap up the concrete steps two at a time to get into the relative safety of the building.

"It's none of your business. You need to stay away from me."

And even though Darryl's words mean nothing, a tiny particle of doubt is lingering as I duck into my classroom, leaving him behind.

Cole never told me about getting kicked off his team. Could that be true? It could, but what difference would that make? He's been nothing but kind to me. On the other hand, my instinct for spotting an asshole is trash.

No. It's fake. I'm fine. I can't let my asshole of an ex get to me. He's already taken up far too much of my life.

Darryl's visit lingered in my mind all day, leaving me a little jumpy. I'm running my gloved hands up and down the thighs of my fleece lined leggings, watching each set of headlights approach and then drive by my apartment building. It's still five minutes until he said he'd be here, so I'm not sure what's got the butterflies dancing away in my stomach.

Cole said he'd drive me back to campus for our first Walk Safe shift together. The kiss we almost shared after bowling last week is nagging at me. I hope he doesn't say anything about it. I need this even more after today. The protection of my fake boyfriend. I can't let anything mess it up.

A car finally pulls up into the curved drop off area in front of our building, and I'm flying out the front door. The pleasant crunch of leaves accompanies me to his car.

The dim lighting under the overhang does nothing to diminish his smooth walk as he exits the car and walks around to hold the door open for me.

"You didn't need to do that."

"My grandfather would disown me if he thought I wasn't opening doors for ladies."

Affection for his grandfather comes through in the warm tone of his voice, and I love that. I'm so close to my own family, and I miss my grandfather so much.

"So you're close with your family."

"Yes. I miss them. My dad, and sisters. My grandpa moved away to live with my uncle in California after gran died, but I still talk to him all the time. He's even learned to FaceTime. To be fair, he's not good at it. More often than not, I'm looking at a closeup of his neck, but he still tries. How about you?"

"Oh, we're close. I miss them. But they're a lot, so I've enjoyed my time away here at school. Figure myself out away from the mass chaos. It's hard to shine and have something that's your own in a big family. You know?"

"Not really. Small family. But I get where you're coming from. It's easy to get lost in someone else when they have a big personality. Does that make sense, or am I way off base?"

"Totally makes sense."

"And by the way, I can't imagine you not shining wherever you are. There's a light inside you that makes the day a little brighter."

I'm not sure how to respond. At first, the compliment wraps around my heart like a warm hug. But Darryl used to say stuff like that to me when we first started dating. And then the nice words became helpful suggestions, which turned into outright criticism. Pretty words mean nothing if they're not backed up by actions. But he's not Darryl. I need to remember that.

He turns back to the wheel, clearing his throat, and I sneak the occasional peek at his profile. The sporadic light of the streetlamps we pass under deepen the shadows of his chiseled features, and he doesn't take his eyes off the road.

I'm not sure if I'm just wary after everything that went down with Darryl or if I've always felt this way. I need to get over it. It'll be weird if I'm shy around my new boyfriend, right?

"Hi, Kenneth." Cole ducks his head, nodding to the thin guy wearing skinny jeans as we get to the Walk Safe office.

"Cole. Jazmin. This is your first shift, right?"

"Yup. You can call me Jazz."

He nods, pulling a yellow lanyard out of his pocket to unlock the cupboard where the phones are kept. The thing he hands me is like a brick encased in a thick protective case. He then hands me my own yellow lanyard with a shiny badge on it.

I wrinkle my nose at the picture. Of course I look like a convict who got caught on the run after shoplifting at Walmart, mouth a thin line, eyes hard. Brushing my hair and touching up my makeup before they took it was a waste of time.

Kenneth flashes his badge at me. His eyes are wide, mouth hanging open, and his skin looks almost ghostlike. "It's ok. I think it's physically impossible to get a good badge picture. My apologies."

I glance down at the other one he handed me. Cole looks dark and brooding, like the hero of a romance novel. How is that possible? That he looks hot even in an ID picture. I bet the jerk looks good in his driver's license photo.

Kenneth tilts his head, laughing. "Except Cole. He's a mutant."

I shove the offending thing at Cole as he comes back over with a couple of safety vests. "How is that fair?"

"What did I do?"

"You look hot in your badge pic."

"What?" His brow is crinkled in puzzlement. "You think I'm hot?"

"What? No, I don't think you're hot. I just mean..." The sentence dies on my lips when I remember our deal. My eyes dart over to Kenneth, but he's busy tapping away on a laptop, so I don't think he missed my slip. Obviously, I'm supposed to think he's hot. He's my boyfriend. "Nobody should look this good in an ID photo."

He shrugs. "Can't help it, Coffee Girl. Comes naturally. Yours can't be that bad. Let me see."

I jerk it back when he tries to grab it. "It's awful. Trust me. You don't need to see that."

"Well now you've piqued my interest. I have to see it." He steps in closer, crowding me, and my breath comes a little faster.

I've got the same trapped feeling as when Darryl had me cornered earlier today. Cole seems to realize though and backs up, raising his hands in the air.

Able to breathe again, I realize I was being ridiculous. He was just goofing around. I close my eyes and hold out the badge for him to see.

"You're right. That's terrible. What are you in for? Selling counterfeit jeans?"

My eyes fly open to see his chest shaking with laugher. I smack him on the arm.

"Shut up."

I grab the vest from him and stalk off, not checking to make sure he's following me.

He easily keeps pace with me, even pulling ahead to hold the door open. The last vestiges of the sun slipped away while we were inside, dropping the temperature by several degrees.

"You know, I don't think of myself as a vain person, and I like bright colors generally, but somehow I don't think neon orange is doing it for me."

Cole laughs, squeezing my elbow through the puffer jacket. "I like it. I'll always be able to find you, in a club, in class..." He stops for a minute. "At my game on Saturday night?"

My heart was already thrumming in my chest, but it kicks up another notch at the question. He's a little hesitant, and it's kinda cute. Does he think I'm going to say no? "Well, I can hardly say no, right?"

His dark brows pinch together. "Of course you can say no. You can always say no."

A gentle breeze slips by, rustling the sparse leaves on the massive tree we've stopped under. "I know. I just meant. Wasn't that the expectation for this whole deal? Show my face at your games?"

He pushes off and resumes our walk around campus, waiting for any calls to come in on the Walk Safe phone he's got hanging off a utilitarian black belt clip. "Yes, I guess. But if you're busy, you don't have to come."

"Let me check my social calendar." I laugh, tapping on my phone and pretending to check my calendar. It's sadly empty, still. Jordan is staying in Chicago with Aspen for the weekend, and my other friends, well, I'm still working on that. I am looking forward to the meetup with my entrepreneur group, but that's on Sunday. "Clear. I'm all yours."

Am I imagining the sharp inhale he takes at my words? Not entirely clear.

"Good. That's good. So I'll get you a ticket. You can sit in the friends and family area, so at least you'll know a couple of the girls. And I'll make sure you get a jersey to wear. That's the most important part."

"Sure." Will it be one of his jerseys? One that he's worn before with that spicy hint of his cologne clinging to it. That makes me think of what it would be like to wear something of his. To have that delicious scent wrapped around me, which makes me think of how close we almost got to kissing.

At least we're walking again. Following the paved pathways around the beautiful campus. It's an interesting mix of old red brick with ivy crawling up the walls, and modern buildings with lots of glass. I loved Lakeview from the moment I stepped foot on the campus. A little pain squeezes my heart at the thought of leaving the place behind at the end of the year. Graduation looms over my head with an insistent pressure.

The need to start my career, and hopefully my own business, is a lot. Leaving behind college is like jumping off a cliff, and hoping there will be a soft place to land on the other side, eventually. My family would take me in any time, but I can't go back there. To the place where I was never my own person. Just one of the Herreras. I want something of my own. To prove that my dreams are just as important as my siblings.

"So..."

"What do you..."

We break the silence at the same time. "You go first." I'm willing to talk about whatever he wants to, especially if it's not that thing that's been weighing heavy on my brain.

He laughs. "I was just going to ask you what you like to do in your spare time? I feel like I should know those things, being your boyfriend and all."

My shoulders relax. "You definitely should. Well. I love coffee. I know. I know. That sounds unbearably nerdy, but my family used to have a coffee farm in Costa Rica, and my grandfather used to talk about it all the time. His love of the land. Growing the trees, cultivating new varietals."

"Coffee grows on trees?"

"Yes. Yes, it does. Where did you think it came from?"

"You know. I'm sorry to tell you. I've never really thought about it before. Tell me about it."

His lack of knowledge doesn't surprise me, but his interest does. Most people zone out when I get into the intricacies of different species, or washed vs semi washed processing methods. "It's ok. Not many people think about it on the regular. They just order their coffee and knock it back to get through the day. That's why I love talking about it. I will warn you, though, that once you get me started, you might end up falling asleep on the bench over there when I don't stop." I gesture to the stone bench off to the side of the walkway.

He slides an arm around my shoulder. "You could never put me to sleep. I love the sound of your voice. Not to mention that little spark of light that glints in your eyes when you get excited about something."

"What are you talking about?" Heat burns a trail up the back of my neck.

He grabs my hand, pulling me to a stop and spinning me around right under the doorway to the library. His hand is a little rough when he slides his fingers under my chin, tilting my head up. I can't help but meet his gaze, and his lips curve up in a slow smile. "That one. Brings out the little specks of gold around your irises."

"Oh." The heat that started in my neck is spreading like a wildfire through my body. Put on the brakes. I pull back out of his grasp. "We should maybe talk about the thing from the other night."

He releases his hold on my chin, taking a step back to give me my space. "What thing?"

He's going to make me say it out loud, isn't he? "The kiss. Almost kiss." I hastily correct myself in a whisper.

His eyes darken. "Yes, the almost kiss. I didn't want to bring it up. Wasn't sure if you'd want to talk about it."

I blow out an exasperated breath. "We should make rules about that. Should we be actually kissing when we're only fake dating?"

"We might need to occasionally. In public, at least. If people are going to buy the whole dating thing, they'll probably expect at least the occasional peck. If you're okay with that. I wouldn't do anything you're not comfortable with."

He makes an excellent point. "But won't it confuse things?"

"I think we can handle it, right? Neither of us is looking for anything real right now, correct?"

I nod. His words are logical. "True."

"Then I think we can handle it, but maybe we should practice. Just once. To make sure we're going to be ok with it before we do anything in front of anyone else. Less pressure."

His beautiful dark eyes are pulling me under. Hypnotizing me with their depths. "Sure."

His lips curve again in that twisty smile that looks happy and a little angsty at the same time. "Really? You don't sound convinced."

Oh, he has no idea how convinced I am that I want to taste his lips, maybe slide that full lower one between my teeth and give it a little nibble. But that would be a terrible idea. "I'm sure."

I'm already leaning in, eyes fixed on his mouth when the phone rings with a call, shattering the spell of the moment, pieces drifting off on the wind.

He groans, grabbing the phone. "Hello, Walk Safe." The husky tone of his voice does nothing to cool the heat of my skin, but that's not what we're here for.

He slides the phone back into the case on his belt. "McKenna building. Let's go."

His gloved hand closes on mine in a comforting squeeze before he starts up at a brisk pace toward the science building we've been called to.

"We'll take this up later," he says.

But we don't. It turns out to be a busy night, full of calls to meet other students, and neither of us brings it up again on the ride back to my apartment. It feels like we missed the moment and I wonder if we'll ever catch back up to it, or if I even want to, because that's not what we're about. That's not what this relationship is about. It's a fraud. An illusion. In a different, more honest way than my last relationship was, but still not real. And that's the way I need it to stay.

CHAPTER TWELVE

ALONG FOR THE RIDE

COLE

T he arena is packed for our home opener. Hockey has always been a popular sport at Lakeview. But after winning the championship last year, the general student body has latched on to ride along on the success of the team. No pressure or anything.

Unfortunately, we haven't closed the gap that was left behind when we lost our entire first line of forwards to graduation. It's what you'd call a building year, and that doesn't work for me. Being less than the best is unacceptable. I've got my family to think of and my reputation to repair. I kept a pretty low profile last year after transferring here, but now with Charlene suddenly appearing back in my life, I'm worried. All I want is to put the past behind me and play my best.

I'm sitting in the corner of the locker room, gear on, eyes closed, head resting on the wall, trying to clear my head before the game when someone sits next to me.

"How's it going? You ready?" Beau asks in the smooth but commanding tone he uses when he's got his captain's helmet on.

I let out a long sigh. "I'm good."

"Listen. I wasn't sure if I should mention it before the game, but I thought it would be better than getting blindsided and losing focus while you're out on the ice. I scoped the arena and that girl of yours is sitting up front. Is that going to be a problem?"

My mind jumps to Jazz's smiling eyes and smooth dark hair when he refers to my girl, but that's not right. My guts churn when I realize he's referring to the other one.

"Not my girl. Not a problem." I hope the words are true, but the churning anger burning me from the inside points to the lie.

"Good. Look, man. I know you've got a lot going on, but the team needs you. You're the top goal scorer on the line this year. The other guys are going to be looking to you. You're going to set the tone for them, and part of that is really being a part of the team. Showing up and participating. I know after what you went through, it's hard for you to trust the other guys, but I need you to get there. Trust off the ice builds trust on the ice."

"Got it." Now that he knows what went down with my last team, it feels like he's in my head, and I'm not a fan. Trust is something you have to build, and I'm not there yet. The trouble is I don't know that I can get there. Not soon enough.

"You sure you're good?" His eyes skate over mine, searching.

"I've got this."

He pushes up from the bench, heading over to join Coach for a little pregame pep talk.

The uneasy feeling that had my brain swirling vanishes as soon as I'm staring down Luchek, my opposing winger. We're playing U Penn for our opener, and they've got the edge this year. We lost a good chunk of our top players to graduation, and even with some promising new talent on the team we're still building. They're in a better place, with only two new additions to their first string.

Luchek's eyes meet mine as the horn blasts setting off a flurry of sticks on ice, and the swish of skates pushing off to get in place. I spin around, keeping my eyes on the action. Grant loses the puck to our opponents, and they drive it toward our net.

Beau and Dev are in place, Dev muscles one of their forwards into the boards with a crash. I skirt the edges of the ice, eyes on Beau as he sneaks in to slip the puck away.

I try not to get too caught up in the noise and distraction of the crowd, but there's a neon yellow sign with my name on it directly behind the spot where Beau is.

The puck shoots straight at me and I'm a split second too slow to pull my eyes back into the game. Luchek takes advantage of my miss to snag it, driving it back up and passing it to their center in a quicksilver move that lights up our net. Fuck. The booing on our side hits me like a right hook, stealing my breath. My skin is tight, and I'm swallowing back bile as my eyes fall back to the cause of my distraction.

She's turned around to talk to someone behind her and her blonde hair brushes her shoulders just above the spot where my name is plastered across her shoulders in glaring gold letters. Heat rises to my head, threatening to suffocate me as my vision goes blurry at the edges.

While I'd love to slam a fist into the face of one of our opponents, that would be a terrible idea, so I slam a fist into the boards instead. The pain jarring my wrist shakes me loose from the clutches of the anger that was my first reaction at my ex's audacity. It dissolves as fast as it came.

"Schaeffer, I thought you said you'd gotten your head into the game?" Beau skates up to me. His tone is stern, but I've never seen the guy lose it. He keeps all his emotions on lock, especially on the ice.

"Sorry, Captain. I'm fine. I got this." And for the first time since she showed back up in my life, I realize I do. I'm practically growling, but it's more of an automatic reaction at this point. Seeing her wear my jersey is still irritating, but it's settled more into a numb disgust than rage.

"I hope so. We're in the middle of a game. An important one. This one is going to set the tone for the rest of the season. Don't blow it. You're not getting paid to play hockey now, but if you don't fuck things up now, you will be next year, and you won't be able to let your emotions get the best of you."

All the sympathy that was in Beau's tone before is gone. He's slipped into captain mode, and he's right. Fuck me if I let her get the better of me. If I let her ruin my lifelong dream. The way I'm going to help my dad and sister out. Get somewhere nice. Stable.

"You're right. I'm sorry."

He slaps me on the back with a gloved hand. "Good. And besides. You've got yourself a real fan now."

He points his stick into the stands, and I follow the neatly taped white tip to see. Her. The sight of her almost knocks the breath out of me, but it's grounding too. Pulls me out of the anger that was building back into my body. The numb helplessness gripping my limbs. I can feel the ice under my skates again, the cool air biting at my heated cheeks, and the noise of the crowd.

She's wearing the jersey I sent over, and it's everything. It's not some brand-new jersey anyone could purchase at the campus store. The rich purple fabric is slightly worn from washing. It's been on my body and now it's draped over hers I'd lament the fact that it's concealing that gorgeous body if not for the fact that her wearing my name feels right in a way I haven't felt in years. Maybe I shouldn't have given her that to wear, but I couldn't exactly afford a brand new one.

I pound the air, heading off the ice for the break. Nervous energy rides me while they get the local kids out on the ice for a shoot off. One of the little ones has a killer slap shot. Maybe one day he'll be out here with the Lightning working his way to the top. That used to be me. And that me would be disgusted that I was threatening my chances at making the pros over a girl. No matter how badly she hurt me.

When our line gets sent back onto the ice after intermission, I'm ready to go. Nothing can stop me. Not the girl who used to own my heart or the one that's threatening to settle in there despite my best efforts.

My vision tunnels to focus on one thing. The puck. I'm constantly tracking it, planning my next move to get ahead of our opponent's defensive line. I've always been good at finding the best spots. Small holes in the other team's defense, weaknesses in the goalie. Penn's goalie is good, but he's been going to his glove side more often than not tonight, and when he has to go stick side, he's a fraction of a second slower than usual. That tiny bit of hesitation looks like a minor injury he's favoring. Maybe a strain or pull. Probably minor, but enough to give me a slight advantage if I can convince my team to pass to me after that shitty lapse in attention earlier.

Grant snags the puck from Luchek when I'm hovering on the wrong side. I slide behind the net while he takes a shot. I know it's not going to make it in before I hear the clang of the puck bouncing off the bar. But I'm there in time. I scoop it up, sending it low and to the left.

Exhilaration fills me as I light it up with a goal that ties up the game.

My team crowds me, and the cheers from the fans fill me up even more, but I can't help myself from zeroing in on that one spot in the stands. The spot where she's sitting, and a warm pride tightens my chest when I see her on her feet, cheering me on.

The vibe in the dressing room is fire. Hail almost started a fight when he snatched the puck from Gillan near the end of the game. But I'm relieved I was able to contribute with my one goal plus the assist. There's so much more pressure weighing me down this year.

"Schaeffer, that goal you snuck in was a thing of beauty."

"I'm the one who scored the winning goal. You may all bow down before me," Hail shouts from across the dressing room.

Dev half rises out of his seat, glancing at Beau. But the captain gives a subtle shake of his head, and he settles back down with a grunt.

"Don't be a dick, Hail. This is exactly the attitude that's going to get your ass kicked if you don't smarten up."

Hail smirks, slinging his gear bag over his shoulder before he struts out. Probably going to snag a girl that will give him the admiration he's craving.

"Anyway, like I was saying. Good goal, Schaeffer. It's like you could see inside his head."

I nod, struggling to pull my plain white dress shirt on over damp arms. As I'm working through the buttons, I look up to spot Beau staring me down as he shrugs into his much fancier plum colored suit jacket. Right. I've gotten so used to keeping to myself that I've forgotten that these guys are my teammates. We're in this together.

"Smolders was favoring his left side. Maybe a slight injury. It seemed like my best chance."

A couple of heads whip around focusing on me. I stare at my fingers, heat creeping up my chest. I may have underestimated how deep inside myself I've hidden since I joined the Lightning. To attract that much attention for one observation.

"Really?" Grant's still got his stick in his hand and he's got his chin propped up on it as he studies me. "That is good information. Coach didn't even notice that one."

"Probably pretty minor. Maybe it was a new thing, but definitely something to keep in mind the next time we play them."

"Hey, Grant." I call at his back as he's walking toward the locker room door.

He swings around. "S'up?"

"Did you ask Summer to make sure Jazz knew where we would be coming out?"

A big, goofy grin spreads across his face. "Sure did. Anxious to see your girl, Coco?"

"She's..." I stop the words before they can get out. As far as my teammates are concerned, she is my girl.

My eyes skate over all the other girls waiting for us to emerge after the game until they land on her. Her loose, black hair is held back by a bright yellow daisy covered headband, and she's clutching her gloved hands around a glittery purple stainless-steel tumbler like it's her lifeline.

She's looking around, shifting from one foot to the other when she spots me. A tentative smile curls the corners of her lips. I return it, moving my legs a little faster now that I've locked on to her.

Summer squeals when she spots her boyfriend, leaving Jazz in her dust as she races over to jump into his arms. I freeze for a moment, not sure how to play this. Obviously, I can't go for an OTT gesture like that, but a handshake isn't going to cut it either. This is unfamiliar territory for sure.

My hands are hovering in the air, unsure of what move to make when I catch sight of the shiny blonde hair that threw me off my game. Charlene is pushing her way through the crowd to get to me.

I close my hands around Jazz's biceps to hide the light tremble, giving them a soft squeeze as I pull her into me.

A delicious mix of coffee and lilacs engulfs me when I lean in close to her ear.

"Do you think it would be alright if I kissed you now? I know we said we were going to do a practice run first, but..."

Her hair tickles my neck as she moves her head up and down in what feels like a nod.

"Cole!" The high-pitched voice is like a jagged knife in my back.

I slide my hands up to the back of her head and pull back to meet her dark brown eyes. They're wide with a tentative look in them that has me hesitating. She glances over my shoulder before turning back to give me a slight nod.

My eyes fall shut as our lips touch for the first time. She's soft under me, tasting of coffee and cherry lip balm. The world disappears as I get lost in my first kiss in a long time. Her hands close over my shoulders, fingers kneading into my achy muscles. There are too many forgotten sensations sparking up. All the silky hair, soft lips, and smooth skin are sending tingles through my body.

"Cole?" That insistent question jerks me out of the moment, and I pull back, reluctantly letting go of Jazz. The reason for the kiss is a firm reminder that it's not real. This is all for show, no matter how good it felt.

I turn around, irritated and also relieved at the interruption.

"I thought I told you not to show up here again, Charlene."

Her red lip pokes out in an exaggerated pout. "Who is this, Cole?"

"Not that it's any of your business, but this is my girlfriend, Jazz." I'm reluctant to let go, wanting to protect her from the flaming daggers shooting out of my ex's eyes. Her waist is soft and comforting under my hand.

"Girlfriend?" She narrows her eyes at us. "I heard you didn't have a girlfriend."

"Well, you heard wrong. I'm tired. We're getting out of here."

I take a step forward, tugging my fake girlfriend with me. It makes me a little uncomfortable to use her as a shield against my ex. But that's what this is all about. We both agreed to this thing.

"Cole. She'll never make you happy. And I'll be here for you when she can't keep you satisfied."

My chest rumbles with a bitter laugh. She says that as if she didn't destroy what little trust I had left by stomping my heart under her heel while I watched her riding my teammate.

"Ow, Cole." Jazz tugs her hand away from me. Shit, I must have been squeezing it too tight.

"I'm so sorry." I pick it back up gently, and flip it over to kiss her palm, trying to soothe the ache I caused.

"It's fine. Just a little tight."

"Sorry. Charlene threw me. I should have been more careful with you."

"I'm not made of glass. Just wasn't expecting it."

We make it out of the arena with no further incidents, and I automatically head for the piece of crap car I inherited from Jacks when he left last year. He was reluctant to leave Mabel behind, but he's probably consoling himself behind the wheel of the brand new Jeep he bought himself with his contract money. Next year can't come soon enough for me.

I'm pulled to a stop when Jazz halts, and I spin around. "What's up?"

She's clutching that coffee tumbler to her chest again. "I should go. I've got to catch the bus home."

"You're not going to come back to the house? The guys are having a party tonight, and it would be nice to have you there."

Her lower lip is tucked between her teeth as she nibbles away, and it reminds me of how good she tasted. I shift on my feet, trying to be subtle about easing the tightness in my pants. Don't want to scare her away. "No. I should get home. Her head swivels around toward the university center.

"That's fine, but you're not taking the bus."

"What?"

"You're my girlfriend now. I'll drive you home."

Her hand flies up to her mouth, so she can nibble on a fingernail. She can't be as uncomfortable as I am after that kiss. I shift again. Maybe she noticed my situation, but it's not like I'm going to jump her on the ride home.

"Not your real girlfriend. You don't have to drive me home."

"Yes, I do, Coffee Girl. What if your ex is lurking around again?" Rage flares up in my chest when I think about the last time I had words with that asshole. No way is she taking the bus. Not on my watch.

It's as if she shrinks into herself, elbows pulled tight into her sides, shoulders hunched, and I want to wrap my arms around her to soothe the fear. The fear that I put there like the dumbass I am.

"I'm sorry. I wasn't trying to scare you. I'll walk you to the bus stop if you'd rather, but I'd really like to drive you home."

Her shoulders loosen a little as she looks back at me. "Yeah, that would be nice."

"Well, I can't promise it'll be nice." I roll my eyes, thinking of my ancient car as she follows me.

I hold out a hand behind me and am rewarded with the warmth of her palm slipping into mine. My pace slows to match hers as we walk through the well-lit parking lot for student athletes.

Mabel looks better than usual when we reach her. All the rust spots and worn paint are not as prominent in the shadow of night. The passenger door lets out a painful squeal as I wrench it open. "But at least I think it's better than the bus."

She laughs, slipping under my arm into the well-worn seat with the mysterious stains on it. I'm just happy to have a ride, though. I've never had my own car. Couldn't afford it.

"It's better than the bus." She pats the beige dashboard.

"How'd you like the game?" I ask her, doing an extra shoulder check as I pull out of the parking lot. The driver's side mirror is a bit wonky.

"It was great. I've come to some games before with Jordan, but this was the first time I had a person of my own to root for. Made it a bit more exciting." She gasps. "I mean. Not that you're mine, but we're friends now, right?"

I chuckle. I kind of liked hearing her lay claim to me. "It's fine. Yes, friends. We're friends. It's nice for me too. My family lives so far away they never get to come to my games. I liked having you out there cheering me on." They used to come watch me. At my old school. Thanks to Charlene and Jeremy, that's no longer a possibility.

"Well, you were amazing. That goal was fire. Had me on the edge of my seat."

Good to hear. "I think you're stuck now."

"What do you mean?"

"I think you're my good luck charm. You're going to have to come out to all my games now."

Her eyes narrow and she pulls back into herself. I'm not sure what I said to cause that. "I can't come to all your games. I've got other things to do."

"I know."

She's struggling with the door even before I've put it in park, so I reach over to still her hand. "Hey, I'll grab it."

I get out of the car, coming around to her side to pull the complaining door open. She scrambles up, but I grab her hand before she can scurry away.

"Thanks for coming tonight. It really was great to have you there. Can we get together sometime this week? Make a little public appearance to keep up the illusion."

Her nod is small and tight. "For sure."

"Great. See you soon, Coffee Girl."

Her lips tug up at the corners at the nickname.

"See you soon, boyfriend."

CHAPTER THIRTEEN

SECRETS AND PIES

JAZZ

T he heavenly aroma of espresso still hasn't taken over the new store smell when I walk through the glass front door of Cool Beans. The board game cafe opened at the end of the summer, and I haven't had a chance to stop in yet. Well-worn boxes line tall shelves around the back three corners of the room.

I take my time walking around the tables, hugging my worn backpack to my chest like a shield. The five of them are laughing, and Rob is dealing out cards. It's been too long since I hung with my friends.

Amira glances up, her face lighting up when she sees me. "Jazz. I'm so glad you came. Which baby unicorn do you want to be?"

My shoulders finally relax at the warm welcome and the matching smiles on the faces of the group. Unstable

Unicorns, of course. I haven't played it in a while but it's pretty easy to pick up on. The main deck is laid out along with a handful of expansions, including the NSFW one. Nice.

"Baby Narwhal, of course. You better not have stolen him, Rob."

"Wouldn't dare," he says, shaking his head.

"I'm gonna grab myself a coffee before I sit down if that's ok." I glance at the menu board chalked onto the wall behind the rainbow-colored counter.

"I got you. Cappuccino, extra shot?"

The last of the tension flows out, and a warm feeling spreads through my chest. "Yes. You remembered. Thank you so much, Amira." Now I'm wondering why I was so nervous about reconnecting with them.

"Not a problem at all. You can buy the chips and guac later. They make homemade chips here, and I've heard they're life changing."

I glance around the table, searching for any sign that they're still mad about my desertion, but there is nothing but kindness here. Molly, Rob, Trinity, and Deacon all look as happy to see me as Amira did.

"Will do."

Three hours fly by in a blur of laugher until we're rushing to clean up the game pieces scattered across the table so the next group can claim it.

"And here I am, bringing my business plans with me and everything. I thought maybe we'd get in a bit of time to chat biz stuff."

"We could take this somewhere else for a little chat if you feel like it," Rob says.

Molly glances over my shoulder at the wall clock, lips pursed. "Wish I could, but I've got a date."

"Yeah, sorry, Jazz. I've got plans too," Trinity says, twirling a brown curl around her finger.

"I've gotta go meet Phil, but you're not going to bail out on me Tuesday to get started on the planning for our charity event, right?"

Amira asked me to be her partner on the project and I'm almost giddy with excitement. We've always worked well together, and I've been looking forward to this project since my freshman year.

Everyone else bows out, leaving me alone with Rob. "Wanna hit group study at the library?" I ask.

"I'm still kind of hungry. How about Ethel's?"

"How could you possibly be hungry? I think I ate my weight in chips and popcorn."

"I'm always hungry. Part of the athlete's life."

Right, he's on the football team. Tracks. He's a huge dude, but I just always think of him as a business friend.

My budget is lean, and I spent my going out funds for the day here, so I'm trying to think of an excuse.

"I'm paying. Come on. Gotta feed the beast."

I nod, the tinkling chimes of the door signaling our departure.

Hay bales, scare crows, and pumpkins nestled on every street corner set the perfect mood. Fall is my favorite season. Give me a fuzzy scarf, a pumpkin scone, and a hot apple cider and I'm a happy girl. And don't get me started on Halloween. Costumes and candy. Sign me up. Unfortunately, I don't have any plans this year.

"It's so pretty along here, isn't it?"

I really have to step up my pace to keep up with Rob's long strides. Rob is a fair bit broader than Cole, but Cole's got an inch or two on him in the height department. Funny how I can always keep up with him, even on our long walks around campus at night. Like he adjusts his stride to match mine.

"Eh. Football season is the only good thing about fall. Other than that, it's depressing. Everything grey and dying. Not my fave."

We turn down Oak St. to get to Ethel's, passing several residential homes along the way. There are a few houses on this street that have gone all out for the season. Dancing skeletons, floating ghosts, and gravestones. I try not to let Rob's words deflate my giddiness.

Thankfully, the yellow curtains hanging in the windows of the diner are straight ahead. The silence was getting a little awkward.

Warmth, and a friendly silver-haired lady greet us as we walk through the front door. The salty scent of french fries coats the place in a layer of comfort.

"Welcome. Come on in. You can hang your coats by the door if you like."

She hustles around at a rapid clip like we're little ducklings she needs to worry into line. Before I know it, she's got my coat hanging on a hook by the wall and we're heading for a cozy round table in the corner. Rob's long leg knocks the table as he settles in, then I pull back when his knee brushes mine. Maybe a little too cozy.

"Why don't we get something to eat first? No need to rush."

I look up from rifling through my backpack, the grant papers I was going to show him already in my hand. "Sure."

He's settled back in his seat full on manspreading when Ethel's granddaughter Gemma walks up to take our order.

"I'll have the double sirloin burger with fries, no onions."

I'm fumbling with the menu. Not ready to order yet. "I'll just have a coke, please."

"You're not getting something to eat? Come on. I told you I'd pay."

I'm not really hungry enough for a meal, but they have amazing pie here. "Hmm. A slice of blueberry pie, please."

"Whip cream with that, or ice cream?"

"Ooh, ice cream, definitely." I'm not one to ever turn down ice cream.

"Good choice."

"Thank you," I say. It's the worst when people don't treat their servers like humans. I have more than enough experience in that department to never do that to someone else.

"My pleasure."

The diner is not too busy right now. There's a scattering of people spread out around the tables, but it's a weird time of day. Not quite lunch, not quite dinner.

Rob's stare has me looking out the window beside us. It lets out into a big backyard that's been converted into an adorable patio, but the furniture is all tucked away to the side. Too late in the season for patio dining in Michigan.

"So, how are you doing? I heard... Sorry, I don't want to pry."

"What did you hear?"

"I'm sorry. I overheard Amira telling Trinity you broke up with your boyfriend. Are you okay?"

Right. Love these guys, but they are all a bunch of gossips. But it's not a secret. I look down at my hands, flexing my fingers to avoid the temptation to nibble on my nails.

"I did. It was the end of last year. It's been a while. I'm fine." Fine is an understatement.

"That's good. I'm glad to hear it." His lips curve up in a small smile. He takes a few big gulps from his water glass, throat bobbing. "Listen, I don't want to be too in your face, but are you seeing anyone else right now?"

"No." The response comes out on autopilot before I remember I am indeed seeing someone. At least as far as anyone else is concerned. "Well, sort of."

"Sort of?" He leans forward on his thick forearms. "Doesn't sound promising."

I lean away from him. "It's new. Very new."

"Anyone I know?"

"Cole Schaeffer. He's on the hockey team."

The smile slips off his face, and his eyes narrow. "You gotta watch out for those guys. They're assholes."

"Some might say the same of football players." I snap back, not liking his automatic judgment. Cole has been nothing but kind to me, and I've seen the way Aspen treats Jordan. That boy worships the ground she walks on.

His eyebrow arches in a question. "Are you calling me an asshole?"

"No. I'm just saying. You're judging them even though you don't know them. I bet people have done that to you before. But you're not just a football player. You're also a business major, and I know you're smart."

His smile is back. "Thanks. But it's not just that he's a hockey player. I've heard things about Schaeffer. He's bad news. Beat the shit out of a former teammate or something. That's why he transferred here. The athletic department isn't that big."

"I appreciate your concern, but I'm good." The spark of doubt that Darryl lit is flaring up into a full-fledged fire. I'm starting to realize Cole only gave me the basics of his story. He's been holding back on the reasons he left his old team.

"Let me know if you ever need any help, or if he does anything. I'm here for you, Jazz. I hope you know that."

He drops a hand on top of mine, and I appreciate the gesture, so I give him a smile and nod. "I will. Thanks, Rob. I've missed you guys."

"I've missed you too, Jazz. Glad to have you back in our group."

The busboy stopping by to clear our table halts our conversation for the moment, so I reach down, fumbling with the worn canvas of my backpack. The clasp is finicky, but I snap it open by the time he's cleared the dishes. I grab my binder and pull it out, placing it on the table in front of me.

There are plenty of tables open, so I don't feel guilty about staying past our welcome or indulging in a free refill of the surprisingly good coffee. Most diners don't know how to brew a good cup, but Ethel is one of a kind.

I drop my hands on the binder, leaning forward. "So, I'm planning for life post graduation, and I've been searching for business grants to start up my coffee shop. I was hoping you'd go over my applications with me. See if I missed anything or if you have any ideas to make them shine. I'm happy to help with anything you're working on in return."

He glances around, then down at the small round table. "How about we take this back to my place? More room to spread out?"

He's not wrong. The place is cramped, but I'm hesitant to go back to his place. "How about the library? We could go to the downtown one. It's just down the street, but they've got those big round group study tables. We can set up camp there."

"Sure." He flashes his blindingly white teeth at me, signaling the server for the check.

"Here you go, loves."

Ethel herself drops the black leather sleeve on the table, and I fumble through my big purse. Of course, my wallet has sunk to the farthest reaches of the void. I should really learn to carry a smaller bag.

"I told you I'll get this," Rob says, brushing my hand away. That gesture itches at the place inside me that's used to being brushed aside as the youngest of six.

I love the cozy corners of the downtown library. I'm always inspired when I'm surrounded by stacks of books. Today, we settle at one of the big tables in the group study area. Rob's sitting next to me, so I can show him the grant applications I've been working on. But he's so massive I have to shift my knee away to avoid him infringing on my space.

"Okay, so this one is specifically for female college students graduating with a business degree, so that's perfect for me." I run my finger down the mostly filled out questionnaire. "The only thing I'm worried about is this section. They're looking for an example of a business project you led that earned a profit. I could use last years from entrepreneurship but I'm not sure if it's strong enough." My nose scrunches up at the taste of the eraser on the end of the pencil I absently stuck in my mouth to nibble on.

He leans his head closer until we're almost touching, then turns his head. His eyes drop to the pencil between my lips. "What's the application deadline? If it's not too tight, you could use the project for Laybourne's class. Who are you paired up with?"

Right. The charity event. It didn't connect in my brain that would be considered profit, but we're going to be making money. Hopefully, lots of it. For a good cause. I've got an idea to run a coffee shop style event with a silent auction. "I'm working with Amira." My eyes run down the application. The deadline isn't until the end of the year. "That'll work. I'm actually really excited about that one. Thanks for the suggestion. So, what have you got going on? Anything I can help with?" I lean back in my chair to put a little distance between us.

"I didn't bring any business stuff with me since it was more of a social thing."

"Oh. Okay. Well, thanks for coming out to help me." I feel a little unsettled. Off balance, but I don't want to sound ungrateful. I'm glad he came out to help me with my stuff, but I'd feel better if I could return the favor. After my last relationship, I've gotten uncomfortable when I feel like I owe someone something. Darryl would always hold it over my head if he changed his plans for me or paid for dinner. I want to pull my own weight whenever I can.

"Any time, Jazz." He takes a sip of his coffee, leaning into me again.

I shift in my seat, gathering my papers. "Okay, I should head home now. I've got some work to do for my econ class."

He stands up while I'm still stuffing things in my bag. "Why don't you come back to my place? We can work on econ together."

Mind's whirring, looking for an excuse. Why do I even feel the need to look for an excuse? I have every right to say no. I hate this doubting side. "Nah, I'm pretty tired.

I'd like to get home, do my work and hit my bed. It's been a long day. I worked an open shift before I met up with everyone."

His eyes widen. "You did? Sorry about that."

Sorry? What's he sorry for? That I have to work to pay for a lot of the expenses of school? Sure, my scholarships help with tuition and books, but my family has six kids. They definitely don't have the unlimited resources to help us all through college.

We snag our coats on the way to the front door.

"Can I give you a ride home?"

"Actually, I can walk from here. My apartment is not that far, but thanks for the offer."

The sky is layered with pinks and oranges as we step out the front door, turning to the left. I didn't realize it had gotten so late.

Rob glances to the right then matches my stride to fall in beside me, feet crunching on the multicolored leaves littering the path.

"I'll walk you home."

"You don't have to."

"It's fine. My legs could use a good stretch after all that sitting, anyway. Plus, I'd feel bad if I let you walk home by yourself."

My tense shoulders ease up. Darryl is making me paranoid. He's a good guy. Making sure I get home safe. And it will be handy to have him with me if my ex pops up again.

"Thanks."

My place is less than a ten-minute walk from the diner, but we fill the silence with talk of our classes, and how the year is shaping up. Before I know it, we're walking up to the glass front door of the small building.

I fumble through my big bag, once again cursing myself for not carrying a smaller bag or at least organizing it better.

When I finally find my key and get the door open, I stumble as it gives way. There's a question in Rob's eyes when I turn around.

"Well, okay. See you in class."

His face falls just a touch, but then he smiles.

"See you soon, Jazz. Let me know if you need any more help with those grants."

"Will do. Thanks again."

My keys jingle as I wave at him, then beat a hasty path to the elevator. Rob's a good guy, but it's not as easy to be around him as Cole. Especially not with his apparent interest in starting something. But the thing with Cole has parameters. Rules to follow. Expectations. That makes it way easier to navigate our friendship. Except, now that I know he's hiding things from me, I'm wondering if I can trust him.

CHAPTER FOURTEEN

BABY PEACH

COLE

I 'm weaving around the orange cones I set up for my drills with Hail, eyes straying to the clock once again to see he's over ten minutes late now. Asshole. Why I got stuck trying to fix his issues is beyond me. And the fact that Beau is dangling my spot is fucking maddening.

The stomp of skates on the sidelines tells me he finally decided to grace me with his presence. He hops down onto the ice and takes off, whizzing around the outside of the rink without even a hello.

I pull off a glove to shove two fingers in my mouth, letting out a whistle shrill enough to stop traffic. His pace slows, and he gives me an irritated look, but doesn't stop his laps.

"Hey, asshole!" My shout echoes across the ice, cutting through the sound of his blades slicing along the smooth surface.

"What?" He calls back.

"I didn't come here to waste my time. I've got some drills planned, and I'm not putting in extra time because you couldn't be bothered to show up when I asked you to."

"Didn't ask you to stay longer. You can leave now if you want. I don't give a shit," he says, but at least he's skating toward me now. "This whole thing is stupid. Why the hell do I need extra work on the ice? I'm one of the best on the team, and I'm only a freshman. I'm going to be out of here with a signed contract before I hit my junior year."

"Not if you keep up that shit attitude. You might think you're god's gift to hockey, but you're a smaller fish here than you were in high school or juniors. And you'll be a freaking minnow when you get to the NHL, rookie. Better to get the sense smacked into you now rather than when you're playing against the greats."

"I'm going to be one of the greats. They'll be looking up to me."

Fuck. I am not equipped to deal with this. I knew he was a cocky motherfucker, but this is way beyond anything. "Excellent. Well, in the meantime, we're stuck together. Both of our spots are relying on me helping you with your teamwork skills. So, let's just get to it. We'll do some drills. Move on with our lives." Hopefully not have to deal with each other much beyond these weekly sessions.

"Why they paired me with you, of all people. In your senior year, kicked off your last team. No contract yet. It's bullshit."

If this is what it's like to have a kid, let that never be my fate. I shut my eyes, taking a deep inhale to stop myself from knocking some sense into his head.

"Anyway. We're going to do some passing drills. I've set up cones. That's your line." I point to the left side of the rink. "Circle a cone, then pass, circle pass, circle pass, and then you set me up to shoot at the goal."

"What? I don't even get to shoot on the net?" His stick clatters to the ice when he hurls it at the ground like the child he is.

"Nope. That's your problem. You always take the shot. You never set anyone up for goals or look at the situation to see what the best option is. If one of your teammates is open or has a better shot, you don't care. You're only looking for the glory of getting the goal."

"I'm just better than them. Why would I risk losing a goal they're not good enough to get it in?"

"And that's why you're here with me. Scoring is not your only job. Yes, it's important, but this game is about working together and meshing as a team. The better a line works together, the better off the team performs. That's how you win the cup. Not by constantly feeding your own ego." Oh, fuck. The words are echoing in my skull in a taunting rhythm. Maybe I understand why Beau gave me this assignment. At least Hail is too self-absorbed to realize how hypocritical they sound coming from me.

"Whatever," he says, skating off to the end of my cones.

Not sure how I'm going to do this all year. Maybe I can get him sorted out by the end of the semester.

We skate in silence, weaving through the cones, the only sounds the clash of the puck on our sticks, and our blades on the ice. We've got a solid rhythm going, passing the puck back and forth, and I'm feeling hopeful. I'll have to come up with a bunch more drills, but I can find those on YouTube. See if Beau has any recommendations. Maybe this will work.

I'm crouched down to the right of the net, waiting for the pass when he scoops it, slamming it dead center with a wicked slap shot. He throws his arm up, fist pumping the air.

"That's how it's done!"

I shake my head. Maybe not. "That's not how it's done, rookie. You're missing the point of the exercise. You get plenty of time to take shots on net. This is about passing. Not taking the shot."

He scoffs. "You can't deny I've got the best slap shot on the team."

I tilt my head to the side. "Grant has a pretty good one too, plus he knows how to work with his teammates. He's got the edge."

I retrieve the puck lining back up behind the cones. "Where are you from, kid?"

"I'm not a kid," he grumbles. "I'm from Pittsburgh. This isn't getting to know you time, though. I'm not telling you my life story and crying into our gloves."

"Wasn't asking you to." His glare is chillier than the air in the barn. "Look, let's just finish up a couple more lines, and then why don't you come back to my place? You can hang with the team." Perhaps a different method of team bonding will help.

He lights up. "I can come hang out at Beau's place?"

"Yes." Hopefully, some of the other guys are home. Seeing as how I usually keep to myself, I'm not that familiar with their schedules. What if I get stuck back there alone with him? Nightmare fuel.

"Okay." He skates over to his section, and we get going again with the exercise, passing and shooting. This time he makes the pass, so I can take the shot.

Five minutes left before the figure skating team takes over the rink.

"Go wild." I leave a stack of pucks and get in front of the net to let him take shots on me.

I'm not a goalie, but I stop a lot of them. He tends to go for the showoffy shots. Drilling them so hard at me I'm afraid I might end up with a bruise or two if I don't snag them. But he's not analyzing me to see where my weaknesses are or shooting for the high or low corners. That's something I'm pretty good at, so I definitely have a thing or two I can teach him in these sessions.

"Wrap it up. Let's shower and get back to my place."

This may be the first time I've invited someone to the team house as if it was my place. I really have been keeping to myself. That's not like me. Not how I used to be. And definitely not a true member of the team. My baby sister was right. I've started mending my fences this year, but

I'm going to have to keep it up and probably work twice as hard to bring this doofus along with me.

Fingers crossed my big bonding effort doesn't end in chaos.

Hail has a Mercedes SUV. I drag in a deep breath of the new car smell still lingering in the air. I've never had a new car in my life. Next year. Fingers crossed. I don't need anything fancy, though. Not like this.

"Nice ride."

He steps on the gas a little too hard, squealing out of the arena parking lot. I'm thrown into the door. Hope this thing isn't a rollover risk.

"It was my congratulations present when I got into Lakeview."

Must be nice. I'm getting a better picture of the rookie now. Spoiled, coddled, getting his superiority reinforced at every turn. Maybe not all his fault he's got an ego the size of Kansas, or Pittsburgh, I guess.

"Why didn't you drive in today?"

"Got a ride with Beau. No use taking two cars. I would have taken the bus home if you weren't coming with me." I stare at my hands, rather than at the bare trees whizzing by at an alarming right. Don't need that kind of stress.

"The bus. Gross."

"It's not so bad around here. I've been on worse."

"I wouldn't do it."

"That's because you've never had to. Next practice, I'll take you on the bus. It'll be good for you. Learn a little patience."

The car swerves a little when he shakes his head. "Nah. That wasn't part of the deal."

I breathe a huge sigh of relief when he pulls up in front of the team house. Not only did we make it here alive, but there are a few cars in the driveway. Looks like everyone is home. Good, good.

Laughter is booming from the small tv room where the gaming rigs are all set up, so I follow the noise.

Beau, JJ, and Grant all have controllers in their hands, and there are carts swerving around on the screen almost as erratically as Hail was driving his SUV. Dev has a well-worn book in his hand, but he's glancing up every now and again over the glasses perched on his nose to check out the action.

"Hi, guys."

None of them try to conceal the surprise on their faces when I greet them. There it is. What I've earned. Surprise that I'm participating at all with the team.

"Hey." Beau smiles his perfect smile at me. All straight, shiny white teeth.

"I brought the rookie home to hang for a bit."

Beau's assessing me, and I don't think he's finding me wanting this time around.

"Nice. Welcome, rookie. Come on in. Grab a controller. We're playing Mario Kart."

"Sweet. My name is Hail, though."

"Nah, you're the rookie for now. Deal with it. Maybe next year you'll earn a nickname of your own, but we won't be around to use it."

Dev snorts at Beau's comment. He's not as invested in his book as he was pretending to be.

"Fine," Hail grumbles. But I'm pretty sure he's just happy to be here. Maybe keeping him at a distance has been part of the problem. Only a tiny part. He's still a ginormous dickhead all on his own.

"I'll sit this one out." There are only four controllers, so I settle into the big red chair off to the side.

"Nah. You can have a turn. I'm gonna order some food for dinner."

I snag the controller before it can hit me in the face when Beau tosses it.

"Who do you wanna be, Coco?" Grant asks, scrolling through the selection screen.

"Iggy Koopa, obviously." I click over to make my choice.

"I'm going to be Bowser," Hail says. "What the fuck?" JJ snatches the controller out of his hand, choosing for him.

"Nope. You're Baby Peach."

I stifle a snort at Hail's glower as JJ hands the controller back to him. "How come he gets to choose his own character?" He tosses a head at me.

"Because he's a senior, and he lives here. You, my rookie friend, have the privilege of visiting and therefore we get to make the decisions."

"Not fair."

I catch Dev's eye as he looks up over the top of the book he's reading, lips pressed together in a thin line as he snorts. We share a nod before I settle back in my seat to focus on the screen that's a little too large for the small room.

Actually, to be fair, five hockey players are a bit much. Six when Beau gets back. Dev is sprawled in a burgundy leather recliner that would probably look big if his massive body wasn't overflowing it. JJ and Grant are taking up too much space on the couch, leaving no room for the rookie while I sink into the other armchair.

I'm almost breathing hard by the time the game is over. Rainbow road is the worst. "That was a tough one."

"Shut up." A pillow hits me in the head to punctuate Grant's point. "You smoked us all. You're a ringer."

I shake my head. "Nobody asked me about my skill level. I've been playing Mario Kart with my dad since I could hold a controller."

"Well, you could have told us that."

"Could have. But it was more fun this way." I'm smirking on the outside, but on the inside I'm warm and fuzzy in a way I haven't been here in Michigan.

"Don't be a sore loser, Grant." Beau walks back in, leaning on the doorframe with a smile on his face. He looks like a king surveying his peasants. I guess he kind of is the king now. Team Captain. Could have been me. In another lifetime.

This can't last, right? In retrospect, my old team in Miami was kind of toxic. I thought we got along well, but looking back, I know my old coach fostered a level of competitiveness that led to backstabbing and trying to steal the spotlight. We still had fun in our off hours, but it wasn't the same as it is here. I've missed so much.

I've been spending so much time remembering those good times and not remembering all the little things that led up to the big, shitty thing that drove me away. There aren't any signs of that kind of behavior between these guys, except maybe the dumb-ass rookie. Everyone genuinely seems to want to work together to make the team better, and I'm for it. But I still don't quite trust it.

CHAPTER FIFTEEN

PLAYING THE VILLAIN

JAZZ

I'm almost vibrating out of my skin as I roll the black tights up over my knees. Halloween is absolutely, without question, my favorite holiday of the year. I'm so glad Cole invited me to the party at his place. I'd go out to the bar, but I don't really have a girl gang right now to back me up. He told me I could invite my business friends along, so we'll see if any of them show up. It would be nice to have some of my own crew there, especially Amira.

The old school buzzer cuts through the poppy Halloween playlist I've got blasting as I dance around, tugging the skirt up over my hips. It's snugger than my usual flowy skirts and comfy pants. I dance over to the speaker box and hit the button.

"Hey, Coffee Girl. It's your boyfriend." At least that's what I think he's saying through the crackly speaker. The boyfriend word has my cheeks heating. It's not even real. Rein it in there.

"I'll be a few more minutes. You can come up if you want." I buzz him up, unlocking the door and hurrying back to grab my top before he gets here. My hot pink bra is cute, but not for the eyes of a fake boyfriend. It gives me a bit of a thrill, though, to think of what those rich, dark eyes of his would look like if they caught sight of me this way. Not happening. That would be a poor life decision. Right? Because I don't need to lose myself in another man.

I haven't even put all the pieces back together that Darryl tore apart. Some of them might be lost forever. I'm not the same person I was before him. My life has been split into two segments, and I need to move forward and figure out who I am now before I even think about letting another man in. No matter how delicious his arms are.

Shirt in place, I grab the crowning glory of my home-made costume. The magenta wig I carefully styled into a stiff long swoosh. I'm sure I'll pay the price later when there are dozens, maybe hundreds of bodies packed into their house dancing the night away, but until then I'm going to enjoy it.

There's a series of quick knocks on the door. Three short, two long and one more quick one.

"It's open," I call out, spinning around to face... a giant snuggly looking Charizard standing in my doorway.

The laughter shaking my shoulders probably ruins the bad ass pout I had going on to fit my character.

His eyes widen then drag down my body in a slow sweep, taking in every inch of my costume, but lingering on the bare strips of skin at my midriff and thighs. It's not a particularly revealing costume compared to some of the ones I've seen worn around campus over the years. But it definitely reveals more skin than I do most days of the year. Especially around here in the fall and winter months.

"Wow."

Pretty sure that's a good wow.

"I'm both turned on and terrified by you."

"Terrified?" My wig weighs down my head when I tilt it to the side.

"Obviously. Jessie is not nice to her Pokémon, you know, and hello." He sweeps a clawed hand up and down his body.

Good point. Jessie of Team Rocket is not one of the good guys. Part of the fun of a Halloween costume. You get to be the villain for a day. But it's only pretend.

"Don't worry, Charizard. I won't hurt you. I smirk at him.

He walks over until he's mere inches away, the heat from his body causing that flush to return.

He reaches a hand up, and my eyes drift half closed as his finger runs along my temple. I'm almost panting at this innocent touch. It has been too long since I've been with a man. Way too long.

After tucking a stray strand of hair under my wig, he backs away, and I kind of wish he wouldn't.

"Anything else you need to grab before we go?"

"Oh, yeah. Follow me."

I put a bit more wiggle in my steps as I walk to the kitchen, knowing the tight white material is clinging to it. If I'm going to have to suffer through this unfulfilled lust, then you bet I'm going to make him suffer a little too, if it's possible. If he's even interested in me in that way.

There are two overflowing plastic bins in the kitchen.

"You're bringing all of that with you?" Even as he questions me, he's bending over to scoop up the bins, testing one, then the other before choosing the heaviest one to carry. "I know you said you were going to bring some stuff for the party, but I was not expecting this."

Did I overstep? "I'm sorry. That one is decorations, and that one is food. It's not my party. You guys have probably got it covered. I didn't mean to..." My tongue can't keep up with my brain, and I'm tripping over my words to get them out. I shake my head, dropping a hand to his forearm. "We don't have to bring it."

He straightens his back, looking at me from under the dark lock of hair that's fallen in front of his eyes. His head tilts to the side. "It's fine, Jazz. Of course I'll bring your stuff. I just meant you didn't have to. We've got some food and a pumpkin. I think Dev put up some lights. But I'm sure whatever is in these boxes is a thousand times better."

It's like he read my distress, and he's going out of his way to reassure me. I jumped immediately to apologizing and backing down. Just like I would have if I slipped up and upset Darryl. But this is Cole. They're not the same. Not even in the same sport, much less league.

"Oh, okay. Good." My smile turns from a small one to a full-on grin again. Halloween vibes back on. "Because that sounds lame. Halloween is the best time of the year. If I'm going to be stuck at the hockey house, I may as well make it perfect."

"So, you're stuck at the hockey house now. I would have taken you out if you wanted. If it's such a hardship." One side of his mouth is quirked up enough to let me know he's teasing.

The fifty pounds of product I had to spray on the wig to make it perfect drags my head down as I shake it at him. "You know I was kidding. I'm actually so happy I can come over to your place to decorate. It's one of my favorite things about my favorite holiday." I grab the lighter bin that holds my decorations. I only put a few things up around my apartment, because it's just not the same when you've got no one to share it with.

There's a full-fledged smile on his face now. "It's my favorite too. Something about being able to dress up, pretend to be someone else for a little while. I've always loved it."

"Me too." There's a happy glow in my chest. I'm always a little suspicious of people who don't like Halloween. Unless, of course, they grew up somewhere where it wasn't a thing. They have my deepest condolences.

He looks up at me from under his dark brows and drops his voice to a growly rumble. "Do you like scary movies?"

I giggle at his attempt to put on a scary voice. It loses all the scare factor when he's swathed in bright yellow fleece. "Yes. Yes, I do."

"Maybe we can watch one later. After the party eases up. I can't promise that'll be too early, though. These guys do not keep normal human hours." He pulls back a fraction, clearing his throat.

Is he asking me to stay the night? And if so, do I say yes? Putting on a show in public is one thing, but what would it mean to be spending time alone together? Would it turn into something more? I thought the flutters of attraction that linger when he's around would dissipate if we spent time together. But they haven't. If anything, they've only intensified the more time I've spent with him.

"And you?" Unsure of how to answer I deflect, but it's a genuine question. I am curious about him. It's like we've shared some of our histories, but we don't really know all that much about each other. And I find myself wanting to dig deeper, to peel back the surface layers one by one.

"I believe in a good night's sleep and, to be honest, I haven't attended a single party they've hosted since I got here. I know that sounds weird since I live with them, but it's the way it's been."

"And before you got here?" I lock the door behind me, and we head down the slightly musty hall to the creaky elevator.

"I used to be more into that stuff. The hockey takes up a lot of time and energy. It's really the most important thing right now. It has to be if I'm going to make it my career."

He's staring at the carpeted wall in the elevator rather than at me as if he's avoiding going too deep on that one.

"If that's the case, what made you decide to go tonight?" The faintest hint of pink creeps up his neck under the yellow hood of his ridiculously amazing onesie.

"You said you had nowhere to go for Halloween. Plus, we've had some issues meshing as a team this year. I've been feeling like I need to get more involved with the other guys."

"That's fair. I'm glad you invited me, boyfriend. And the best part is you get to help me with the decorating. It's going to be so much fun!"

I don't know what I was expecting from the serious hockey boy, but I don't think it was the look of childlike excitement on his face. Maybe I was expecting something more akin to terror, but he looks genuinely excited to be doing this with me, and I'm glad. That closed off distance is on his face more often than not. But this has brightened him up, softening those hard lines of his features into something more open.

The drive to his place goes by way too fast with all the talk of our childhood costumes and favorite candy.

He glances at the phone I'm busily tapping away on as the car rumbles along. "Are you catching Pokémon right now? Hardly seems fair since I'm stuck here with my eyes on the road."

His lower lip is sticking out in a pout that has me tucking my own between my teeth, imagining what his would feel like against my tongue. Bad Jazz. You're just a little horny after your dry spell. He's your fake boyfriend. Emphasis on the fake. But try telling that to my needy brain. Although I think he's to blame. He's the one who planted the idea in my head of us cuddling on his bed, wrapping an arm around me and tucking me into his side when there's a jump scare on the screen.

"You still there, Coffee Girl?"

Right, yeah. The Ghastly breaks out of its pokeball and vanishes in a poof. "Yes. And that is a passenger perk. Catching them all. Fun fact. It's also one of, no the only perk to riding the bus. I can catch and spin to my heart's content, and I even pick up miles when the bus is going slow enough."

"Interesting. Maybe I'll have to take the bus with you sometime."

His engine gives a little shiver, as if it's pre-emptively jealous of him taking the bus. "Might be sooner than you think, from the sounds of it. This poor girl seems like she might be close to retirement." I pat that dashboard. I've never even owned my own car, so I can appreciate her while still realizing she might not have that much life left in her engine.

He shrugs. "I appreciate every mile I've gotten out of Mabel. When Jacks graduated last year, he entrusted me with her, but he said I had to return her the minute I signed my own contract and bought myself something newer. You know Jacks, right?"

"Of course. Big, sunny smile, terrible design skills. At least that's what Jordan always bemoaned about him. No flare for the visual is I believe how she put it."

"Sure. Anyway, he's the only one on the team I got to know, and honestly, I wouldn't have if he hadn't pushed the issue. I'm trying to expand my horizons a bit more this year."

"Sounds like a fantastic plan. I've just reconnected with my entrepreneurial group at school. We hung out last week, and it was really nice. Rob even helped me a bit with my grant applications."

I can see his chocolate eyes flicking toward me while the rest of him still faces the windshield. "Rob? Who's that?" There's a slight edge of wariness in his tone.

"He's in my program. We're in a lot of the same classes and he's part of my little group of six I made friends with in first year. Everyone else had to bail out, so he took me out for food and to the library after."

"Just the two of you?"

"Yes. Is there a problem with that?"

He jolts back into his seat, brows drawing together. "No, but maybe you shouldn't be seen with him alone out in public. What if someone saw you? What if our exes saw you? Our entire story might unravel."

My hackles are rising. Is he trying to stop me from seeing my friends? Just like Darryl did? I really didn't like that little thrill that raced up my spine when he mentioned our exes, either. Was he trying to scare me into not seeing Rob? "It was just a school thing. I'm allowed to have my own friends and my own life. You don't get to tell me who I can and can't see, Cole."

His shoulders slump, and his tense grip on the steering wheel eases up. "Of course not. I'm sorry if I made you feel that way. I don't even know what I was thinking. Just the thought of you with... never mind. Let's not let this ruin our night. This is Halloween, after all. Best night of the year."

I drag in a deep breath. "Not technically. It's only the 29th."

"True, but I don't think we should wear our costumes to our Walk Safe shift on Monday, do you?"

A laugh ripples through me at the thought of him prancing around with a safety vest over his Charizard costume. "Probably not."

Mabel squeals to a halt in front of the beautiful house the hockey players live in. I would love to sit on that porch swing wrapped in the fuzziest of blankets, with a steaming cup of coffee and a book. That's my idea of a perfect day. Oddly enough, in this ideal picture in my head, someone is sitting next to me on that swing, arm wrapped around me, dark head resting on my shoulder.

I can't even look him in the eyes when he opens the door for me, afraid he'll guess the untoward thoughts that were traipsing around in my head just now.

He holds out his hand to help me up, and I have to smooth my tight skirt down and squirm out of the car awkwardly to avoid flashing him.

I'm stopped in my tracks by our attached arms when I start to move around the car. I glance over my shoulder to figure out why he's not moving, and intensely aware of his calloused palm gripping mine.

"Before we go in, I just want to say something."

My heart picks up its speed. Where is he going with this? I nod, swallowing hard.

"I don't know what this party is going to be like. It could get wild. Whenever the hockey team throws a party, it draws a crowd. If you need to escape, we can sneak off and hide in my room. It is, in fact, one of my specialties. Maybe we should make up a safe word."

My shoulders are shaking by this point in his speech, and I shake my head at him. "I'm sure I can handle a few college students at a party. You've seen the customers I occasionally get at work." That makes me think of him rescuing me from the asshole. Worst customer of the year so far. That was only the first time he rescued me. Maybe what he's trying to say is that he might need an escape route. "Cole, I'm sure I'll be fine, but if you think it'll get out of hand, we can do that."

His inky lashes are impossibly thick, resting on his cheeks when he closes his eyes, nodding. "Good. What's something that wouldn't come up in regular conversation?"

"Umm, Lechonk?" The chonky little piggy is one of my new favorite Pokémon. Charizard is my ultimate fave, but obviously that wouldn't work, given Cole's costume.

He shakes his head at me. "That could totally come up in conversation. How about..." He taps a finger against his lip. "Snowball."

My nose wrinkles up as I study him. "Snowball?"

"Right. It's Halloween, so obviously we're not going to be talking about Christmas. No snow on the ground yet. Plus... that was the name of my pet bunny when I was a kid."

My laugh goes full-blown cackle. "You had a bunny named Snowball? Aren't you from Florida?"

"Hey, she was fluffy and white, and my younger sister named her."

I shake my head in a slow swing. "Sure, she did. Snowball it is. If I need to escape these silly little hockey boys and their friends, I'll ask you if you're up for a snowball fight."

"Perfect. I think you're ready."

He hoists both bins up in his arms, twists the door handle, shoving it open with his hip. Too bad the Charizard costume isn't the slightest bit more form fitting. I wouldn't mind seeing all those muscles flexing with the effort.

CHAPTER SIXTEEN

FEEL THE HEAT

COLE

T he guys seem determined to prove me right when we walk through the front door, and I almost turn around and go right back out. Beau's got JJ shoved up against the wall, one hand gripping the collar of his shirt. He looks extra menacing in his Negan costume. A shiver rips through me every time I see him casually swinging a barbed wire wrapped bat with his other arm.

"You keep my sister's name out of your filthy mouth, asshole."

JJ's eyes are wide with terror, and he's got his hands flung above his head as he dangles a few inches off the carpet. "I'm sorry, captain. I was just joking. I would never touch your sister. I swear."

Dev's got his arms crossed over his massive chest, leaning against the far wall to observe the interaction.

Grant lounges on the couch, one leg slung over the arm while he tosses popcorn in the air, catching it in his mouth as if he's enjoying the spectacle.

"See what I mean?" I turn to Jazz, leaning back to whisper in her ear. "Sure you don't want to nope out of the situation right now? I wouldn't blame you."

Her magenta lips are pressed together, shoulders shaking with mirth. "I'm good. Maybe Grant will share his popcorn. Looks like a good show."

I blow a breath out, cutting through the nonsense to drop her food bin off in the kitchen. After that's settled on the counter, I take the other one back into the living room. Jazz has made her way over to Grant, and she's got her hand in his bag of popcorn. An uncomfortable heat swells in my chest at the sight of her laughing with him. Not real. Gotta remember that. And Grant has a girlfriend. I need to chill the fuck out.

"Where do you want this one, Jazz?" I lift the bin.

She purses her lips. "Right there is fine." Her hand waves at the wall beside our half empty bookcase, then she claps her hands together and marches over to where Beau is still glaring at JJ. At least his feet are on the ground again, but Beau's still got his fist clenched around his collar.

"Alright, boys. Enough with the shenanigans. The party starts in five hours. No time to waste. I'm going to need you all on board to help get set up." Her hand looks small when she places it on Beau's shoulder. "Beau, you need to let go of JJ. He's not going to touch your sister, and I need both of you to help me out."

His hands slowly release their grip on his teammate, and he turns around, running a hand through his blond hair to straighten it out. "I'm sorry, Jazz. You shouldn't have seen that. What do you need from us?"

The rest of the boys stand up, pull themselves together and step forward as if they're drawn to her. It's impressive really that the chaos of hockey players is listening to the girl they're towering over.

"What can we do?" Grant asks.

"First of all. You can clean up all the popcorn that missed your mouth." Beau's mouth twists in disgust when he glances over at the couch scattered with white puffs.

"Will do," he says, ducking his head down.

"Who is the best in the kitchen?"

We all point to Dev, who continues to stand by the far wall, glowering under his brow. I don't think he's a huge fan of Halloween, but he stepped up and assembled a throwback Dwayne Johnson costume complete with fanny pack and gold chain. The contrast of his crossed arms and frown with the ridiculous get-up is too much. Not what I was expecting to see.

"Perfect. Can you unpack the food bins? Put away anything that needs to go in the fridge and lay the rest of the stuff out on the counter. I'll get it all organized closer to the start."

"Who wants to be in charge of music?"

"I will." JJ jumps up, completely recovered from the incident with our team captain.

"Okay. I need you to put together a killer playlist. Halloween songs, and spooky vibes. Enough songs to last us all night. Can you handle that?"

He nods.

"Excellent. Beau, Grant, Cole, you can help me unpack the decorations and we can get the place ready to go."

I step right up, opening the bin, and pulling stuff carefully out. It's like some kind of clown car. Granted, it is a huge bin, but it's packed with stuff. Skeletal hands, pictures with regular people that look horrifying when you look at them from the right angle. There's a fuzzy rat, caution tape, gel-like blood splatter, and disembodied body parts packaged up like meat at the grocery store. Gross.

Jazz doesn't touch a thing. She strides around the room, telling us all what to do and where to put everything. I like this side of her. It's hot watching her boss the guys around, and I find I don't mind it when she directs it at me either.

"No, no, no. You can't hang that ghost there. People will bang into it on the way to the kitchen. Hang it over the coffee table."

I nod, fixing the mistake as she directs JJ on the perfect placement of the blood drops on the big front window.

Her hips wiggling around in that tight white skirt are too tempting to resist any more, so I sneak up behind her, closing my hands around them. She glances over her shoulder at me with a smile, so I squeeze her in a tight grip, pulling her back against me.

I lean into her ear. "You're good at this."

She spins around in my hold, dropping her arms casually onto my shoulders. "I told you Halloween is my favorite holiday."

"I meant more the organizing and decorating. Directing the guys, transforming this place."

I look around. The decor of the place is upscale and neutral, so it doesn't really have much of a personality. Which is usually fine. A house full of college hockey players has plenty of personality without adding loud decor to match the loud mouths. But she's turned it into a fantastically creepy space. Eerie orange lighting in all the right places. Unexpected scary surprises in every corner.

"I enjoy this kind of thing. My family is big and loud and there's always some party or celebration going on, but I never get to do the organizing. That's all on my older sisters and mom. That's one of the things I love about being away at school. I get to be in charge. Make the decisions. I don't get to do it often enough, though. My apartment isn't exactly big enough to host parties. And honestly, I don't have that many friends."

"But you invited your business group, right?"

Her smile lights up her entire face. "I did." Then it falters a little. "Not sure if they're going to be able to make it, though. It was kind of late notice."

"I'm sure they'll come. Who would want to miss out on this?" I glance around, and of course Beau and JJ are bickering in the corner again now that they don't have tasks to accomplish.

She laughs. "Good point. You boys are not boring, that's for sure."

"True. Well then, event planner extraordinaire, what's next?"

"I think you guys have earned your dinner."

Beau didn't look like he was paying any attention to us, but he proves me wrong, swinging back in our direction. "I got this. Everyone good with pizza?"

"Thank fuck! Yes. All the meat," Grant says.

"What do you want on yours, Jazz?" he asks.

"Whatever is fine. I'm not picky."

I shake my head at her. "That's not the correct answer. What are your very favorite toppings?"

She scrunches up her cute nose. "My tastes are unusual, but like I said, I'll eat pretty much anything, except sausage. Not a fan."

JJ steps toward us, clearly eavesdropping on the conversation. "Oh, you don't like sausage? Clearly, Cole is doing something wrong. I bet I can convince you."

He gasps as if it's a surprise when my fist flies out, smacking him in the arm and sending him stumbling back. "Don't be a dick."

"Tell me what you like?"

"Pineapple, hot peppers, and bacon." She shrugs.

"Sounds delicious. Did you hear that, Beau? Get one with pineapple, hot peppers, and bacon on it."

"Got it," he's typing away on his phone.

A shiver runs down my back as she toys with the back of my fleecy hood. "You didn't have to do that. I know it's weird."

"It's not weird. Don't be ashamed of something you like."

"Darryl said..."

My fingers tighten on those thick hips of hers. "What did Darryl say?"

"Nothing. He just didn't like those things, so we always got the deluxe."

"Well, I'm not Darryl. That guy sounds like a total moron. I will one hundred percent try your pizza, but even if I hate it, I wouldn't stop you from getting the things you want. Especially not after you've done all this work to get the place looking great for the party. I haven't even had a chance to look at the food you brought, but I can't wait. I bet it's amazing."

I love the happy, smiling side of her. "Thanks."

"No problem. You can always ask me for anything." I lean in closer, dropping my voice so the guys don't hear. "The dating thing might be fake, but I'd like to think that we're friends now." It seems like an inadequate name for what we're becoming, but I can't think of a better one.

"Break it up," Grant steps toward us.

"Go away, Gigi." I use the name JJ likes to call Grant.

Her strange pizza topping combination is surprisingly good, although my mouth is on fire. Especially after she snagged some hot sauce that I didn't even know was in our fridge to dab on top.

I snag one last slice as Beau is snapping the cardboard box shut, jamming it into my mouth as we pull food out of the fridge, setting it up around the place.

The doorbell rings at seven thirty while we're still scrambling around to get everything in order and in walks the rookie, as well as Mack and his girlfriend.

"You're early, assholes," Dev says.

"Oh, sorry," Mack says, glancing back at the door as if he's going to turn around and walk back out to return in half an hour.

"Lucy's just fucking with you. Come on in guys." Beau pops his head out of the kitchen to wave them in.

"DJ JJ, can you get the tunes pumping?" Jazz directs the order at our goalie, who is dancing around the room even without music.

"Yeah, I got it." He bounces off to do her bidding, and the Monster Mash is pounding out of the big speakers shortly after.

People trickle in. The team first, and then Jazz's friends promptly at eight o'clock. They're all dressed in costume except for the biggest guy in the group. He's wearing a snazzy black suit that stretches tight across the barrel of his chest. The pair of dark shades he's got on is the only sign that he's got some sort of costume on, but it could be any number of things.

"Cole. This is Amira, Trinity, Deacon, Molly, and Rob. They're my biz family. And this is Cole... my boyfriend." She pauses as if it's hard for her to get the lie out to her friends.

"Nice to meet you." I shake their hands. Rob squeezes my hand in a fuck you grip as if he's trying to assert his dominance. Ah, he's that kind of guy. I'm vaguely familiar with the football players. He's a decent player, but not going to make the NFL by any stretch of the imagination. I guess that's why he's getting a business degree. He's one of the ones who has a life plan after college sports are finished.

If I don't make it in the pros, I'll probably go back to school. Get my masters, maybe my PhD in philosophy. Become a professor. But that's not what I want. I love studying philosophy and trying to figure out the why behind human actions, but that's not where I want my life to go. I've dreamed of playing in the NHL since I was a tiny kid. It's always been my dream. Not to mention the things I can do to help my dad and siblings once I get that sweet paycheck. Dad won't have to work two or three jobs anymore to send his other kids to school.

"Need a drink?" I ask Jazz, wiping an arm across my forehead to catch a couple of errant drops of sweat. She's deep in conversation with a pretty girl with long dark hair wearing a Barbie costume. Amira, I think.

The number of bodies packed into every room on the main floor has the temperature verging on Florida in August levels, complete with damp humidity emanating from all the sweaty bodies. My Charizard onesie is pulled down off my arms and tied around the waist by this point.

"I'll take a cola or something," she says, turning to me with that gorgeous smile of hers that lights me up in a way that has me shifting uncomfortably on my feet.

I head upstairs to hit the bathroom first, stopping when I hear voices at the end of the hall.

"You shouldn't be here, and you definitely shouldn't be wearing that." Beau's tall form is blocking my view of the girl he's talking to, and my protective big brother hackles rise. Who is he talking to like that?

"Your roommates invited me, and our parents own this house. I have just as much of a right to be here as you. Even if you wouldn't let me move in."

The hackles settle. It's the infamous Cecelia, his twin sister, who transferred to Lakeview this year. I still haven't met her yet, even though I think she was at the last game. He's keeping her away from his hockey team on purpose. The knee-breaking threat he issued at the beginning of the semester wasn't enough. Go near my sister and... insert menacing glower.

"The house is full, and would you really want to live with a bunch of hockey bros, anyway?"

She snorts. "I dunno. Some of them are pretty hot."

"Cecelia." Her bright laugh outshines his growl.

"Don't worry. I'll leave your precious teammates alone. I know you're worried I'll break them."

"That's not what I..."

She ducks under his arm, popping out to reveal a skintight Spider-Gwen bodysuit with the hood and mask flipped back. Her tousled blonde hair and blue eyes match her brother's, but she's over a foot shorter than him.

"Hi." Her bright blue eyes lock on mine, and she gives me a smile so big it scrunches up the corners of her eyes.

"Sorry. I was just going to use the bathroom. And hi."

"Don't even look at her, Cole," Beau says to me. "Ouch. Fuck."

I press my lips together to avoid laughing at him when his sister lands an elbow in his ribs, and I throw my hands up in the air.

"Hey, I wasn't doing anything. I've got to get back to Jazz, anyway."

"Is that your girlfriend?" She asks my back. "Can I meet her? I need to make more friends at this school I've been banished to. A girl always needs more friends. Come on, take me down and introduce me."

She hops over, ignoring her brother's glare. I shrug at him. What am I supposed to do against the enthusiastic force of nature that is his sister?

He shakes his head, swinging the door to his room open. "Please, don't do anything that'll get you in trouble, Cecelia, and no hockey players."

"Whatever you say, bro. Don't worry about me."

She tugs on my arm, skipping down the stairs and taking me with her in the wake of her personality. Not what I was expecting.

"You'd think I was wearing nothing but lingerie by the way my brother is going on. This is a perfectly legitimate costume. Not even a hint of skin. Not that it's any of his concern." She waves her arms up and down the white and black suit that looks like it could be painted on.

In general, I'm not about shaming women for wearing anything they choose, but thinking of either of my sisters wearing that does make me a little uncomfortable.

I scrunch up my face. "I have sisters, so I get where your brother is coming from."

She scoffs at me. "Of course. You guys have all got to stick together. So, where's this girlfriend of yours?" The heat and noise intensify as soon as we hit the first floor.

"I told her I'd grab her a drink, so I'm going to hit the kitchen first."

She trails behind me as I head for the big blue cooler where Dev stashed the non-alcoholic stuff, and rifle through it until I find a Coke. "Want one?" Soothing cool water drips off the can as I shake it at Cecelia.

She snorts. "No thanks. This is a party, after all, right?"

I wince as she heads for one of the blue coolers that has all the booze, but since I was planning on grabbing myself a beer, I guess I can't be judgy.

She pulls out a White Claw, and it lets out a slow hiss as she snaps it open. "No laws."

"If your brother asks me, I'm claiming ignorance of where you got that."

"I'm a grown ass twenty-one year old woman. I can make my own decisions. Thank you very much. Thinks he can control me, since he's two minutes older."

"That's all well and good, but he's my captain, and I can't afford to inspire his wrath, so I'm pleading the fifth." Especially since I've been riding this careful line between really going all in with the team and remaining on the outside. But the more time I've been spending with the time, the more I realize how lonely I've been. It's a good feeling even though letting them in scares the shit out of me.

It's hard to identify anyone amid all the writhing bodies, but Jazz's bright white costume stands out in the crowd. She's on the dance floor and at first all I see are those full hips swaying to the pounding beat. When it registers that there is a pair of large hands resting on the bare skin at her midriff, a burning knot settles in my gut. I can feel the anger swelling up that I try my best to keep on lock down.

I drag in a shaky breath, counting down from five to one in my head. The anger is still simmering when I get to one and open my eyes. I shove through the crowded bodies stuffed into our tv room until I get to Jazz. Her back twitches under the hand I place on it, and she tilts her head back, smiling and pulling out of Rob's grip when she sees me.

"C'mon, Jazz. You promised me a dance. Aren't you going to at least finish the song?"

I see red when he grabs her hip again and my hand is trembling with the urge to karate chop his hand.

"Hands off my girlfriend, man. I've got someone who wants to meet her."

He mutters something under his breath but releases his hold on her. I grab her hand because it helps ease the shaking, pulling her back through the crowd to find Cecelia.

It's not hard. Didn't take her long to find someone to piss her brother off with, which seems to be her goal in life. She's got her arms twined around the neck of some guy as she slithers around in that slinky suit. If Beau saw her now, he'd probably drag her off the dance floor and lock her up, but she's not my sister. I tap her on the shoulder, and she immediately releases the disappointed looking guy, spinning around and clapping her hands together.

"Is this Jazz?"

Jazz quirks her brow up with a curious assessment.

"Yup, wanna hit the kitchen. Or maybe the porch?"

"Porch would be amazing. I'm sweltering." Jazz says fanning her face that's gone pink with the heat and exertion.

A blast of cool air hits us as we step outside. I'm surprised there's no one else out here, but the large deck in the back has more furniture, so maybe that's where the other partygoers who need to cool down have congregated.

Jazz makes a beeline for the big wooden porch swing, giggling as it slips out from under her when she tries to sit down. I throw my arms out to catch her before she hits the ground, my hands catching on her top causing it to ride up her torso. A tantalizing amount of bare skin and a hint of pink lace have me staring for too long. Fuck.

She glances down, mouth popping open, so I grip the slippery fabric and yank it back down to cover her. I lift her up to settle her on the seat, sitting down next to her as far away as I can get.

She sprawls out, dropping her arms behind the seatback and tilting her head back to reveal the long, lean line of her neck. My eyes lock on that exposed skin and my tongue darts out to lick my lips. All I can think about is how she'd taste under my tongue, my lips. Whether she'd like some soft nibbles under her jawline.

"Maybe I should leave you two alone out here?"

The bright voice breaks through my trance. Good thing. I'm pretty sure I was seconds away from discovering just what she tastes like.

Jazz's head snaps back up, and her wig tips forward to her brow. "This thing." She mutters, yanking some pins out and fumbling to pull the wig off. She's got a hairnet containing the waterfall of her shiny black hair, but there are stray bits poking out all over.

"We're good. This is Jazz. Jazz, this is Beau's sister Cecelia. I ran into her and her brother upstairs and she wanted to come meet you. She's new to Lakeview this year."

"Nice to meet you." My girl straightens up in her seat, giving the other girl all of her attention. "What's your major?"

"You can call me Cece. Only my family calls me Cecelia. Beau calls me Sissy when he's not being an overprotective doofus. I'm in marketing, but what I really want to do is animation. I create my own comics in my spare time. How about you?"

"I'm taking business management with a focus on entrepreneurship."

"Amazing. Love that. Look, we definitely need to hang out some time, but in the meantime, I'm gonna head back in there." She looks over to the window at the dark shadow behind the curtain. Must be Beau waiting for his sister to get back. "Let me airdrop you my deets."

The girls tap their phones together, and then she's off, slamming the front door behind her.

"That was kind of weird, but she seems nice."

"Yeah. It was the first time I met her, but I'm sure she's great. I think Beau has been keeping her away from the team."

She laughs. "That doesn't surprise me in the least after what he was doing to JJ when we got here."

Her shoulders shudder, and she crosses her arms over her chest. The chilly air must be hitting all that exposed skin. Goosebumps have popped up on the exposed expanse of flesh at her midriff.

I act on impulse, dropping an arm around her shoulder and tucking her into my side. I haven't had a girl this close since, well, since Charlene destroyed me. But there's no room for her in my head right now. For the very first time since she shattered me, I feel like maybe I'll be able to heal. Maybe one day I'll be able to let someone back in.

CHAPTER SEVENTEEN

BLURRED LINES

JAZZ

T he crisp air felt good on my overheated skin when
we first got out here, but after my internal temperature leveled out, the chill set in. Cole must have caught
my shiver because he closed the distance between us,
pulling me in close to share his body heat. I nuzzle in,
dropping my head to his chest, and he rubs a hand up
and down my arm. The gesture sends a different kind of
shiver through my system.

"You want to go in?" he asks.

"No. I'm kind of liking it out here. It's peaceful." I love
a good party, but sometimes you need a break from the
peopling and now that I'm the arms of my fake boyfriend
I'm reluctant to leave them. Who knows how long it'll
be before I'll be able to get this kind of human contact?
Should I start dating again? The problem is when I think

about it, the only face I imagine sitting across from me is his. Everything is getting all jumbled up in my head. The lines between real and pretend blurring like the veil between life and death this time of year.

The side of his finger strays a little to the left, brushing the side of my breast through the tight fabric of my costume. My nipples ache, and warmth stirs in my neglected lady parts.

"I'm so sorry."

I tilt my head up to look at him. His eyes are glazed, and I place a hand on the one he tried to pull away from my arm. "It's ok." I stretch up, his liquid brown eyes dragging me in, pulling me toward him like a magnet.

His lips part and he dips his head down inch by slow inch as if he can't resist me, either. The memory of his lips on mine at the game is seared into my brain, and I want to experience it again. Maybe it was a fluke. The one-off passion of two lonely people. Maybe if I let myself kiss him again, I'll be able to move past this restless need that's been riding me.

I stretch up in my seat until we're so close I can feel the heat of his breath. He makes the final move, closing the last gap between us. His lips are soft and warm, just like I remember them. My eyes drift closed as we move against each other in a gentle dance of give and take. I need more. Tingles run from my lips to my hardened nipples and my pulsing core.

Our mouths part in sync, and he pulls my lower lip between his teeth, tongue swiping against mine. I swing around, throwing a leg over his thighs. His long, steely length is ready for me, and I gasp into his mouth as it presses against me in just the right place.

My hips grind against it as my hands slip up the shorn hair at the back of his head until I can reach the longer locks on top, tangling my fingers in their silkiness.

He traces a swirling line down my back until he reaches my hips, digging into the flesh and pulling me closer until we're shifting together in a desperate grind.

"Jazz," he moans out.

"Cole." I trace my tongue along his, rubbing my chest against him, wishing his hands would slide up to touch me there, craving the friction.

"Wait." He pulls back, hips stilling their movement. "We shouldn't."

I'm panting and desperate by now. "Why not?"

"Because this isn't what we agreed to. I don't expect this."

I sit back on my thighs, needing a bit of space between us, but I can still feel him between my thighs. "What if we change the rules?"

His mouth parts, brow tightening. I can see the conflict in his eyes, and I want to chase it away. Take advantage of this moment, and each other. I haven't been with anyone for too long. Haven't wanted to. But here, now. I want to, but only if it's with him. Because I feel safe with him. There are boundaries and respect and even friendship between us. And I trust him, which is something I wasn't sure I would ever feel for a guy again.

"I don't know. Is that a good idea? Wouldn't that mess up everything we've got going here?" He raises a hand to his hair, and I follow the movement. The softness felt so good sliding between my fingers. I want to feel it again.

I give him a smile that I hope is a little sexy and a little sassy. "Tonight is Halloween, after all. Technically, we're not even Jazmin and Cole. What if we explored things just for tonight? See how it goes. If we don't think it's going to work, we can move on and go back to our previous arrangement. Unless... unless you're not interested?"

What if he's not actually into me like that? A mortifying heat threatens to set my face on fire, and I squirm a little. But the groan that rumbles through his chest at the movement seems like pretty solid proof.

"Trust me, Coffee Girl. Attraction is not the issue. I haven't felt like this since..." He trails off, dropping a set of impossibly thick inky lashes over his eyes.

Since? I'm not sure I want to ask that question. The answer might be too much. I'm sure he's slept with other girls since he broke up with her, so whatever he's talking about might be a little too much for me right now.

I'm shifting off his lap, ready to put some distance between us when he grabs my hips, yanking me back until I'm pressed so tight against him, I can feel his heart beating. He shifts, opening those eyes again to show me their liquid depths.

"Okay."

"Okay?"

"Yeah." His hands slide below my thighs and he's on his feet in one swift movement that sends the porch swing rocking. "Let's go up to my room."

I'm bouncing in his arms as he heads for the front door with a determined stride. Seems like once he's made up his mind, he means business.

I smack at his shoulders. "Put me down, Cole!"

"No." The firm tone of his voice jolts straight to my already overheated pussy.

"Seriously, you can't carry me through the party like this?"

"Why not? You are my girlfriend, aren't you? At least to everyone in there. It'll really drive that point home. Good PR, you know."

I reach down, tugging at the spandex fabric of my skirt that is riding dangerously high on my thighs. Another inch and way too much of my ass is going to be on display given the thong I had to wear with the tight skirt.

"Everyone is going to see my ass."

He glances down to the place where his hands are gripping my bare thighs. "Well, shit. That won't do. I'm the only one that gets to see this juicy ass tonight. Sorry about that."

He lets me slide down his body, which stokes the fire inside, but I at least feel a little more comfortable now that I can tug the skirt down over my exposed cheeks. He even helps me tug it a little lower, smoothing his palms down my legs as he goes. The rough skin sends another shiver through me.

I loop my arm through the elbow he's holding out for me, and we head back into the fray to run the gauntlet of partygoers. Not sure if it's just the contrast with the still night air or if the party did in fact increase a few decibels since we left, but I'm happy to see that everyone is having a good time.

Amira and Trinity make a beeline for us. "Hey, Jazz. We got tickets to Niche tonight for their big Halloween bash, so we're going to head over there now. Thanks so much for inviting us, though. We had a great time. You too, Cole." She smiles at him. "It was great to meet you."

"Thanks for coming."

Her right brow arches in a slight curve as he tugs me in closer, sliding a hand around my waist over the sensitive bare skin.

"Have fun," she singsongs.

The heat that's been simmering creeps up my neck.

"Good night, Amira, Trin. Have fun at Niche."

"Will do."

The door shuts behind them with a soft click and I turn to Cole, nibbling on my lower lip. "Maybe I should go back to the party. Find my other friends. I invited them, after all. Wouldn't it be rude for me to just ditch them with all these strangers?"

He snorts. "They're grown adults, Coffee Girl. I'm sure they can occupy themselves at a college party. They wouldn't have come if they weren't up for it."

"I guess. I just hate to be rude."

He squeezes my biceps. "I get it and I love how much you care for your friends, but now that you've put the offer on the table, I can't stop thinking about tearing this costume off of you. Especially if this is a one-night pass. But if you want to, I'll go back with you."

He shifts on his feet, looking uncomfortable at the idea. It seemed like he was enjoying himself, but he does always seem more at ease when it's just the two of us. Shoulders lighter, smiles more free and easy.

I glance over his shoulder one more time, searching. Rob's massive figure is hard to miss. He's dancing away, surrounded by a crowd of girls and a couple of other large guys that I don't recognize. I nod. They're good. Cole's right. And honestly, I think it's time I take something for myself. I want this. He wants this. What the heck am I hesitating for?

"Let's go." His lips curl into a smile that crinkles the corners of his eyes, painting his face in an innocent joy I haven't seen too many times before.

He grabs my hand, bringing it to his mouth, and a shiver runs through me at the soft press of his lips on the sensitive skin.

That's it. I'm his. At least for tonight.

He slides his hand down my arm, twining his fingers with mine as if he needs the contact just as much as I do. I follow him away from the crowd toward the stairs.

My heart gallops as we make our way up. His fingers trace a ticklish pattern on my palm.

I barely notice the hallway as he leads me to a white door. My hands wrap around his waist as he fumbles with the key to let himself into his room.

"You get a lot of intruders in your house?" I ask, wondering why he needs to keep it locked.

"It's usually fine. My roommates can be nosy fuckers, but they wouldn't go in my room without permission. But when there's a party, you never know who's going to end up in your bed. I learned that lesson in my freshman year. A threesome. Had to wash my sheets three times. Never again."

"Gotcha." Makes sense. At home, I had no privacy. Always sharing a room and never knowing when someone would decide to barge in and borrow my favorite sweater when I was out. That's why I've lived alone since I got to college. I love my private space. Even if my apartment is a shoe box, and I could save some money by sharing. "I have my own place, so I never thought about it like that. Not exactly party central. It must be hard for you."

He swings the door open, one hand sliding down to my lower back as he guides me in ahead of him.

"It's alright. I've got headphones, and I really don't mind people. Unless they're spreading their bodily fluids all over my bed. My social skills might be rusty, but even I know that's just fucking rude."

"It seems like we're both in our introvert years. I've left behind the chaos of my family to figure myself out, and you've isolated yourself from your hockey team."

His dark brows pull together, and there's a faraway look in his eyes. I want to reach up and smooth those lines away. This was not what I intended. How did we get here? All the flirtation and teasing has evaporated with the seriousness of a conversation I'm not sure we should be having. This is all supposed to be easy. Fake, right? These things? These are real. Too real for my comfort.

"I don't know how we're even having this conversation right now. How can I possibly take you seriously in that bright yellow onesie?"

He glances down as if I've surprised him, letting out a laugh. Like he got so lost in our conversation he forgot where he was, what he's wearing. I think I did too for a moment.

"You're right. I'm completely ridiculous. Get over here, Jessie. I think it's time I let you catch me."

I feel anything but trapped when he reaches over my shoulder, boxing me in against the door as he clicks the lock. It sounds very final. Very official. Like there's no turning back. I know that's not true. There's no doubt in my mind that if I told him to stop, he would, but I want it so much. Too much, probably, but there's time to worry about that later. Tonight is Halloween, when anything is possible, and you can pretend to be anyone you want. So I'm going to pretend I'm a brave seductress, and hope he doesn't laugh at my efforts. I wish I wasn't so unsure of myself. I never used to be. Before... But he is the last person I want to be thinking about right now.

I take a deep breath, flick my eyes up to the dark chocolate depths of his and let my lips curl up at the corners in what I hope is a sexy smile. My hands grasp the hem of my top and I drag it over my head in a swift move that pulls his gaze to my chest. The sheer lace of my pink bra hides nothing. His tongue darts out to lick his lips and I seize the invitation, leaning in to taste it for myself. He tastes like chocolate and salt.

His lips press back, but his hands remain braced on the door on either side of my head, as if he's afraid to move. Looks like I'm going to have to help him out here. I wiggle out of the tight skirt, and he swallows hard as the tiny piece of fabric falls to the floor.

"This needs to go," I say, pulling back to grab the zipper he pulled back up to his chin when we were on the porch. "There is absolutely no way I can fool around with Charizard."

His laugh turns into a groan as I rip the zipper down and slide a hand down the satiny smoothness of the shorts he's got on underneath. He's impossibly hard under the fabric, and large. Holy shit, he's big. It swells, twitching under my touch.

"Shit, Jazz. Keep that up, and I'll lose it in my shorts."

"We wouldn't want that, would we?" I say, reluctantly releasing my hold on him to pull the rest of the fleecy costume off.

That's better. He's got on a tight white compression shirt that hugs the sculpted perfection of his chest and biceps. Loose blue basketball shorts do a poor job of hiding his hard on. And it's all for me. His hands grip my arms when I go for the gold again.

"Seriously, Jazz. I meant it. I'm going to need you to keep your hands to yourself. At least for a little while. It's been a long time since anyone else touched me and I don't know how good my self control is."

I nibble on my lower lip up, flicking my eyes up to look at him, but his eyes are closed, head tilted back to reveal the length of that neck I want to nibble on.

"How long?"

"What?" he asks, rubbing his hands up and down my biceps.

"How long has it been since you were with someone else?"

He finally opens his eyes to look down at me. "A year and a half."

A year and a half. Wait, so that means... "You haven't been with anyone else since your ex?"

He shakes his head, and I watch his Adam's apple bob as he swallows hard again. "I've never been with anyone except her."

The confession rocks me back like an explosion. "You've never been with anyone else?"

He winces. "Nope. Was that weird? Did I just fuck this up?"

I'm frozen in place, thoughts racing while I try to gather them enough to form a coherent sentence. A college senior athlete who has only been with one person? It doesn't seem possible.

I finally get myself together enough to shake my head. "No, but are you sure you want to do this?" I don't know what I was expecting, but it wasn't this. Everything I've heard about the hockey team is that they're a bunch of players. Even Aspen had his share of women before he finally gave in to his feelings for Jordan.

"Yes. I'm sure."

"Can I ask why?" It's not like I've been sleeping around, but I hooked up with an old boyfriend over the summer. I was in a low place, after running from Darryl, and I fell into his arms. It was a terrible idea. He was not as bad as Darryl, but he never treated me right, either. If anything, it intensified my fear of getting involved with someone again. My judgment with men is obviously less than stellar.

"I haven't wanted to. Until now. Until you. I've never been interested in sex without getting to know someone first. Not my thing. I used to think maybe I was broken or something, but now I know it's just the way I'm hard-wired."

I cross my arms over my chest, feeling vulnerable with all my skin on display now that the conversation has taken a turn.

"But we're not together together."

"But we have a connection. A friendship and apparently that works for me."

"I don't want to make you do anything you don't want to do." My arms squeeze tighter around my chest. He seems to realize how uncertain I am, because he reaches a hand up to tilt my chin so he can meet my eyes. He peels my arms apart, getting a firm grip on my hand and dragging it down his front until I'm touching his dick again. I think it may have swelled even larger if that's even possible, straining against the confines of his shorts.

"Oh, I want to. You have no fucking clue how badly I want to feel your hands on my cock, your tits in my mouth. I feel like I'm going to burst out of my skin if I don't get a taste of your sweet pussy. Never doubt the effect you have on me."

Before I can respond, his large hands slide under my bare thighs, yanking me off the floor until I wrap my legs around his waist. My back hits the door with a thump and his cock crashes into my pussy, grinding against me through the fabric. Too much fabric.

My fingers are drawn back to waves of hair on top of his head, tugging on them to bring him closer as he dips down to suck my nipple through the thin lace. I tilt my head back, moaning at the sultry heat of his mouth on my tight bud. My back arches, seeking more, and I'm rewarded when his fingers close over my left breast, pinching and toying with my other nipple.

Liquid heat shoots from my breasts to my pussy. I grind into him, and he spins me around, the world shifting as he carries me to his bed, dropping me with a soft bounce.

"Please." I beg, missing the feel of his mouth and fingers.

"Please what?"

"Please touch me." I squirm underneath his gaze.

"Oh, I will. Lift." He commands, his fingers hooking in the waistband of my matching pink panties.

I obey, lifting my hips off the bed so he can drag the fabric down my legs. He takes his time, placing small kisses on the inside of my thighs and down my calves as he goes, dragging them over my feet agonizingly slowly.

His hands slide up my freshly shaved legs as he takes his sweet time, moving back toward my center. Nerve endings light up one by one as he goes, and I'm not sure I'll make it. Death by anticipation. Feels like a good way to go.

Finally, finally, he's so close I can feel the warmth of his breath brushing the tops of my thighs. So close and yet still way too far away. I slither toward him, seeking some much needed pressure on my aching core.

"Cole." Is that breathy whisper even my voice? Hard to tell.

"Yes." He looks up at me under dark lashes.

"I need." I don't even know what I need. Fingers, tongue, yes, I want to feel his tongue on me. I bet it'll be amazing.

"This," he says, and he uses his tongue all right, but it glides up the inside of my thigh, instead of the place I need it the most.

"Stop teasing me."

He ignores the request. Licking up the other side until he's there. Almost. Inches away from sending me to heaven.

I don't think I can handle it anymore, but then he's there. A wash of hot breath has my pussy clenching around nothing and then he gives me what I need with one slow, almost lazy lick with the flat of his tongue.

I gasp, arching up to meet his licks.

Small swirls send heat through my entire body until I'm burning up. Ready to combust. And I'm almost there already. The rhythmic laps of his tongue and small swirls have me panting, helpless with need.

But a gentle flick to my clit has my legs trembling, pushing me higher than I've ever been. One of the hands gripping my hips loosens, and he reaches down to toy at my opening, circling the edge, slipping just the tip into my dripping channel. It slides in with ease, helped my slick heat. His mouth latches on to my clit at the same time he finally slides that finger in all the way. In and out. The rhythm of his plunging digit matches the gentle pulls on my swollen nub until I'm gasping and pleading.

Every part of me is burning and shaking.

A second thick finger pushes in beside the first and the thrusts get faster, harsher, until lightning, thunder, fireworks. My world implodes around me, arching my body off the bed as if I've been shocked.

I collapse back on the bed, limp and more satisfied than I've ever been in my life.

"You did good." His voice is a husky rumble edged with his own need.

"Holy shit. That was fanfuckingtastic."

He chuckles, stretching out beside me on his bed, dragging my lifeless body farther up and tucking a pillow behind me.

One arm slides over my torso and his head drops onto my shoulder. That's when I realize the bra never even came off and he's still fully clothed. That's no good. I want to see what's under that shirt. Those shorts that have still got a massive tent going on.

He shudders under my touch as I slide a hand down his chest, over his impossible abs, and lower. But a soft weight drops onto my exploring hand, preventing me from reaching my prize.

"It's okay. I'm good," he says, and I'd almost believe him if the straining length of his cock doesn't take that moment to jump, pulsing against my thigh.

"I want to feel you." I roll over on my side. "Can I please? Unless you don't want me to." Maybe he's not ready for that. If he hasn't been with anyone other than his cheating girlfriend, maybe he's not as ready for the touch of another woman as he thought.

He groans. "I want you to. I want your hands, your mouth, your pussy. Whatever you'll give me, but don't feel like you have to."

"Trust me. Getting a taste of this." I slide my hand under his shorts and finally feel that silken skin under my palm. "Won't be a hardship."

"Fuck, Coffee Girl. I'm going to blow before I get my dick anywhere near that gorgeous pussy if you keep touching me."

CHAPTER EIGHTEEN

SILK AND SUNSHINE

COLE

"I don't mind." The slight twist of her soft lips is mischievous as fuck.

Those words break me. Every last ounce of self control I had left snaps and I'm tearing my shirt off over my head, desperate to feel her skin against mine. She's all over me. The sweet scent of her intoxicating pussy, the taste of her coating my tongue. I didn't know if I'd ever feel this way again, but now that I'm here, it's so much better than I remember. So much more.

I drag the cups of her bra down, pushing those beautiful breasts up. Her fingers dig into my back as my mouth closes over the delicious mounds. My tongue flicks at each dark brown tip in turn, and her fingers close around my cock. A shudder runs through me, pressure building in my balls already.

I suck in a deep breath to keep myself under control as she strokes along the heated length.

"Please. Don't. I want to be inside you. If that's okay."

"Yes. Yes. Please. I want it all." She releases me, pulling at my hips again.

I sit up, jerking my shorts and boxers off in one swift move and tossing them to the floor. I twist back to see her lying there. My eyes devour every inch of her light brown skin. Those curves. Fuck. I roll over until I've got her underneath me, desperate to get inside. I'm almost there. So close, brushing her liquid heat.

"Fuck!"

She looks up, startled, as I sit back on my heels.

"Condom. I don't have a condom." I drag a hand through my hair, swearing at myself internally for not planning ahead. Not that I was expecting this to happen tonight, but I should have been prepared. I should have known something like this would happen. I've been thinking about her naked underneath me almost every day for the last few weeks.

Her lower lip pushes out in a slight pout. "It's ok. We can do other things. I'd love to get a taste of you." My cock twitches as if it can feel her eyes drifting down to check him out.

As much as I'd love to feel her mouth around me, I'm not sure if I'm going to get this chance again. As real as this is starting to feel for me, I know it's not part of the deal. She said we could have tonight because we can pretend to be other people. Less broken people. And if this is all I'm going to get, then I want everything. I want to sink so deep inside her she'll never forget me.

I drag a hand through my hair, glancing from the door to her beautiful body laid out before me. Those boys are prepared for everything. I just might be able to find what I'm looking for.

"Hang on a sec."

Pushing myself up and away from her is difficult. I don't want to leave her even for a second, but I do. "I think I've got this."

"Okay." Her lazy smile stretches in a contented yawn.

Snatching the shorts off the floor, I unlock it and cautiously push it open. The muffled noise from the party downstairs roars back to life as I creep down the hall, breathing a sigh of relief when I don't run into anyone.

The hall closet is a treasure trove. I don't know if it's Beau or someone else who keeps it stocked, but there's a basket full of hotel sized extras. Flowery shampoo, and tiny bottles of body wash. I root through the baskets, pushing aside tampons and toothbrushes still in their packaging. C'mon, c'mon.

"Whatcha looking for?"

The sound of Beau's voice freezes me like a kid caught climbing on the cupboards to reach the chocolate stash on the top shelf.

"Nothing. I'm good."

He moves closer. "Cole. I thought we'd been over this. You're part of the team and you live in this house. What do you need?"

My face scrunches up as I debate my options. Didn't exactly want to share with the class, but I really, really want to go back to that girl in my room, and I don't think he's going to let me go until I fess up.

"Condom," I mutter under my breath.

A brief laugh bursts out of him, and I can feel him behind me before he claps a hand on my back. "Nice. I gotcha covered." He reaches down to the bottom shelf and moves aside a stack of towels to reveal not one, but four unopened boxes of condoms. Ambitious.

"Take what you want. I'll put my headphones back on. Enjoy."

He leaves me with burning cheeks, and I snatch up the first box my fingers close on.

I slink back to my room, booty in tow as his door shuts behind him. I guess he's done with the party.

Jazz is sitting up when I get back, legs pulled up to her chin, eyes wide as she gnaws on that plump lower lip of hers. I hope she's not having second thoughts.

"You good?" I ask, closing the door, but hesitating before I strip the shorts off even though the loose material feels like it's strangling my dick and I'm dying to tear them off. Maybe we'll have to spend the night together in a different way. My pained cock isn't pleased with the idea. He deflated a little during the incident in the hall but came roaring back to life as soon as we spotted all that bare skin again.

"Yeah. Did you find what you were looking for?"

I give her a slow scan, drinking in every inch. Long legs, thick thighs, plump hips and those tits, peeking out behind her knees. When I get to her face, I study every inch from her slightly upturned nose to her rosy cheeks and sex-mussed black hair. "Oh, I definitely did." My eyebrow arches.

The pretty hint of a flush in her cheeks spreads to her chest.

She turns away. "I mean..."

"I know what you meant, gorgeous." Her mouth falls open as I waggle the box at her. "And I got an entire box. I may never let you leave this room again."

She glances back at me. "Are you going to tie me to the bed and hold me captive?"

That's an interesting thought. Not something I ever would have tried with... Don't think about her. Fastest way to slay a boner. "Did you want me to?"

Her giggle has an uncertain edge to it. "Maybe."

Interesting. "Maybe not tonight. Tonight, I need to feel every inch of you, wrapped around every inch of me."

"That's a lot of inches."

"Why thank you."

"Enough talk. Get over here." She's all talk. Brave, bold words while she still sits there clutching her legs.

Dark eyes intensify as they trace a trail down my body when I drop the shorts. The box of condoms bounces beside her, and I jump up to kneel in front of her.

Her skin is silky under my hands as I untangle her fingers, kissing each palm before placing it down on the bed beside her. I part her legs, pushing her knees apart to reveal the prize. Drinking in the sight, I slide a finger in her mouth, letting her get a taste of her essence still lingering. When I trace it down between her breasts, over her soft tummy and through the light thatch of dark hair between her thighs, she shivers. And when I reach her lower lips, I part them, pressing her thighs further apart to get a good look at her as I sink my finger into her depths. I groan when I find her still dripping with her release. Still ready for me.

"Perfect."

"Cole." She cries out.

I grab at the box, fumbling with my left hand, reluctant to leave her empty, and she snatches it out of my hand.

"I got this, don't stop." Who am I to argue with this gorgeous fucking creature?

Adding a second finger, I scissor them inside her, stretching her out to get her ready for the width of my dick.

The sound of paper tearing accompanied by her soft moans spurs me on even faster until I can feel a distinct tingling at the base of my back.

I still my fingers, taking a minute to compose myself.

She shoves a shiny foil packet in my face, and I snatch it, pulling away from her.

My fingers slip and I feel like an inexperienced teenager again, fumbling with the packet as I tear it open and slide it over my length with trembling hands.

Sliding forward, I lick first one, then the other nipple, pressing my tip to her entrance. She squirms under my touch.

"You ready?"

"I've never been more ready in my life."

Plunging forward with one hard thrust, I'm finally there, deep inside her hot channel. She feels like silk and sunshine and everything that's good in this world, and everything clicks. I think I've shared more with her than I have with anyone else in my life. There's been an intimacy between us as if we were old friends from our very first conversation, so everything about this closeness feels right. As if this was our inevitable destination.

Shivers skate down my back when her fingers clutch at me in a desperate hold to bring me closer, but I'm not going to last long with her touching me. I grab her wrists, never ceasing the plunging rhythm that has the headboard slamming into the wall. Twisting my fingers with hers, I slam her hands back, holding her down as I fuck her relentlessly.

She gasps, lifting her hips off the bed to meet me. Sweat slick bodies slide against each other as we keep up the dance. Push and pull. Grasping, seeking that place of perfection.

My entire body is tingling, dick pulsing, and balls drawn tight up to my body, but I want to make her come one more time before I let go.

Her head tilts back, chest arching up toward me as my thumb circles her clit. I can't resist the temptation of those swollen nipples, bending to capture one in my mouth as her thighs tremble beside my thrusting hips.

"I need you to come." I'm begging now and I don't care I need this so bad. The release. The closeness. The beauty of spilling inside her. Connecting us for real.

She gasps. "I can't. It's too much. Too sensitive."

"Yes, you can. And you will." I insist, slipping a finger down to feel myself as I move inside her. She's soaking me, so I move that lubricated finger back to her sensitive bud and resume my insistent swirls. "Come for me."

My teeth sink into her breast in a nip bordering on painful and I press down on that button at the same time, sending her screaming over the edge.

My body seizes, pleasure ripping through me like a tidal wave as I give in. Her pussy clenches around me as I continue to pulse inside her, spilling into the condom.

Small thrusts work me through the last of the orgasm and I reach up to hold her chin so I can stare into her eyes. Her beautiful brown eyes are wet with moisture.

"Are you okay? I didn't hurt you, did I?"

"No. It was..." she trails off as if she can't find the words, but I've got one for her.

"Perfection."

A stray hair falls across her eyes as she nods, and I brush it back with care as if she's fragile as glass. A shiver still ripples through her sensitive skin at my touch.

My body is spent, but I'm still reluctant to pull out of her. I could stay inside her all night, but we should sleep. I have to at least get rid of the condom.

The slight wince as I pull out gives her away, and I stroke her cheek again.

"You sure you're okay?"

"I'm fantastic. You're just so big and it's been a little while. I'm going to feel that for a while."

"Good. Every time you get a twinge down there, you'll remember how fucking good it was having me stretching you out. You'll think of me every day. Just how I want it."

"Mmm." Is all she can manage.

I can't even get up. My legs are like jelly, so I tie off the condom and toss it into the bin beside my desk, stretching out beside her to tuck her up against my body. She feels so right there. The curve of her ass tucks perfectly against my sated cock, and she snuggles into the hand I've got curled around her torso.

I'll get up and clean us up in a bit. For now. I need this. This intimacy fills me up, recharging me, so I soak it in while I can. Who knows when I'll get this again?

That thought leaves my overheated body cold. I've missed this so much, but not with just anyone. I want it with her. My fake dating idea doesn't seem like such a good one anymore. Could we make it real? What would that mean for me? For her?

It would mean trusting someone, letting them see me at my most vulnerable. Giving them the power to destroy me. I don't know if I could live through it if someone hurt me again like that. but she wouldn't do that to me. Right?

CHAPTER NINETEEN

ANYTHING FOR YOU

JAZZ

Soft snores rumble under my chest and I smile, looking up to see the harsh lines of Cole's face softened by sleep. A sliver of moonlight sneaks through the window to highlight every ridge of muscle exposed by the sheet.

I glance around, disoriented, in the unfamiliar room, and spot the red light of a digital clock on the bedside table. It's only three, not time to get up yet. I should go back to sleep, but I can't stop staring at him.

I trace a finger down his chest, circling his pecs and each groove of his abs. The soothing rhythm finally eases me back into a sleepy state. It's fine. I can worry about the details in the morning. We said this would be one night, and it was an incredible one. I'll just enjoy this man for now and see where it goes later.

"What is that incredible smell? Did I die? Is this Heaven? Cause if so, I take back every sin I've ever sinned."

Of course it's JJ's voice that rings out louder than the rest. The boisterous enthusiasm from behind me is a little much even for me this early in the morning, and I consider myself to be a morning person. Given an adequate supply of caffeine, of course.

"What are you searching for, JJ? Coffee or breakfast?"

"All of the above."

I spin around. "There are fresh scones baking in the oven, and I've got some bacon and eggs frying up. They won't be long. Help your self to a cup of coffee. You guys had some good stuff there, so should be tasty." They actually have a full-on fancy espresso machine in the kitchen, but I didn't exactly feel like playing barista on my day off, so I made a regular old pot of drip.

"You can stay over any time you want. I could kiss you right now."

"Not if you don't want to lose a limb or two." Cole strolls into the kitchen, sending his roommate straight to hell with his glare.

I brush my hands down the front of the apron I found in the drawer. "Nobody's losing any limbs. There's plenty of food and coffee for everyone."

He frowns at me, walking up to slide an arm around my waist and dropping a kiss on my forehead. I guess it's still on, at least for the day. "But he said was going to kiss you. Not allowed. Mine."

"I don't belong to you, Cole." That possessive tone sets off alarm bells in my head, and I shove at his arm. I know it's just his roommates, and he's teasing, but I had more than enough of the jealous, possessive, controlling boyfriend bit to last a lifetime. Not looking for any more of that.

He bends down to whisper in my ear. "Not what you said last night. Last night you were all mine."

"Well, it's not night anymore. And during the day, I'm my own person, so back off. Don't worry, you'll get a treat too." My shove this time is more playful. I know he's just posturing around his roommates. That's the whole vibe of this house.

His smirk is evil. "Really. A treat just for me?"

If I rolled my eyes back any farther, they'd end up in the back of my skull. "No. The scones are for everyone."

"Scones?" Beau steps into the kitchen, followed by a grumbling Dev. Even the big man lights up a little when he stumbles through the door, rubbing a hand over the closely shorn hair on top of his head.

"Yes, I made blueberry scones from scratch. I hope you don't mind I stole some of the frozen berries."

"It's fine. They're for smoothies, but we can get more."

"Perfect. I've gotta flip this bacon and look after the eggs before they burn."

Cole follows me back to the stove, stepping in close and slipping his hands around my waist as if he needs the touch as much as I do.

"I've got things to do. If you're not going to help, then back off."

"I can think of several things I'd like to do to you." His breath tickles the back of my neck, raising the hairs. "But if you insist on finishing this cooking, then I can help you."

I tilt my head up to him. The doubt must be very clear in my expression.

"What? I can totally cook. I used to cook for my younger sisters all the time while my dad was at work."

"Okay then. Grab the tongs and flip that bacon over. I'll finish these eggs up." I toss some fresh chives into the mix as well as some chopped tomatoes.

He gets to work, keeping his hands to himself as we work together, moving about the kitchen with ease as if we've done it a million times before. I'm used to a crowded kitchen, and as the youngest of six girls I was always given the mundane tasks like chopping vegetables and tossing salads together, but I actually enjoy the work. It's soothing and reminds me of the best parts of home. Food has always been an inextricable part of our life.

"I miss my family."

"Me too. I wish I lived closer, but it will not get any better after I graduate, unless some of my siblings attend a school closer to where I end up."

"That's gotta be tough. Not knowing where you'll end up."

"It is, but it's worth it. The things I'll be able to do for them after I get a contract will all make it worthwhile."

He yoinks a slice of bacon off the tabletop griddle, dropping it and blowing on his fingers. "Fuck."

"Serves you right. You should know better. Is that why you want to play professional hockey? To look after your family?"

He nods his head, pulling his burnt finger out of his mouth. A flutter of desire wakes up as if I'm still not satisfied, even after the mind-blowing sex we had last night. Greedy. Now that I've had a taste, I'm not sure I'm going to be able to back off.

The oven lets out a long beep to give us the one-minute warning, so I serve up eggs on the pristine white plates I found in the cupboard. Cole adds a couple of slices of bacon to each one and then pulls the perfectly baked scones out of the oven.

The guys are lounging around the big dining room table, but Beau shoots to his feet at my approach. "I'll grab cutlery and napkins."

It's a nice little group. I don't quite understand why Cole kept to himself after he got here, but it looks like he missed out on so much. They seem like good guys.

Everyone is seated at the table about to dig in when I spin around to head back to the kitchen, but I run straight into Cole in the doorway. He grips my waist. "Sit down."

"I need coffee. Very important."

"I'll get your coffee. What do you take in it?"

I'm very particular about my coffee. "Just a pinch of sugar and like half a milk. Just enough to cool it down a bit."

"A pinch?"

I swat at his hand when he pinches the skin at my waist.

"I can get my coffee myself if you keep that up."

"No way, Coffee Girl. It's your day off. I'm looking after you today. Especially after you cooked breakfast for this group of idiots. You didn't need to do that."

"I know, but I enjoy cooking for people. It makes me happy to see them enjoying my food. Part of why I want to own my own place someday.

"Ah, now the truth comes out. Need the glory of compliments to keep you going."

"Sure, that's it."

He boops my nose. "Now go sit down. I'll get your coffee, and if I don't make it perfectly, feel free to talk to my manager."

I shake my head at him and go to sit down. Judging from the almost indecent moans of appreciation, the guys are all enjoying them.

Yup. I did good. The pastry is buttery and flaky, almost melting in my mouth.

"These are so good, Jazz. Thank you so much for baking for us. You can stay over any time."

"Glad to see you made use of the stash last night." Beau's eyes flick up over my shoulder.

"Oh my god, Beau. Shut up," says Cole, placing my coffee in front of me.

I eye the dark brown liquid critically. It looks about the right color. I lift it to my lips and take a small sip.

"Perfection."

"Yeah?" Cole asks, sitting down beside me.

"Yes. You did good."

"Excellent. I'll make you coffee any day you want."

"Me too," JJ pipes up. "I'd do anything for another taste of your scones."

My stomach flips over even as I'm laughing at the goofball goalie. Now's my chance to ask them about the auction. I've been putting it off, even though Amira asked me to look after it.

"Anything?"

"Yes. These are fucking delicious. If you ever decide to leave Coco, I'll be here waiting for you and your baked goods."

"Okay. This is a bit of a big ask, but I've got this event coming up in a few weeks. It's for one of my classes. I have to plan an event to raise money for a charity of my choice."

"I'm sure it will be great. What can we help with?" Beau says.

"Well. I have to make this one really stand out. Make a splash and make a big profit for the women's center I've picked. This is going to be a project I'll use on my business grant applications."

"And? What do you need?" Cole drops his hand onto my leg, giving it an encouraging squeeze.

I focus on his face. It's easier to direct the question at him. "It's a coffee shop style event with live music and a silent auction."

"Silent auction. So you need donations? We can do some signed jerseys for sure."

I toy with the hem of the shirt he lent me, and his tongue darts out to lick his lips. "That would be great, but also Amira suggested we add in a different kind of auction for another stream of revenue. A bachelor auction. I know maybe it sounds a little wild. But she knows I have a connection with the hockey team, so she begged me to ask if any of you guys would be willing to participate. She came up with it on the fly, so it's totally short notice. If you guys can't do it. I'll understand."

I'm so fixated on Cole that it's easy to see the subtle tightening of his shoulders at the request.

"I know it's a lot to ask, so zero pressure, but I promised her I would. Rob said he could probably get a few of the football players on board anyway, so I'm sure we'll have enough bachelors." I'm squirming in my seat, staring into my coffee.

The hand on my thigh tightens. "I'll do it," Cole says.

"Really? I'd understand if you don't want to. No hard feelings." I don't want them to do anything that might be uncomfortable.

"Of course I will. That's what boyfriends do." He puts a little extra emphasis on the word, and it sends a tingle skating across my skin.

"Getting auctioned off to a hot chick? Yes, please. I am in." JJ pushes out of his chair to do a little dance, punching the air. It makes me laugh and eases the tension.

"I'm sure we can get a bunch of the guys on board," Beau says, crossing his arms over his chest and scanning the room. "We can do better than the football team, right?"

"Woot!" Grant calls out. "But if my girlfriend doesn't win me, she's going to serve me my balls for dinner. Don't make me eat my own balls."

"What do we have to do with the winner?" Dev asks.

"Give her the use of our sticks all night long, hopefully." JJ says, bobbing an eyebrow.

Jazz throws her hands up in the air. "No, no, no. I'm not running an escort service." I can feel heat rising to my cheeks, and I duck my head. "Just an innocent date."

"We'll be there." Cole says, rubbing small circles on my back that are making me want to drag him back upstairs. It's not even actually Halloween yet. Couldn't we enjoy each other a few more times without messing up this thing we've got going on? "I'm there for you."

I blow on my coffee to cool it down and take another small sip, avoiding that look on his face. That look that says he means every word he says. And when he says things like that, it makes me want it. Someone in my life to look after me, the way I look after others. Someone to look at me like I'm precious to them. But that can all change far too quickly to something darker, more possessive. I can't afford to let someone become my entire world. I've got my own dreams and goals, and I can't let myself get lost in someone else. Not like I did before.

Chapter Twenty

Mixed Signals

Jazz

I t's been three days since the party. Three days since Cole and I finally gave in to the need that's been pulsing between us since we started hanging out. Now here we are strolling around campus on actual Halloween.

A lot of the students did their partying on the weekend, but this is a college campus parties happen every day of the week, especially on Halloween.

There are quite a few fairies dancing across the lawn under the eerie shadows of bare branches. The last of the leaves are fluttering to the surrounding ground. Witches, devils, and angels run around in groups giggling in costumes that barely cover their assets.

Since I was on duty tonight, I couldn't go all out in my full costume, but I threw on some leopard ears and a tail to keep up with the spirit of things. Cole has on a set of sequined devil horns and a forked tail. I can't help but laugh every time I look at him.

Things between us are fine. Not as weird as I thought they'd be after our naked shenanigans. It's almost like it never happened, except I can still feel him between my thighs. He really meant it when he said he'd make sure I could feel him for the next week. All it does is make me want a repeat, though.

"So, Sarah. Are you doing anything for Halloween?" I ask the blonde girl we picked up at the library. We're walking her back to Eastdell, the apartment style residences on the other side of campus.

She adjusts her glasses, fidgeting with the straps of her backpack. "No. I'm not really into dressing up. My parents wouldn't approve."

"You could still go down to the UC to hang out and do some of the activities they've got going on there." If I hadn't volunteered to work the shift tonight, I'd probably be there. In fact, Cole and I might still be able to make the midnight showing of Friday the 13th once our shift is over.

"I don't know. I don't really know anyone who's going to be there."

I remember being a nervous first year like her. Not knowing anyone on campus and feeling weird about going places by myself. I made my little group of friends pretty quickly though, and things got fun. It must be hard feeling alone a couple months into the year.

"Maybe you can convince one of your roommates to go with you." The Eastdell units have four or six bedrooms that are joined by a common space with a kitchen. I lived there in first year too. That's where I met Amira. We were the only freshman in our unit, so we stuck clung to each other like we were attached with Velcro for the first few weeks.

"They're probably going to be drinking and partying."

"Got it." It's hard when you have to share space with people that don't really share your interests. I should know. "I'm sure you'll find your people, though. That's what college is all about." I give her a reassuring smile as we reach the front doors to her building, and she pulls out her key to let herself in.

"Thanks, Jazz. It was great to meet you." Her face is a little lighter, and she flashes me a shy smile as she waves goodbye. Forget the barista as a therapist thing. Apparently, this job is all about counseling people as well. Maybe I chose the wrong field.

Nah, I think of my grandfather and the stories he used to tell me about growing up on the coffee farm. The beautiful sun shining down over the glossy green leaves and bright red cherries ripe for picking. I feel a connection to him every time I open a fresh bag of roasted beans and inhale that sweet scent. Every time I serve someone a perfect cup and we have a friendly chat. I love the connection of the place. And it's going to be so much better when it's my own cafe.

"That was nice of you," Cole says, breaking through my reverie. "Encouraging her like that." He's looking at me with those eyes again. That admiration that borders on something more.

"I guess I know what it's like to be her. I was so nervous my first few weeks after I got here. Afraid I would never make friends. But I was lucky enough to get assigned a room next to Amira. We bonded almost immediately and then made some more friends over the first few weeks. But I can totally picture myself in her place if I hadn't made those immediate connections. A couple months into my first year and still scared, with no one to fall back on."

"I guess I always took it for granted. Being part of a team meant I always had a built-in network of friends. I'm not saying I've been super close to all my teammates, but I always had them. It was kind of easy. Until it wasn't. Until I realized I'd relied too much on the bond of sport without really looking deeper into the character of some of the guys I was hanging out with. Just because we like the same things doesn't mean we share the same values. It was a hard way to learn the lesson, but it really stuck."

"Did something happen with one of your former teammates in particular?" I don't know why I haven't asked before. I've been assuming it was the Charlene thing that made him push everyone away, but the way he talks sometimes makes me think there's more to it. I place a hand on his elbow as we continue our stroll along the cobbled walks, waiting for another call.

His eyes shutter, and that faraway look is back on his face. The one he always wore when I first met him. I thought we were past that, but now I'm not so sure.

"Yeah."

I pause for a minute, waiting for him to expand on it, but he keeps his silence, staring ahead, and pulling his hand out of mine to rub the back of his neck. My stomach lurches, but I check myself. He doesn't need to tell me everything.

"But you know not everyone is like that, right?"

He places a warm hand over mine, turning to me. "I'm starting to realize that. As I've been working with Hail, I've been remembering the importance of trust and team-work. And spending time with you. Listen, Jazz."

I'm forced to stop as he halts in his tracks, spinning around to look at me. "I've been thinking..."

He swears softly under his breath as the cell goes off again, signaling another call.

The rest of the night is hopping with calls and there's no chance to catch our breath, much less resume that dangerous conversation. I can't honestly say how I'd re-act to it. How I'd respond to a request for this to be something more. Something real. If that's where he was going. I think, though. I think I might have said yes. With Halloween in the air, and our passionate night together, still imprinted in my memory.

There was too much time to obsess over the things he's potentially keeping from me, and the ways he could hurt me. I'm all edgy and uncomfortable by the time we turn in our vests.

He slips an arm around shoulders, pulling me in to drop a kiss on the top of my head. "Wanna go see that movie?"

The stomach flutters kick up another several notches, and I chicken out, feigning a yawn. The fake yawn turns into a real one. "I'm pretty tired. Think I'll go home and hit my bed. I've got an early morning tomorrow."

His shoulders droop a little. "No worries, I'll give you a lift home and text you tomorrow."

I nod into his shoulder, afraid he'll spot the lie on my face.

I wasn't lying when I said I had an early morning tomorrow, but as I'm getting ready for bed, my mind races, and I don't think I'm going to be sleeping anytime soon.

I'm in my tiny kitchen, heating milk to make a hot chocolate, when there's a knock on the door. My heart picks up its pace, and flutters start up in my stomach. Cole? Did he come back to finish what he started? And how do I feel about that? Judging by the huge smile that I can't even try to dim, I think I know the answer.

I swing the door open, and a cold sweat breaks out, replacing all the fuzzy feelings that were spreading through me.

"Darryl. What are you doing here?"

His eyes are a little glazed, and his hair is mussed up, sticking out from under the skeletal mask he's got perched on the top of his head.

"Jazz."

His breath comes out in a boozy wave, and I pull away from him, trying to slam the door shut. But he jams a foot in the doorway before I can shut it. I'm no match for his bulk.

"What are you doing here, Darryl? I need you to leave."

"Jazz. Come on. I came all the way over to see my girl."

That's right. Another thing he used to make me feel guilty for. The fact that my apartment is so far from his. He made it out like it was a huge hassle to come pick me up and that's how he usually convinced me to stay over at his place. It got to the point where I was hardly sleeping at my own apartment anymore.

"I'm not your girl, Darryl, so you don't get to come over here. Please leave." I try to put as much steel into my voice as I can despite my trembling fingers, but I can't control the fearful quaver.

"Jazz. Please. I can't live without you. I've tried but seeing you with that hockey guy. It makes me livid. How dare he put his hands on you?"

I glance around, looking for my phone. Shit, where did I put it? Bathroom counter maybe. If I make a run for it, maybe I can lock myself in there, but what if I didn't leave it in there and then I'm trapped with him inside my apartment waiting me out? I'd give anything to be at that scary movie with Cole right now. Reality is so much more terrifying. My breath is coming faster, fingers going numb.

He seems to read my move, grabbing my arm in a painful hold before I can dart off. My heart is racing out of control now as he leans over me.

Chapter Twenty-One

The Enforcer

Cole

I drive Mabel around the neighborhood aimlessly, trying to gather my thoughts together. Students are spilling out on all the sidewalks downtown, stumbling and laughing, and it feels like a fun house. I'm in my own personal hell of regret. Wishing I had told Jazz how I feel, asked her if she could maybe give me a chance.

Finally, I turn around and park in front of her building. Trying to gather to courage to go in. Yes. I need to do this. If she says no, then that's it. I'll leave her alone and we can be just friends as painful as that might be. But if she says yes. Everything inside of me is hoping that she does.

She gave me the code to buzz into her building, so I let myself in, climbing the scuffed stairs two at a time, too impatient to wait for the old creaky elevator.

As I shove through the heavy fire door, I hear her voice shaky with fear. "Darryl, let me go. You need to leave."

Burning rage rips through me like a wildfire at the sight of that asshole towering over her. My girl. It's so much more intense than the rage that had me pounding on Jeremy's face until it was far past the point of "you asshole, you slept with my girlfriend."

"Get your fucking hand off my girlfriend." I growl, advancing on my prey. He's gripping Jazz's arm in a hold that has her struggling to escape.

He doesn't even turn around until I grab the back of his shirt and yank him away from her. Then makes a wild swing at me that sends him reeling on his feet. A bitter laugh rips from my chest.

"Really? That's all you got?"

He's too stupid to read the dark promise of pain in my eyes. "She was mine first."

Jazz is shaking all over as she turns to me with gratitude in her wide eyes. "Cole."

I should comfort her, pull her into my arms, and call the cops. Instead, I turn back to the worthless piece of shit, punching him in the gut so hard he doubles over.

"She was never yours, you pathetic excuse for a man. She's mine, and you will never touch her again." I slam an elbow into his back, and his legs give out. He hits the floor with a satisfying thud. I give him an extra kick in the ribs as he scrambles to get up.

A dark sense of satisfaction fills me as he curls in around himself on the floor, but I'm so not done with him. I drag him to his feet, holding him up as I sink another knuckle cracking punch in the face. Hot blood spurts from his nose, splattering my hand, and there's a satisfying crunch.

"Leave my girl alone. Don't even fucking look at her again."

I'm about to land another hit when a soft whimper behind me jerks me out of the red haze, and a hand lands on my back. I spin around, all senses on high alert as the adrenaline races through my blood. My arm is drawn back, ready to take another swing when I spot my attacker. It's Jazz. No. There's terror in her eyes.

I'm shaking all over as the fear on her face washes away the rest of the anger at her ex. Fuck. I've scared her. What was I thinking? Why did I come here?

I drag in a few deep breaths to get myself under control. There was a reason I came here. I was going to ask her to be my girlfriend for real. But now. Now she's looking at me the same way she was looking at him. I can't blame her.

"Cole?" Her eyes are wide.

"Jazz? Are you okay?" I drop my voice to a whisper, wanting nothing more than to pull her into my arms. That would be the only thing that could soothe me right now. I reach out for her, needing to touch her. To reassure myself that she's okay, but she backs away and I cringe in on myself.

"I need to know you're okay. Can I see your arm?" I'm pleading now.

She shakes her head.

"I should call the cops." I reach for my phone, even though I'm sure I'll be the one that comes out looking like the bad guy in this situation, but I think it's the right thing to do. To make sure this guy doesn't try anything with her again. And maybe it was foolish of me to think we could keep him away with the fake relationship thing. Maybe I've made things worse for her. Set off his jealousy.

She shakes her head. "No. I'm sure he'll leave me alone after that." She waves her arm at his bleeding nose.

"Don't call the cops." He has the audacity to beg for leniency. "I'll leave. I won't bother you anymore, Jazz." He swipes at the blood dripping from his nose. Just as I thought. He's a bully, but only with people he thinks are weaker than him. No way he'll try anything again if I'm around. Joke's on him, though. Jazz is stronger than both of us. She broke free from him. Told him to hit the road and leave her alone, and I'm sure she would have figured a way out of this situation even if I hadn't showed up. But I'm still glad I did. I'm glad I was able to protect her.

He staggers a couple of steps away.

"How did you even get in here, Darryl?" Jazz asks.

"I walked," he mumbles. "Was at Niche for a party. Thought you'd want some company on Halloween. Turns out you're still the stuck-up bitch I thought you were."

"Are you fucking kidding me? Was that not enough for you? Want some more? I could do this all night, asshole." I advance on him again, and he backs away, hands in the air.

"No, no. I'm going."

"Apologize before you go." Jazz grabs my arm as I take another step toward him. "Apologize to my girlfriend, shit for brains."

"I'm sorry. I'm sorry." He says, his entire body clenched in fear.

"Good. And don't come back here. Ever. Don't look at her. Don't come near her or I'll make sure you don't walk out of here on your own two feet next time."

He finally fucks off and I step into her apartment, the door rattling in its frame from the force of me slamming it shut and locking it behind him.

I run a shaky hand through my hair, afraid to look at her. Afraid of seeing that look of terror in her eyes again.

"Let me just..." She walks away, while I stand there unsure if I should leave or sit down. I'm definitely not doing the thing I came over here for now.

I hear the water running while she's in the bathroom and then she emerges, looking much more composed than before, with a bright red bag in her hands.

"Sit down."

I obey her, collapsing on the couch. My knees were about to give out on me, anyway. She pulls my hand away from my head with a gentle touch and I hear the zipping sound.

"Look at me Cole."

I finally do. Opening my eyes to see her staring at me with concern as she holds my large hand in her small, cool one. She's got an antibiotic wipe which she swipes across my cracked knuckles. I hiss in pain at the sting, but at the same time I relish it. Pain in my body helps ground me, taking my mind off the anger still gripping me.

The fear is gone in her eyes, but so is the lust and the soft anticipation that was there earlier. She's wary of me now. I wish she'd never seen that side of me.

"Thank you. I'm glad you showed up. I don't know what would have happened if you hadn't."

"I'm glad too. Glad I could be there for you."

She wraps a bandage around my knuckles, giving me a soft smile.

"You're all patched up. You should probably head home now."

"Are you sure you don't want me to stay? Do you want to talk about it? I really hate to leave you like this." The truth is, I don't want to be alone with my own thoughts right now. I need to be here with her. She keeps me calm and level.

"I think I need to be alone right now."

The words are a blow to my gut, taking my air away. It may be what I was expecting, but that doesn't make it hurt any less.

"Are you sure? That was a lot."

"I know, Cole. That's why I need to be alone." Her tone doesn't allow for any argument.

"Okay, I'll go."

I stand up to leave, and she stops me with a hand on my shoulder. "I'll message you with the details of the auction."

Right the auction. We agreed to participate for her, and she still wants me there, so that's a good sign. Maybe not what I was looking for, but at least we're still something. Friends, fake boyfriend and girlfriend, but at least it's something. I'll take any crumb right now.

Although the thought of standing up there in front of a crowd and letting some girl bid on me is not appealing. Not if it's someone other than her.

"Let me know if you need anything else from me before then," she says. And it feels a little too close to a goodbye. Leaving it up in the air whether we'll see each other or talk to each other before the auction.

"I'll text you." I promise her. I may not get an in person meeting, but at least I'll text her. Remind her I'm still here for her whenever she needs me. God, how did things get so fucked up so quickly?

"Good night, Cole.

"Night, Coffee Girl." I want to steal a kiss. One more before I go. Taste her lips. Let me know she's okay after all that happened, but I don't have that right.

She's pale and a little shaky, and every cell in my body is aching to reach out. Comfort her. To explain why I lost it like that. Finding him towering over her, touching her. All my protective instincts came roaring to life. Seeing her threatened like that intensified the feelings that have been growing ever since she walked into my life.

My palm falls to the door after she shuts it, and I linger there for a minute, ten. I'm not sure, but it's a struggle to leave her here by herself, and vulnerable.

CHAPTER TWENTY-TWO

MISTAKES WERE MADE

JAZZ

"Okay, so this is the list of silent auction donations I've got set up so far. I'm waiting to hear from the Blue Bottle downtown. I think they're going to donate a voucher for a prix fixe dinner for two and it looks like Salazar's is going to offer a VIP tasting and tour. Where are you at?"

I lean back against the comfy yellow couch in Amira's shared house, pulling a stack of papers out of my bag. I rifle through them, searching until, yes. Those are the ones I was looking for. I hand them to her. "I've got us all setup with the Bean Bar for their coffee cart and snack service. And Jordan has hooked us up with Lena Gold for a book signing, so that will draw a good crowd of the bookish girlies, and we've got several special edition signed copies ready to go for the auction as well. The space is rented, and our insurance is all set up."

The closer we get to the event, the louder the buzzing running through my veins gets. I'm a chaotic mess of nerves and excitement. It's going to have a totally different vibe from a fancy charity gala, but with some similar components. More casual and eclectic with the coffee shop, bookstore vibe. Totally up my alley and perfect for the college crowd we're trying to bring in. It feels perfect to me, but what if it's too eclectic for my professor?

"Fantastic. We're at about fifty percent capacity for the ticket sales and once we get our line up of bachelors firmed up, I think the rest will fly." She's nibbling on the end of her pen. "How's it going with the hockey guys?"

I blow out a breath. "They said they were on board when I asked them last Saturday, but I haven't finalized the details about who is for sure going to be there." Procrastinating? Who me? No way. My last interaction with Cole has been running through my head on a continuous loop, and it is not helping the nerves.

Amira is pretty perceptive, though, and she must catch the slight hitch in my voice. "Trouble in paradise?"

The list of book donations in front of me is suddenly very fascinating.

She reaches out, placing a warm hand on mine. "Hey, is something going on with Cole? If it's a problem for you, we can get by without them. I'm in this for you."

Her words ease my shoulders a little. I know I've been avoiding contacting Cole after everything that happened. The incredible sex and closeness we shared that was blown away when I saw that ugly edge of jealousy and possessiveness. That's exactly the opposite of what I need in my life right now. Another controlling man in my life.

I sigh. "Everything is okay. Something happened with Darryl and Cole got all defensive and it freaked me out a little."

Her eyes are narrowed to suspicious slits. "Did he do something to you, Jazz? Are you okay?"

A hard knot settled in my chest after he left, and it hasn't left. I've been keeping everything locked down so tight, but I need to talk to someone. I need a friend. I'm used to relying on myself because there wasn't always enough space for my thoughts and needs in the crowded house I grew up in. But it's time. It's time I let go a little. "Darryl showed up drunk at my house on Halloween. I opened the door, thinking it was Cole coming back after he dropped me off. Darryl got handsy and pushy. He wasn't taking no for an answer. Turns out, Cole came back and came charging to my rescue. He yanked Darryl away from me."

Amira gasps. "Did he hurt you before Cole showed up?" She squeezes my hand.

"He grabbed my arm, tried to kiss me, but then Cole got there." That first moment after I laid eyes on him, something clicked in place. So much relief, but then when he called me mine, he claimed me. It was suffocating.

"I'm so sorry that happened. Did you call the police?"

"No. He ended up leaving, but the problem was, Cole took it too far. He really laid into Darryl. At first, I was relieved and a little smug, but then it was scary. It turned into a pissing contest of male dominance, and I'm not an object to claim. I didn't really like that side of Cole. I didn't want to be alone, but having him there was overwhelming, so I sent him home, and haven't seen him since. It was my fault. I know better than to open the door without checking who it is. I was just so excited to see Cole again." There's the real truth. I was looking forward to seeing him and it made me foolish.

"Jazz!" The harsh edge to her usually soft tone jerks me up from the paper I'm staring blankly at to find her focused on me, brow pinched together in anger. "Listen to me. You are not responsible for what they did. You're not responsible for Darryl harassing you and you're definitely not responsible for the way Cole acted. They're both grown ass men who should know better, and if they can't handle their own emotions, that's their problem. Did Cole hurt you?"

I shake my head. "No. It just scared me a little seeing him like that. And... Can I tell you a secret, Amira?" I look around as if to make sure no one is eavesdropping, even though I know there's no one else here.

"Of course."

I check out the ceiling, the picture of a galloping white horse on the walls. Anything but her. This sounds weird even to me. "Cole and me. We're not really dating." A sharp twist of pain squeezes my heart as I hear myself saying the words.

She doesn't say anything. Only the arched brow tells me she's almost as confused at my confession as I am.

"We were fake dating to keep Darryl and his ex off our backs."

Her nose scrunches up and I can't say blame her. "Fake dating? But I saw you together at the Halloween party. None of that looked fake. Are you sure you didn't go into the wrong program? Maybe acting is your calling."

"Yes. We got to know each other and realized we both had a problem. Obnoxious exes who kept interjecting themselves in our lives. His crazy ex moved all the way from Florida to be near him again."

"Okay, but you're friends, right?"

"Yes, we were." This is all coming out so jumbled. I don't even know where my own head is at.

"Were?"

"Yes. Just friends who pretended we were more. Until after the party. I'm really attracted to him. I have been almost since when we first met, and I thought I could keep that in check. But I was wrong. That night I couldn't help myself. I went for it. And he did not protest." A sizzling heat crackles through me at that memory.

The hint of a smile curves her lips. "You slept together?"

"Yes, we did, and let me tell you. It was incredible." If only I could open a window. I could use a gust of fresh air to cool down my heated skin.

"Well, that's good, right? Or was he not on the same page as you?"

"Oh, he was on the same page. A hundred percent. And the way he started talking. The things he started to say made me think he might be interested in something real.

And if he had asked before Wednesday, I probably would have said yes. But now. I'm not sure. I got scared and I don't think I want to put myself in someone else's power like that again. Am I crazy?"

Her dark hair swings in a smooth waterfall with the vigorous shake of her head. "You're not crazy. You know what's right for you. You know what you can handle. And if the red flags are flying, maybe you should stay away from him."

"Right." I nod. "That's what I thought." I rub at my chest, trying to ease the vice tightening around my heart.

"Not so fast. There's a caveat. Make sure that it isn't just your fear that's stopping you from pursuing something with him. I don't want to make this about me, but I was dating this guy in first year. Brendan. Everyone told me not to commit to someone so early in my college years, so I blew him off and threw away something good. Turns out there are way too many mediocre players on the field. Out of all the guys I've dated, no one has come close to what I felt for him, and I regret breaking it off." She squeezes my hand.

I remember. Brendan was a great guy. He's been dating someone else in our program for the last couple of years. It must be hard for her to see them together all the time if she still feels that way. "I had no idea, Amira. I'm sorry. I've been a shitty friend. So wrapped up in my own life and problems that I haven't paid enough attention to you."

She picks up a random stack of papers, shuffling through them. "It's fine, Jazz. You don't have to put every-thing on yourself. That's not what I want. I was embarrassed, so I didn't talk to anyone about it, even you. And just so you know, I still consider you my best friend here at this school."

"Even after..."

"Even after you bailed on me for Darryl. I don't blame you and you shouldn't blame yourself. He offered you something you needed at a time you needed it, and you didn't realize how deep in you'd gotten until it was too late. But you recognized the signs. You realized what was happening, and you got yourself out. You are strong, and you need to embrace that. That's how I know you're capable of making the right decision on your own about Cole. You've been the one spending time with him. You'll be able to tell if he's bad for you."

I shake my head, still not able to trust myself, but it helps. Sharing with her. Helping each other. "Thanks." I'm so glad I have her back in my life. "And just so you know, you're my best friend, too."

I lean in to give her a hug, dropping my head to her shoulder. This is totally what was missing in my life. Now if I can figure out the rest, I'll be golden.

"Okay. I'm going to text him to figure out which guys are in for the auction, and we'll finalize this list so we can get it published. I have a feeling these tickets will sell out in under a week once we get some of the star hockey players on the auction block. After all, who is more eligible at this school than a member of the championship winning hockey team?"

"Don't feel obligated. I wasn't trying to pressure you into it."

"I know. But it doesn't matter what's going on between Cole and I. Friends, fake relationship, real relationship. We're something, and honestly, some of his friends seemed excited about it. It shouldn't be hard at all for him to convince them to commit."

Amira flips her laptop open as I tap away on my phone.

> **Hey Cole. Just wanted to finalize which guys are in for the auction. They've got to be fully on board, and I need a list if you can get that to me. Thanks so much, Jazz.**

There. That's fine, right? Friendly. Not weird. Or maybe it is weird. I have no clue any more how to navigate this thing between us now that we've crossed so many boundaries.

CHAPTER TWENTY-THREE

POST GAME HIGH

COLE

I can't help myself from constantly checking out the small crowd as I whiz by the glass during our warmup skate. There is still an abundance of empty seats, but people are continuously streaming in to fill the seats. This is an important game against North Chicago. Hopefully, it'll be the one that turns everything around, giving us the momentum to climb the ranks. So far, we're at two wins and two losses for the season. Not exactly a stellar record. But NCSU is at four wins and zero losses, so if we can pull it together and beat them, it'll be the message in the sky that lets everyone know we're coming for them. Our play during practices has been improving. We're starting to mesh as a team, but we've still got our weaknesses, and I can't afford to be one of them.

And I don't want Hail fucking things up and making me look bad, either. We've had a few more sessions together and I think some of my wisdom, if that's what you'd call it, is sinking into his thick skull, but he's still fighting me at every turn.

I push up from my stretches, skating over where he's taking shots on goal. His favorite pastime. Every now and again, he glances over at the crowd to make sure they're watching him.

"Hey, Hail. Toss me the biscuit."

"Get your own puck." He doesn't even bother to turn around as he shoots me down.

"Hail. I thought we were getting over this shit. This game means a lot, and I want to make sure we're working together like I know we can." Look at me being the advocate for teamwork. I never would have thought it, but then I wouldn't be doing this if I hadn't had my spot threatened by the captain. I hate to admit it, but I think the sessions might be doing me good as well. I've been finding spots easier and communicating on the ice with more accuracy. Look at me. I've always scanned the opposing team for their strengths and weaknesses but haven't taken as much time to use that skill on my own teammates.

"I don't need your advice, Schaeffer. Keep it to yourself. I'm sure you could use it." He goes back to shooting pucks and I notice he's gone back to his old habit of shooting toward his favorite spot in the top left corner. So much for progress.

"You keep shooting there and Grimes is going to read you like a book. He'll be blocking your pucks without even straining a muscle."

"Whatever," he mutters, yanking his stick back again, but the next shot goes low and to the right. Look at that. He might never admit it, but he is listening to me.

"Toss me the puck." I repeat my request, hoping I can convince him this time.

He whips it at me in with an angry swipe, but he's clearly underestimating me if he thinks he's going to make me chase it. I snag it, slapping it straight to the back of the net.

Skating over, I retrieve it and send it back his way.

"Four touches and then a shot," I tell him, and we spend the remaining warm up time on the drill that has my muscles loose and vision sharp for the start of the game.

There are lightning bolts flashing across the ice now and the arena is probably about three quarters full. My eyes scan the crowd, skipping by Charlene. She's standing near the glass, waving frantically at me. There's no anger left in me for her anymore, which makes it much easier to ignore her desperate bid for my attention.

There's only one person I really want to see out there. I'm still worried she won't show, even though she said she'd come. But we've been texting again, and I managed to snag her for lunch a couple of days ago. Sure, all she wanted to talk about was her event that's coming up next week, but I don't mind. I know how important it is to her and how stressed out she's been getting all the details in perfect order. I m glad she wanted to share it with me.

We seem to be back on the friendship track we were on before the Halloween party. Before the incident with Darryl. The fake relationship is still on, which is a good thing. At least I keep trying to tell myself that even as I rub at the knots in my shoulders. They haven't relaxed since she kicked me out of her place, and I lost my right to tell her how I've been feeling. And now every time I'm near her, there's a tingle of awareness that I can't tamp down no matter how hard I try.

It's a constant presence that I've grown used to, but it's nothing like the shock of lust that almost knocks me off my skates when I finally spot her. She came, and she's got the rich purple fabric of my jersey draped over her stunning body. I don't think I'll ever be able to see that comfortably. It hits me somewhere deep and primal. An urge to claim her. Take her as mine. Unfortunately, that's precisely the attitude that scared her away.

The swish of our skates slicing across the rink soothes the ache a little as we race against each other to clear the ice for the last Zamboni run. I can't help myself from stopping by the glass near her section and banging a glove on it. She looks down at me with a tentative wave, and her dark-haired friend giggles. Amira.

"Okay, boys, this is it. Our chance to show everyone out there that we're more than a team struggling to get our shit together. I need to see you put everything on the line out there. We need this win. Especially you seniors. There could be scouts in the audience today or any day from now on."

Like I need the pressure of that reminder. My entire future is on the line any time we hit the ice.

"No fucking around, no showboating." He levels a glare at Hail. "And trust each other." I get the brunt of his captain's glare on that one. "So get out there and do this thing!" He shouts, pounding a fist in the air. I narrow my eyes, taking in the shaking hand he's swiping through his blond hair. Is he okay?

The crowd is as worked up as us. I think they need the win just as much as we do. Prove that their faith in us is warranted. We're going to do this for them.

I hit the ice on a smooth glide, skating a casual circle around the edge of the rink before settling into my position across from their extra tall winger. He's gotta be six foot seven. I wouldn't be surprised if he's the tallest in the division, but I'm not scared of a little extra arm span. I can skate circles around him or anyone on this team. I'm not even being cocky. I've watched so much tape, I know I'm the fastest one in the division right now. But what I've been learning recently is being the fastest isn't the be all and end all I once thought it was. I need to rely on my team just as much as they need to rely on me.

We snag the puck off the face off and work it down the ice. They've got an excellent defensive side and they're blocking us at every turn. Not a chance of a shot.

We've been battling for every inch, every pass. Fighting this hard is mentally and physically draining. We're better than this, and we've got objectively better players than NCSU, and still we're struggling. The score is tied at one all when we have a line change up shortly after the beginning of the third period. The crowd is getting restless, stomping, and calling out tips and insults. There are cheers too, but not quite enough to lift morale. I whip my helmet off, running a hand through the sweat-soaked strands dripping down my forehead. I gulp back some water before turning to Hail again. Not everything that's been going on is his fault, but there were a couple of times when he could have passed it and chose not to.

"Hail. You need to be aware of when someone has a better shot than you and pass it. Grant could have snagged a goal on that last play."

He snorts. "But who's saying he would have? I've got more precision."

"Maybe so, but he had the better spot to take a shot." Something is rumbling in my chest. Anger and frustration that the kid won't fucking listen to me, no matter what I say. No matter what the proof is. Not to mention Beau's promise that if I can't get him in line, it'll be my spot in jeopardy.

"Stop ragging on me. You missed a pass, too." He turns to me, hostility in his blue eyes, knuckles white, they're clutching his stick so hard.

"I'm aware of where I went wrong, Hail. That's not what's in question. All I want is for this team to succeed. I'm going to graduate next year and move on, but you'll still be here and if you don't get over this shitty attitude, you're going to sink the team."

My eyes are tracking every single play, even as we have this conversation. I gasp when our defense drops the ball and Chicago gets a solid shot in. The breath of relief

I take when JJ stops it is echoes down the bench and throughout the stands.

"I carried my entire team last year. I have no problem doing it again."

Maybe that's the root of the problem. He was allowed to dominate, and he learned to do it. He's not used to playing on a team or trusting the other guys. Fuck. Who am I to be giving this fucker advice? I've been doing the same thing since I joined the team. Maybe not trying to snag the glory for myself, but definitely light on the trust.

"Maybe so, but that will not cut it if you want to go pro. I know you can do it. You've got the eye and the passing skills. Just please try. We need this."

He sighs, smacking his thigh. "Fine."

Thank fuck. Not sure if he'll actually take that agreement out onto the ice, but I can dream.

When we get called back out, I glance over at my new good luck charm one more time. I've always played for myself. Maybe for my team too in the before times, but I've never played for someone else. Now seeing Jazz sitting there waving at me with a huge smile on her gorgeous face, I find I want to play for her. Look at all the epic shit she's doing for her charity event. If she can do that, then I have no excuse for not playing my best. After all, this is the thing I live for. The thing I've was born for. The thing that ignites that same passion under my skin that I see when she talks about her business plans.

I put every ounce of my speed into my blades, pushing off to clear the pack and give myself an opening. Hail races toward me with the puck and I can see the indecision on his face. He really wants to take the shot, but he's got two D-men on him. Don't fucking do it. I try to send the message through my glare.

I slam my stick into the ice as another player races toward me. Every second counts in this game and if he doesn't send it my way, I'm going to lose my clear shot.

I shake my head at him, but he comes through, sending the puck my way. Goalie is better on his glove side, so I go stick side skating the edge between sneaking it into the net and slamming it off the bar. My gamble pays off as it slips past him, lighting up the net and the arena.

Everyone is on their feet, screaming my name. My teammates pile onto me and even Hail looks grudgingly happy. When it comes right down to it, all we want is to win. All of us. It doesn't matter who scores the goal and who gets the assist.

I pump my fist in the air and search for my girl again, pointing my stick at her to let her know that one was for her and her alone.

"Good job." Beau claps me on the back, and the game starts up again because it's not over until the bitter end. Anything could happen and we can't let one goal make us cocky.

My goal boosted our morale and possibly it's shaken our opponents as well. Grant snags another goal within the next few minutes and then there's a bitter fight to keep the game in our favor.

Chicago fights hard, but with only thirty seconds left on the clock, Hail gets his chance for glory, skating behind the net and leaving himself nice and open for a rebound shot. Grant sends it pinging off the bar and Hail snags it, shooting it back in for our fourth goal of the game and a resounding win.

This is what I'm talking about.

The crowd absolutely loses it, thumping and chanting for their home team. We pile on for a congratulatory hug before skating off to celebrate the turning point in our season.

Everyone has already cleared out of the dressing room, and I'm anxious as fuck to take off. I want to see if Jazz is waiting out there for me. It feels like too much to ask for, but since we are still maintaining this fake relationship thing, I figure she might show up for me. But Beau asked me to hang back a bit, so here I am sitting on the bench, knee bouncing as Dev takes his sweet ass time leaving.

I spring up as soon as the door swings shut behind him.

"What's up, Captain?" His hand falls on my shoulder as I stride off to wear down the floor.

"I just wanted to tell you that you're doing a great job with Hail. I'm not sure what you've been up to, but it looks like it's working."

While I appreciate the compliment, I feel like it's not deserved. "He definitely wasn't hitting it during the first two periods. I can't say anything I'm doing is working on that guy."

He pulls on my shoulder to turn me toward him. "Don't dismiss your progress. I heard you talking to him during second period. and it definitely woke him up. You were both playing better by the end of the game, and did you see the effect it had on the rest of the guys? The entire team played better when you guys were working together."

He has a point. My jitters ease as I look him in the eyes. He still seems a little on edge. There's some tension creating lines beside his mouth, but I'm glad I could do my part and take a little of the weight off his shoulders. I nod. "I've been trying. I'm glad we pulled it off. It feels good to be on a functional team again." I pause, weighing my words. This shit is hard to talk about. "I don't think I realized how disconnected I was last year."

White teeth flash through his movie star smile. "About fucking time, man. I knew you had it in you."

"Gee, thanks."

"You've been doing much better since you got with Jazz. I think she might be a keeper."

I glance around, even though everyone else filed out ages ago. "Well, I'm not so sure anything's going to come of that."

"What are you talking about? Are you fucking around on her?" The captain looks perturbed by the idea. Not sure what he's so pissed at. I've never seen him with a girl more than a few times.

"No. It's just..." I can't help searching the corners of the locker room again. "It's not real."

"Not real? What does that even mean?"

"We're fake dating." It sounds even worse when I say it out loud. No way is he going to understand any better than I do, even though I was the one who suggested it.

"Fake dating? What even is that?"

"I asked her to pretend to be my girlfriend. She had an ex who was harassing her, and I had Charlene. We were getting along, but neither of us was looking for an actual relationship. It seemed like a good idea at the time. Perfect match." I let out a bitter little laugh.

"That's fucking weird, but alright. So, what did you need the condoms for?"

Shit, yeah. Did not think this through. "We ended up having sex. The thing is, my feelings for her are not so fake anymore. And I thought she was starting to feel the same way, but I fucked that all up, so we're back to the fake thing."

"This is way too complicated for me. Totally killing my post game high. Let me know if I can help you out, but honestly my advice is just suck it up and tell her the truth. If you want to date her for real, man up and let her know. End of story. Doesn't have to be complicated."

"Sure." I shake my head. Easy for him to say.

My ears prick up at the shuffling sound from the direction of the shower area.

"What the fuck, man?" Nobody else was supposed to be in here. No way I would have spilled my secret if I thought someone else was in here. It was hard enough dragging the words out to share with Beau. I'm building trust with the rest of the team, but Beau is the only one I feel comfortable having that sensitive information.

He looks as confused as me, though, as Hail comes sauntering out of the back, a white towel hanging from his waist.

"What the fuck were you doing back there?" I ask him, chin in the air as I storm toward him.

"Showering. The fuck is your problem?"

"I didn't hear any water running."

I hit the sauna after. "Not that it's any of your business, nosy fucker."

Well, at least he couldn't hear our conversation if he was in the sauna. But what if he's lying? I take another aggressive step toward him, wanting to shake the information out of him when Beau grabs me by the elbow, jerking me back.

"Leave him alone, Schaeffer. Go see your girl and calm down."

I count backward from five in my head, eyes closed, until the anger eases up and back away. The thought of seeing Jazz's smiling face is enough to calm me down this time.

"Fine. Good game. Catch you later." I nod to them, grabbing my bag and shoving out the door.

That took way too long. If she was waiting for me, she's long gone. Disappointment drags my shoulders down, and I head for the back door that leads out into our section of the parking lot.

But it's all washed away in a rush of euphoria when I spot her standing there, arms wrapped around her jersey-wrapped torso, shifting nervously on her feet.

"You waited?" She looks up from her feet at the question. My voice is a little husky.

"You asked me to," her smile is tentative. A warning not to do the thing I really want to do, which is run over there and scoop her up in my arms. Give her a kiss she won't forget. I've got to take my time. See where it goes from here.

"I just wasn't sure if this thing was still on. If you were still okay after..." I'm fiddling with the crooked knot of my tie. "You seemed a little distant when we had lunch the other day."

She presses her lips together. "It's okay. We're good. You stepped in to get Darryl away. Emotions were raging. You said things you didn't mean. It's fine. I thought about it, and I know you don't really think I'm your actual girlfriend. You just said that to get him to back off."

The words slam into my chest like one of Hail's slapshots, almost robbing me of my breath, but I nod. "Right. You got it. I'm glad we're good."

"And also," she grabs the lapels of my jacket. "I wanted to congratulate you on a great game. You were fantastic."

"Thanks. Wanna grab a bite to eat?" Pride helps ease a little of the hurt, and I know I probably shouldn't invite her out, but I can't help myself.

She looks apologetic, but it doesn't take away the hurt of her shutting me down. "I can't. I told Trinity and Amira I'd go out with them tonight."

"That's too bad. Where are you going?"

I loop my arm around her shoulder in a casual gesture, and she allows it, but her shoulders tense at the question. Is she hiding something from me?

"We're going to Niche. Dancing. Girl's night. Is that..." She trails off, checking herself. "I mean, I'm excited."

"Sounds good. I'm glad you get to spend some time with them. You've been working so hard lately at your event. You need to let loose."

Her shoulders shift under me as she twists around, looking at me with a curious expression. "You're okay with it?"

Now I'm just confused. "Of course. Why wouldn't I be? You're not bringing your other fake boyfriend with you, are you?"

Her coat rustles as she shakes her head. "No. It's just... Never mind."

Now it's dawning on me. That prick of an ex of hers didn't like her going out with her friends. What a royal asswipe.

"Jazmin, look at me." She does and I can't help slipping a finger under her chin to tilt her head up. I want her looking me in the eye when I tell her this. "I will never stop you from going out with your friends. As long as you stay safe and look after each other, I'm happy when you're happy. Any guy that is jealous of your friendships is a sorry excuse for a man and doesn't deserve to stand next to you on a street corner, much less date you."

There's still a hint of doubt shadowing her gorgeous brown eyes, but she looks much brighter, and the excitement is back.

"Oh, I'll be safe. We always look out for each other."

"Good." I drop a kiss on her nose. "You have fun."

She babbles excitedly about her plans for the auction next week on the drive home and I'm happy to sit back and listen to her. I'm still a little nervous about having to auction myself off, but for her, no questions asked, I'm there for her. A hundred percent. Even if I can't have her for real, I support her all the way. I know how important this is for her plans.

CHAPTER TWENTY-FOUR

BOYFRIEND FOR SALE

JAZZ

The best part of running this event as a casual coffee shop instead of a grand gala is the comfy clothes. I'm wearing the burnt orange jumpsuit I thrifted along with the all-white platform Adidas runners I save for indoor occasions. White shoes are pretty, but not exactly practical for everyday use.

Wearing comfortable shoes helps on one level, but it doesn't ease the buzzing anxiety that's been zipping around my belly since we started setting up this morning.

"Coffee cart is here. I'm going to get them settled into their spot before I come over to help you finish up the florals." It's kind of surreal speaking into the earpiece like I'm a secret agent or something.

"Gotcha. I'm dealing with the auction item delivery. I'll meet you by the front entrance in ten or so." Amira's official voice crackles in my ear.

A tall woman with her dark hair smoothed into a tight bun pauses, eying up the door frame as I'm hurrying over.

"Hi, Shanna. Let me get that for you." My fingers make quick work of the latches set into the side of the double doors to open the left side.

She gives me a bright smile. "Thanks, Jazmin. I've had to muscle this thing through all kinds of spaces, but why work harder, right?"

"I've always thought that was a great theory." I reach out to shake her hand. "I can help you get you all settled in."

"Thanks." Her smile turns apologetic. "My assistant got stuck in traffic, so he's running a bit late."

"Well, I'm here for you."

Between the two of us, we get the cart set up on the far side of the atrium.

"This is a beautiful space for an event." She says, locking the brakes in place.

We've got it tucked away in the back left corner of the space, leaving plenty of room for people to wait in line for their coffee. Or they can roam the edges of the room to get their books signed or browse the silent auction items. The bachelor auction seems to have turned into the main attraction, though. Once we started blasting out emails and posting signs around campus about it, the tickets sold out in a few days.

I glance over at the massive windows that stretch from floor to ceiling around the curved walls. It's a beautiful day too, the sun shining down to warm the space. Not that it will matter for the actual event, which doesn't take place until the evening, but it's nice to soak in some sunshine while we get things all set up.

"Anything else I can help you with here?" She looks up from her phone. "Nope. Jeff finally made it, so I'll get him to help me unload the van."

"Great. I'll be around getting everything sorted, so let me know if you need anything else."

"Will do." We part ways, heading in opposite directions, and I find Amira arguing with a harried looking guy by the back door.

"What's up?" I ask.

She turns to me. "We're missing two boxes of our auction prizes, and he won't go back to pick them up for us." The poor guy shrinks back under her glare.

"I've got to get to my other job. I picked up everything that was set out on the porch."

"Do you think they got stolen?" I ask.

"Actually, I'm wondering if they got left in the prof's office. They got delivered later than the rest."

"Okay, so it's not his fault." I turn to our delivery guy, who's trembling harder than a leaf in a hurricane. "What was your name?"

"Todd."

"Thanks so much, Todd. We can handle it from here."

"What are we going to do, Jazz? That's all the way across campus and Laybourne is probably not going to agree to come in on the weekend."

"I'll handle it. You set up everything we've already got, and I'll deal with this." I head off to a quiet corner to make a couple of phone calls.

I can't exactly leave the venue. There are so many last-minute details to oversee, but Cole and his guys are planning to come early to help direct traffic as we get going. If I can just get Laybourne to meet them at his office, we can make this work. I send off an urgent email to him and a text to our TA, Annie. If he isn't checking his email on the weekend, I'm sure she'll be able to get in touch with him.

"Jazz?" He picks up before the first ring has finished. "Is everything okay?"

"Hey. Everything's fine. I just have a small favor to ask you guys." I'm pacing the small hallway that leads to the office area.

"Anything. What's up?" There are shouts in the background. "Hang on, let me go up to my room. These guys are out of control."

There's a steady thump and the background noise dims to silence. "Sorry. We were playing Call of Duty. What's up? How's the set up going?"

"It's going well. I think it'll all come together, but we're missing a couple of boxes of our auction items." Now that I've got him on the phone, I'm second guessing myself. Darryl couldn't even be bothered to drive to my apartment. Why would Cole, my fake boyfriend, go out of his way like that? "Um, I was wondering if you guys could pick them up from our prof's office on the way in. He's in the Harbor building. If it's too much trouble, you don't have to worry about it."

"Of course I can. No problem at all. Shoot me the time and room number and we'll be there. I'll have to hustle the team to get ready faster, but that shouldn't be too much of a problem. Except maybe Beau. The captain won't leave the house unless every hair is in order."

I'm not ready to breathe a sigh of relief yet, but at least that's one piece of the problem handled. "Fantastic. I'm waiting to hear from my TA to see if she can let you in to the office. Fingers crossed, I'll have details for you soon."

"Perfect. And if there is anything else you need. And I mean anything, just let me know. I am, after all, already selling my soul for you."

"You're not selling your soul. Just your hot body." Heat creeps up my neck as I realize what I just said, but he barks out a laugh.

"I was not informed that you were auctioning me off like a prized stud. I thought this was an innocent, platonic date."

The burn moves inside, leaving an unpleasant trail of acid down my chest at the thought of another girl's hands on him. "I take that back. I don't know what I was thinking. I'm making you a hands off the merchandise sign to take up on the stage with you."

The silence on the other end stretches a little longer than I'm comfortable with. What is wrong with me tonight? I keep blurting stuff out.

"Better."

"Jazz, there you are." Amira comes barreling down my quiet hallway with what looks like another fire to extinguish. I'm going to need a week off after this. Yeah, right, but it's nice to have dreams.

"I gotta go. Amira's calling me, but I'll text you the deets. Talk to you later."

"Can't wait to see you."

There's a huge smile on my face as I turn to Amira. It doesn't even fade at the slightly panicked look on her face. Whatever it is, I can handle it.

The room is cast in a soft pink glow as I'm doing my last check to make sure every single detail is in place. I straighten out a vase full of colorful gerbera daisies for the third time, when I hear a sound that quickens my heart. Never thought loud male voices arguing would do it for me, but I know they're a signal that Cole's here. And he brought his chaotic crew with him. The stars of the show.

"Looks like your man is here," Amira says, throwing up air quotes. I don't love that. I'm glad I confessed to her, but I'm not so happy about the reminder.

I break out into a jog, weaving around the tall tables to get to the commotion at the door.

"Hey. Did you get the boxes?" My body pitches forward as I catch my foot on a stray bit of extension cord that needs to be taped down. Even the comfy shoes can't save me from that.

Hail catches me, setting me back on my feet.

"What the fuck, man? Hands off." Cole and Dev walk in, carrying the goods.

"Not my fault your girl fell for me," the rookie smirks, but he releases his hold on my waist, throwing his hands up in the air.

Cole looks furious, dropping the box in his arms and taking a step forward.

"I tripped, he caught me. Not a crisis situation."

My stomach lets out an angry rumble to further dispel the tension. Cole and Dev are surrounded by the comforting smell of fries. Maybe I'm so hungry I'm hallucinating.

He shakes his head, picking his box back up. "Right. Sorry. Thanks, rookie."

I pull myself back together. "I'm happy you're here. You four go report to Amira." The boys are back to shoving at each other and bickering quietly as I point to my friend, who's doing a sound check on the stage. "And you two, follow me." I wave Cole and Dev after me.

I hustle off toward the auction table, doing a quick time check. We've got fifteen minutes until the doors open. Beau must have taken his sweet time, like Cole said he would.

"You can put the boxes down here and I'll get them set up." The bidding sheets for the auction are already laid out, so I just have to match the item to the correct sheet.

Cole sets his box down, pulling a bright red box of fries out of it. "I got you some fries. I figured you might not have had time to eat with your busy day."

He's right, and the pain in my stomach is proof. "Thanks so much. I haven't eaten since breakfast." And to be honest, all I could force down then was a single slice of toast. The nerves have been on high alert all day. "Let me get this stuff set up first."

He helps me place the items in their spots, and our hands brush a few times as we're reaching in the box. Shivers run through me with each touch and I'm having trouble remembering why it would be such a terrible idea to make this thing between us real.

Dev wandered away with a grunt after he set his box down. So, it's just Cole and me after we get the last item on display. I take my time fluffing the cellophane to make it look perfect.

He reaches out a hand, pulls it back and then grabs the box of fries, handing it over to me. "They're cold. I'm sorry."

I snag a few golden sticks and the hunger monster roars again as soon as the salty goodness hits my tongue. "Best thing I've ever tasted."

He's smiling, watching every bite when my fingers hit the empty bottom. "Ugh. I was hungrier than I thought. I ate those way too fast."

"Gotta keep your strength up. I can't have you fainting in the middle of the auction. You've got to bid on me. You are going to bid on me, right?" There's a hint of desperation in his expression.

"Of course I will. I've got to go clean up my hands." I pop them in my mouth to lick the grease off, holding them up in the air so I don't accidentally wipe them on my outfit.

His eyes track my fingers to my mouth, and a pulse of need courses through me. I need to get him out of here before I combust.

"You need to go find Amira. Get yourself settled with the other bachelors."

He nods, giving me one last lingering glance before he turns around to find my friend. My gaze falls to his ass, and I have to shake myself back into motion.

After I wash my hands, and dab a little cool water on my flushed neck, I head out to check on Shanna and her coffee cart.

"I knew in theory that college students love their coffee, but I don't think I quite predicted how much until now. I'll definitely have to think of some ways I can draw them to my events, or hit spots with a college heavy presence."

"Oh, I could have told you that. I'm glad things are going well for you, and thanks again for your contribution to the shelter. You're totally going above and behind." Shanna is incredible. She owns her own business that she started from the ground up. A successful woman in business who also cares about her community. She offered to double the percentage of her sales that's she's going to donate to our charity. Kicking ass and giving back.

"Hey, I just want to pass my success on. I wouldn't be in the place I am today if my family hadn't had help from this community. I'm paying it forward."

"You rock. I hope we get a chance to catch up later, but it's going to be super busy tearing down and cleaning up. If we don't get the chance, I'd love to meet up with you to have a chat."

"Of course. Any time. You've got my info." Her smile is radiant. Such a positive force.

Amira's voice comes through my earpiece. "Time to get the boys locked and loaded."

Shanna tilts her head when I can't stop the laugh, so I point to the headset, rolling my eyes. "Gotta go. Duty calls."

"Me too." She turns back to her cart, where her assistant is looking a little frazzled.

I give her a wave and start weaving through the crowd. The nerves that had settled down as the evening moved on smoothly are back in full force at the final auction that's coming up. Hopefully, this will bring in a last chunk of donations to meet our goal. Although at the rate things are going, I think we're going to crush our initial fund-raising goal.

"You're killing it, Jazz." Trinity calls out, grabbing my hand as I pass by. I nod to her and the small group of students from our class that have been helping tonight.

"Thanks, Trin. I've gotta go, though, get the bachelor's in line." She giggles as I wink at her and hustle on.

It seems like every few steps someone wants to stop me to talk. This must be what it's like to be a minor celebrity, or athlete. Come to think of it, this is probably the kind of attention that's waiting for Cole if he lands a spot in the NHL. But probably on a much larger scale. Not really my thing, but I'll take it for the night. I'm pretty proud of what we accomplished here, and I can't wait to present a check to Women's Place once the finances are all sorted.

I could drink a dozen shots of espresso and not experience the level of jitters that are dancing through my stomach now that it's my turn at the mic. Amira is doing most of the emceeing, but I said I'd handle one small but very important announcement.

The last of the bands we were showcasing just wrapped up their set, so they're tearing down their instruments as I ascend the few steps up onto the small stage. Please don't fall. Please don't fall. I really hope I can make that happen with words alone, but I'm extra careful with each step just in case the mantra isn't enough.

Everybody is out mingling as I make my way to the mic, and I slide the earpiece out. No need to deal with any potential interruptions from that end.

I drag in a deep breath, closing my eyes and finding my center before I pick up the mic.

"Everybody, I've got an announcement to make if I can have your attention." I wait a few minutes for the buzzing conversation to die down enough to be heard.

"First of all, I want to thank you all for coming out tonight. Are you having a good time?"

The crowd responds with an enthusiasm that has a big smile stretching my face and some of the tension in my shoulders easing up.

It takes a hot minute for the claps and cheers to die down. "Glad to hear it. I'm Jazz, and I'm so happy to see you all here tonight. Thanks for your support. The main event is coming up shortly, but I wanted to give you a ten-minute warning on the silent auction items. I've checked out the bidding sheets and it looks like we've got some fierce competition on some of the prizes. If you want to snag that weekend at the Waterfront, or a tour of Salazar's, get your last-minute bids in. We'll be collecting the sheets promptly at 8:50."

A handful of people sneak off to get their last bids in before we shut it down.

"I hope you've all visited the table for Women's Place to find out about all the amazing work they're doing to support women and children in our community who need a safe place to land and a helping hand. Thanks so much to Fran and Ginnie, who came out tonight to share their work with you."

"You know what's coming, right?"

The cheers are even louder this time and I'm not even sad that the bachelors are getting louder cheers than I did. More interest means more money raised.

"Who are you most excited about? The star quarter-back, our regional championship winning debate team members, or maybe, just maybe, you've got your eyes on the hockey captain."

The clapping rises to a crescendo as I go on, and Amira sidles up beside me.

"Fantastic. I'll be handing off the mic to my partner in crime, Amira, and I'll go wrangle those guys up for you. Don't forget to get your last bids in, but don't spend all your money. Save some for our boys."

"Now I'm going to pass you off to Amira, who will be the host and auctioneer tonight. I promise she's going to make you laugh while you're opening up your wallets, or Venmo apps, I guess. Give her a cheer."

I'm happy to relinquish the mic to my friend. Her fingers are tipped in beautiful coral polish, and she's got on a matching flowery dress.

"Give it up for Jazmin. This night would only have been half as awesome without her. She drapes an arm around my shoulder, pulling me in for a hug. My eyes are already focused off the stage on my next task, wrangling the guys, but I give a shy smile before heading off at a brisk but careful walk when she releases me.

I finally make it back to the hall I was in earlier. We've got the guys set up in a couple of small meeting rooms. Loud and familiar laughter points me in the direction of my boys. When did I start thinking about them like that? But I stop by the other two meeting rooms on my way to check on the other bachelors. There's a few from the football team, a couple from the swim team and some from the soccer team as well. We even got a couple from the Robotics club and the debate team to round out the bachelor offering. I'm sure intelligence will appeal to some of our bidders. It's not all about athletic ability.

One of the massive football players has another one in a headlock when I peek in the first room. "Boys. Ease up, you're going to mess up your hair."

They both look up, matching startled expressions on their faces that immediately turn sheepish. "Sorry, Jazz."

Rob waves and smiles at me. He's looking good in a pin-striped dress shirt and crisply ironed grey pants.

"Save the shenanigans for later. I'm going to call you out to line up for your turn to shine. George, you're up first. Smooth out that hair."

He obeys, swiping a hand over his mussed up blond locks.

There's some sort of argument going on in the next room about which battle bot would win in a fight, but at least it's not gotten physical, so I move on.

My hockey boys are surprisingly chatting nicely.

A warmth oozes through me like honey when Cole's dark eyes meet mine. Why do I forget all the reasons I shouldn't be thinking of him like this whenever he looks at me? It's like all my common sense and life experience melts away under the heat of that gaze. Remember Darryl, remember that possessiveness the other night. I already know I can't trust myself to make good decisions about my love life.

"Are we up?" Grant looks at me. "You told your friend not to let anyone buy me except my girlfriend, right? She'll murder me if someone else snags me, and you don't want to be responsible for depriving the world of this face, do you?" He bats a set of lashes at me that many a girl would be jealous of.

"Don't worry, Grant. She's got your back."

"Good." He nods, the wrinkle between his brows smoothing out.

My phone vibrates in my pocket. That's the two-minute warning. "Ok Grant, you're first up from the hockey team. Time to empty your girlfriend's purse. There are three guys ahead of you, but I'm going to get you lined up and ready to go when your names are called. Follow me."

The guys are shuffling around like a group of kinder-gartners waiting for the bell to ring, with Rob at the front of the line.

"You're up. Knock 'em dead." I pat Rob's shoulder as he heads out. He ignores the stairs, leaping onto the stage in a move that would definitely land me on my ass, suffering from a wardrobe malfunction if I tried it. His smooth bow has the crowd cheering, and the bidding commences.

Grant's girl wins him, and he jumps off the front of the stage to give her a huge kiss, lifting her off her feet to spin her around. The crowd loves that, and I'm pretty impressed myself. Definitely worthy of one of Jordan's book boyfriends. I search the crowd, spotting her crim-son waves off to the side. She couldn't make it out earlier in the day, but she came to meet her author friend and make sure everything went smoothly with her set up.

Hail is in his element when his turn rolls around. He's the only one who showed up in his jersey, and I'm pretty sure one of the girls in the front row almost fainted when he flexed.

Every few minutes I'm back getting another couple of guys lined up when I glance down at my list, realizing I've reached the last three guys. Dev, Cole, and Beau.

"Can you try to smile when you get up there?" I ask Dev before I send him off.

"Not part of the deal," he grumbles. To be honest, I'm impressed I got him here at all, so I guess I'll take it. Some girls love the brooding athlete, right?

He stands there, tatted arms crossed over his muscular chest, brows drawn together, and he still goes for a price that I wouldn't be able to afford.

"Cole." I grab his arm. "I don't think I'm going to be able to afford you."

"I won't go for that much. It'll be fine."

"But what if I can't?"

An uncertain look crosses his face. "It'll be fine. I think."

He bends down toward me, reaching a hand up to hover over my cheek, and the heat emanating from his skin soaks into me.

"Cole Schaeffer!"

Amira shouts his name into the mic, and enthusiastic clapping starts up.

"Cole is the right winger for our very own Lightning. They took the championship home last year, and you've only got two more shots at picking up your own trophy tonight. Can we start the bidding at ten dollars?"

I turn to Beau. "You good if I go out there?"

He nods, brushing a hand down his pristine white shirt. He's one of the few who went for a collared dress shirt, but it suits him.

"Thirty dollars? Do I have thirty?"

I raise my hand, sneaking in at the side of the crowd hanging around the front of the stage.

"Thirty to the lovely lady in orange."

"Fifty!" The color drains out of Cole's face, and I search the crowd to find the source of the bid. It's his ex. Everything has gone so well tonight, something had to happen to throw it off. I was really hoping she wouldn't come. She's still been showing up at his games but hasn't made any other kind of moves since she confronted us at the first one. I kind of thought maybe the fake dating thing was working, and she was backing off. Apparently, I was wrong, and he's the one who's going to pay for my mistake.

"Fifty to the lady in red. Can I hear sixty?"

Amira turns to me with wide eyes.

"Sixty," I call out, already higher than I was hoping to go, but he looks so desperate up there.

"Sixty-five." Charlene has got a malicious gleam in her eyes when she turns to me. Does she really think that winning him in an auction will do anything for her cause? He's not going to suddenly fall back in love with her because he's forced to spend a single date with him. It'll probably have the opposite effect.

"Seventy." I say, already thinking about the ramen I'm going to have to eat for a couple of weeks if I have to put that much money out.

"Seventy-five." Amira can't even keep up with the bidding. She's just nodding and pointing at us in turn.

"Eighty." I close my eyes and pray. That's it. That's the highest I can go, even if I dip into my saved tips from All Capps.

"Eighty-five." Charlene pipes in right away.

The silence following her bid is heavy. Guilt weighing on me that I'm letting Cole down.

Amira focuses back on me, but I shake my head at her. She knows I can't do any more than that, so she turns back to the crowd, and I rush off, blinking away tears. Why is this affecting me so much?

It's only one date. He'll be ok. I'll make it up to him somehow. There are a couple more shouts behind me, but I don't turn around to see what's going on. Apparently, someone else has joined the bidding, but I'm sure Charlene will not let this opportunity slip through her fingers.

Beau is shifting from one foot to the other when I get back to him.

"Sorry, I shouldn't have left you here by yourself."

"It's fine. I'll be fine," he says.

I'm not sure I believe him. There's a slight hitch in his voice and he's tapping his fingers on his thighs in a repeating rhythm.

I reach up, placing a hand on his shoulder. "If this isn't ok with you, you can back out. No hard feelings. The last thing I want is to make you feel uncomfortable."

He shakes his head at me. "It's fine. I have to go to all kinds of events like this for my family. I can handle it."

Save me from stoic boys who have to tough it out regardless of how they're feeling, but he's a grownup. He can make his own decisions.

I send him off with an encouraging smile. "You got this."

Bidding starts out high for the golden boy hockey captain. He's the whole package, athletic talent, good lucks, and a trust fund that would set him up for life even if the hockey career doesn't pan out. But that's not who I'm looking for. I search the crowd for the dark hair that I know feels impossibly soft under my fingertips.

The bachelors are back in the crowd, mingling with everyone else now that the evening is almost at a close. Something dark unfurls, spreading its vines through my soul when I do spot him. There's a tic in his tight jaw, and he's leaning away from Charlene. Her fingers rest on his arm, and she's leaning in. One of the invasive vines twists tighter around my heart. It's jealousy. I'm jealous of this girl who has her claws on my boyfriend. A decidedly real kind of anger has me marching over to them.

"Hey, hon," I say, stepping in beside him and slipping an arm around his waist.

The urge to kiss him is strong. Make my public claim and warn this other girl away from my man. The taut coil of possessiveness is uncomfortable. Is this not the very thing I freaked out on him about?

I lean in closer, and a wash of the spicy musk of his cologne engulfs me. That does it for me. I stretch up on my toes to plant a kiss on his cheek, but he turns his head at the last moment, and our lips clash in an awkward touch that melts into something sweet. It sure feels real to me whenever we're joined like this.

He steps in closer, lifting a hand to the back of my head, random girl forgotten.

She huffs and steps away, but I don't pull back even though my point has been made. I can't. He's my new addiction, and I can't get enough of him. His fingers tangle in my hair, pulling me into him, and our tongues meet at the same time, like we've got a connection deeper than surface. Like we can read each other's thoughts and needs.

A wave of loud applause breaks out around us, shattering the moment. The illusion of privacy I had when the world faded away at the touch of our lips.

I pull away, wincing at the pain in my scalp when he can't untangle his fingers in time.

"Sorry," he says in a husky tone.

"Not your fault. Listen, I've got to go join Amira up on stage to deal with the last speech and then we've got a lot of work ahead of us to get this place cleaned up."

"I'll stay to help out. I'm here for you."

"You don't have to."

"I know, Coffee Girl, but I want to. I'd wait for you way longer than the couple of hours it's going to take to clean this place up."

A shiver runs up my spine, and every part of me wants to stay here in his arms. My lady parts are especially insistent, throbbing with need, but I can't. Not yet. We've got the rest of the night to sort things out. It can wait.

CHAPTER TWENTY-FIVE

WASTED SECONDS

COLE

The guys stayed to help out. Even Hail, although I think he was more interested in finding some fresh blood among the bidders than cleaning up, so he bailed early. Still, it's progress. He's stepping up for the team, and the way everyone rallied around me tonight really shook up all the doubts I've been having since I got burned by my former best friend. Real bonds can exist, and I've been an idiot to hide from them for so long. If Hail can change his ways, then so can I.

But then there's the reminder of from my past that keeps popping back up in my life. A churning dread at Charlene's win left me cold even as I was celebrating Jazz's success. I'm happy for her, but the thought of spending even an hour or two with my ex is unbearable. I wish Jazz could have bought me, but I get it. Money is tight, and the way the price skyrocketed near the end of the bidding blew my mind. Maybe I shouldn't have agreed to this. Put myself in this position, but Jazz needed me, and I'm finding it very hard to refuse her anything. She could ask me for my signed Zetterberg jersey, and I'd pluck it off my wall.

Dev carries the last table into the crowded storage room at the back of the atrium, leaning it against the others before walking back out to join us. Most of the heavy lifting is done, and these guys have been an immense help.

"Thanks so much for everything."

"We're your teammates. Of course we're going to be here for your girl," Grant says, and a ribbon of guilt twists around my guts.

"I really appreciate it anyway, but I think we're good here now. You can head out. I'll help Jazz with any last details and give her a ride home."

"I bet you will," JJ says, throwing a hand up in the air for a high five. "Am I right?" He turns to the team.

"Grow up, and leave poor Cole alone," Beau says. "He's got to save his energy for later."

They all burst out laughing, and I roll my eyes. Figures. For a mere second, I thought Beau was going to be the voice of reason, but he devolved into macho nonsense, just like the rest of them.

"Get out of here." I tell them, but I say with a smile.

"Bye, Jazz. Great event," Grant calls out to her. "Thanks for looking out for my balls."

I turn around to find her walking toward us, shaking her head. "Thanks, Grant, and you're welcome. I guess. Are you guys leaving?" She turns to me, her lips twisting down into a little frown I want to kiss away.

"They're going to head out. I'm here until the bitter end. What's left?"

She shakes her head. "Not much. Just have to load up the van with the tablecloths and glasses. Then we're good to go. Don't feel like you have to stay. It's been a long day. I can get a ride home with Amira."

"Don't be ridiculous. I wouldn't leave you here after all your hard work. I'll give you a ride home."

"Perfect." Her smile is a little tired, but still just as beautiful.

Soft snores are rumbling out of Jazz when we pull up in front of her building, rivaling Mabel's old engine. I hate to wake her up, so I pull around to the visitor's parking area in back, sliding into a spot and cutting the engine.

I lean my head back on the headrest, turning to drink her in. Moonlight is cutting through the window, highlighting the curves of her cheeks, and her slightly open mouth. She's always beautiful, but in the dark of night there's a vulnerable quality to her beauty. Like her defenses have all been washed away in sleep. All the hurt she's experienced in her life, the doubts and fears are gone, and what's left is peace and contentment.

"Cole." My name on her lips has power. Especially in her sleep when she's not second guessing herself or our relationship, whatever that is.

"Oh, Jazz." I sigh, reaching out to brush a strand of black hair behind her ear. She blinks awake, brown eyes taking a minute to focus on me.

She clears her throat, throwing a hand up to cover her yawn. "I'm sorry. I didn't mean to fall asleep. It's been a long day."

"It's all good. I didn't want to wake you, but the car is getting chilly. Let's get you inside and you can get a proper sleep."

I hop out, tracing a path around the front to open her door.

She reaches out, twining my fingers through hers as if it's the most natural thing in the world as we pass under the dim light on the side of her building. I don't love this place. The thought of her coming home here at night by herself sets me on edge. Anything could happen, especially if her ex decides that my lesson wasn't enough of a deterrent.

"Good night, Jazz." I mumble into the top of her head as she opens the front door. I don't want to leave, but I should. She's exhausted. I am too. Plus, I really don't want to be alone. I'll only dwell on my future date with Charlene. I don't even know if I'm angry with her anymore. Just tired and numb.

She turns to me with wide eyes. "Come up with me."

My heart skips a beat or three. I want nothing more than to come up with her, but only if she's saying it for real. Not because she's tired, and a little vulnerable from sleep. "Are you sure?" I should ask her the question I've been thinking about since Halloween. Ask her if she'll be my girlfriend for real. But I'm scared of the answer. What if she says no? I don't want to risk that hurt. If she doesn't let me in. If she does let me in, and then destroys me.

"I've never been more sure of anything. I want you to come upstairs with me. I want you to stay the night and I want to wake up next to you."

Sounds fucking amazing to me. "Okay."

I'm still scared to touch her. If I lay hands on her on the way up, I don't think I'll be able to let her go, and she said nothing about wanting more than just my company. It wasn't exactly a blatant invitation for more. Besides, I don't think I want to go any further with this if it's just for the night.

She pulls me through the front door, and my fingers trail through hers, sliding along her palm until the tips slip off.

"Make sure you lock the door." I can't help the request, even though I know she's been looking after herself for years. But after Darryl invaded her space, I'm a little paranoid for her.

"Oh, don't worry. I've been on hyper alert since you were here last." I resist the urge to reach out to smooth the lines of her scrunched up forehead.

Now I'm doubly sure I shouldn't have broached the subject. Now she's remembering the last time I was here when I made her ex bleed, when I said she was mine. It might have been effective, but I scared her, and that's the last thing I want to do.

"Maybe I should go." I don't want to, but I also don't want to be the one who puts that look on her face.

"No." She shakes her head, straightening up. "I don't want you to go, Cole. I want you to stay the night."

"It's been a long day. You must be exhausted." Not sure why I'm trying to cock block myself, but there it is.

"Listen." She steps into me, placing her hands on my chest. "I don't know exactly how you feel after a game. But I imagine you're all hopped up on adrenaline, heart racing, energy coursing through you that you need some sort of release for."

Her head tilts to the side as she studies me.

"Yeah. That sounds about right."

"Well, that's how I feel right now. I did this huge thing. Despite a few hitches, everything went smoothly. We raised a bunch of money for a great cause. Now I'm restless. I need to work this off. I need you." As if to emphasize her point, she trails a hand down along each ridge of my abdomen.

I want that so much, but not like this. My palm closes over her wayward hand, and I lift it to my mouth in an apology. I don't want her to feel rejected, but I can't do this. At least not like this.

"I can't, Coffee Girl." I swallow hard and glance at my feet to avoid the disappointment in her eyes.

"Sure looks like you can," she says, undeterred, and I can feel my cock twitching under her speculative look.

"It's not that I don't want to. Just not like this. I don't want to be a release for you. I want to be more, because this thing we've got going on..." I step closer to her until we're a hairsbreadth away from touching. I want nothing more than to close that last slim gap between us, but I resist. "This relationship is a lot of things. It's fun, and easy, and challenging. It's become so much more to me." I take a deep breath, closing my eyes, but I can still feel the heat from her body, and it drives my words. "The next time my hands are on your body, I want you to know who you belong with. I want you to belong with me. I want to kiss every inch of you, touch every curve, and know that you're mine and I'm yours and we're in this together for real. Because you want to, not because you're trying to scare off your ex, or keep mine away. This is real for me, and I can't sleep with you again if you don't feel the same way. It would hurt too much."

Everything about her softens, her mouth goes slack, eyes wide and shoulders sinking. Even her proximity isn't enough to warm my numb fingers. Great, this might be it for us.

"Yes."

What does that even mean? "Yes?"

"Yes. I'll be yours for real."

Hope swells in my chest like an over-inflated balloon. "Really?"

"Yes. I want you too. After I saw you with Charlene. I wanted to rip her hair out."

She throws her hand up in front of her mouth as if she's embarrassed she said that, and I clasp it in mine to peel it away. I want to see her face. "You were jealous? But it's not just about that, is it?" All my insecurities are swarming to the surface. I know what it's like to be jealous, but I don't want this to be a gut reaction from her.

"No, but it made me examine my feelings a little more closely. I've been denying my feelings because I was scared after the way Darryl controlled me. I thought that if I gave into them, I would lose myself again, but that's not who you are. That's not what you do. You let me be myself. And more than that, you help me. You encourage me to work for my dreams, just like you're working for yours. And that night, even after you freaked out. Even after you called me yours, you left. I asked you to leave, and you did. Gave me the space I needed to process. I'm not denying it anymore. I'm yours."

The happiness is almost painful. Knowing that she wants me as much as I want her is incredible. Not something I ever thought I'd want again. I duck away when she leans in for a kiss.

"Wait. I have to do this right." I slide down her arms until I've got both of her warm hands grasped in mine. "Jazmin, will you be my girlfriend? For real this time?"

A white flash breaks through the serious look on her face. "Yes, I will."

"Well then, let's not waste another second."

Chapter Twenty-Six

Light It Up

Cole

We slam together in a mess of heat, and I can breathe again. She's my air. I'm fumbling at her waist as my lips catch hers, sealing the deal with a kiss. "How the fuck do I get this thing off?"

I can feel her laugh vibrating through my chest. "Zipper," she says.

"I wish you were wearing a dress so I could flip it up over your ass and slide my dick inside that pussy. I bet it's already wet for me. Is it?"

"Yes," she pants, trailing her fingers up my back to grasp at my neck, sealing me tighter to her lips.

My hands close over her hips to spin her around, revealing the plump curves of her ass straining against the fabric. Did she really go out in public wearing this? Nobody else should get that view except for me.

Her skin is smooth and hot under the kisses I plant on her back as I slowly drag the zipper down. The fabric parts to reveal an expanse of caressable light brown skin. She shivers under my touch as I slip the material off her shoulders. It falls to the floor in a smooth cascade, leaving her standing in nothing but an electric orange bra and matching thong. The little triangle of fabric at the top dipping between her cheeks is the only thing between me and heaven.

"Fuck. I take it back. You can wear this anytime."

A breathy laugh is her only response.

I'm too awkward, fumbling with the clasp in my rush to touch her, so I give up on her bra, sliding my hands under the cups. My girlfriend. My cock jumps and I moan at the feel of her soft mounds overflowing my hands, and I knead the soft flesh, circling each taut nipple.

Her hands flutter at her sides as I pass over the soft curve of her belly, traveling toward the prize. Her neatly trimmed mound is soft under my touch as I inch ever closer underneath the front of her thong. Damp heat welcomes me in.

"I was right. You're wet for me, dirty girl. Wet for your boyfriend."

That word feels almost as good as her pussy. Maybe better.

I circle her clit a few times, as she arches into my other hand that's taking turns pinching and teasing her breasts. She's slick with need by the time I reach her entrance. I breech it with the tip of one finger, testing her out, and she clenches around me, trying to draw me in.

"Not yet. Be patient." I move her forward until we reach the edge of her couch, pressing her down over the arm, and yanking the panties off. I need to see all of her.

"Spread for me. Show me that gorgeous pussy." I tell her.

She's shuddering under me already and I've barely gotten started, but she doesn't obey me, so I kick her legs open, putting her on full display. I drink in the sight of her. Lips damp and ready for me. Ass up, waiting for my touch,

I drop to my knees, and she screams when I bury myself between her legs.

"Holy fuck, Cole."

She was on fire for me before we got through the door. I lap at her sweet juices, and finally give her what she's looking for, sliding a finger into her welcoming heat. She pulses around me, and I find the needy little bud that's swollen for me and me alone.

She's writhing under the alternating strokes of my tongue and fingers on every sensitive spot. I alternate between sucking on her clit and curling my fingers deep in her channel. Her hips buck back, driving me deeper.

When I feel her tremble. The first sign of her orgasm has me pulling away from her.

"Cole. No. I need you."

"There's plenty of time to feel you coming on my face, pretty girl. Right now. This first time as my girlfriend I need to feel you coming around my cock. Sound good?"

"Yes, please."

"Good, but I want to see your face while I make you come. Let's take this to your room."

"No, wait. Sit down." She pushes against my chest until I collapse into the seat of the couch. It doesn't take much effort on her part. My legs are weak and wobbly with need.

She reaches for the hem of my shirt, yanking it over my head and tossing it aside, so she can trail her fingertips over my chest. Flames light up my skin as she traces every curve, every ridge of hard muscle, and then she dips lower, flicking open the button on my jeans. The sound of my zipper rips through the sounds of our panting breaths, and I lift my hips to allow her to slide the pants and boxer briefs over my hips.

"Wait." I plead. If she goes any further, I'll forget everything. My mind is already half gone from just the taste of her lips. "Have you got a condom?" I fucking hope she does, because I certainly didn't plan on my night ending like this.

"Yes. Yes, I do." I stare at her bare ass jiggling as she darts to her bedroom. My hand slides to my cock, giving it a few lazy strokes while I wait for her, eyes locked on her doorway.

Her little tongue slips out to wet her lips when she spots my hand, and she drops to her knees. I groan. Pretty sure I can't handle her mouth on me, but I'm willing to try.

"I want to thank you for all your help tonight."

"You don't need to thank me."

"Oh, but I want to. I can't wait for a taste of this. It's been a long day and I'm hungry for my man."

I shudder as her tongue flicks out to lick the bead of precum off my tip. Then the heat of her mouth closes over it, sending a shock wave of pleasure tingling through me. I bury my hands in her hair as she bobs up and down, licking and sucking me until I'm impossibly hard. My hips twitch, wanting to slam down the back of her throat. But that would push me over the edge and, like I told her, I want to be inside her pussy, staring into her beautiful eyes when I come this time. I tug at her hair, trying to pull her off.

She presses forward, her tongue making little swirls around my dick.

"Jazz, please. I need to be inside you." I tell her, tugging again.

She finally obeys, sitting up on her heels and swiping a hand across her mouth.

I'm about to stand up when she places one thigh on the couch beside mine, swinging up to straddle me. She's hovering over me, so close I could slip inside her with a single thrust of my hips, but her hand presses down on my chest.

Orange lace still covers her tits, and I want to see them, to touch them, so I reach around behind her, flicking open the clasp. The satiny straps are the next to go, slipping off her shoulders. I pull the cups down over her luscious breasts, leaning forward to close my mouth around one.

She gasps, jerking her hips forward until I'm poised at her entrance, when I flick my tongue over the stiff peak, and her hand moves from my chest to my shoulder. She braces herself on me, breathing hard, eyes glazed.

Her fingers are clumsy on the wrapper, while we both stare at each other. Desperation high. I can't take it anymore, grabbing the foil, ripping it open with my teeth, and sliding it down over my aching length.

I grip her hips, yanking her onto my cock. She's like heaven. So wet it eases my passage as she stretches around me. Nothing has ever felt better. Slick, tight, with little pulses fluttering around me as I sink balls deep into her channel.

I squeeze tight, and she gasps, but it's not pain, it's need that has her clenching as she rides me hard and fast. I let her nipple slide from between my lips, shifting my mouth to suck hard on the delicate flesh.

She dances under me in a rapid rhythm that sends me spinning faster than I'd like. I need to feel her coming around me. I need us to share this moment. This first time as real boyfriend and girlfriend. I crave that connection more than anything.

My thumb finds her swollen clit, and it slides easily over the needy bud. She's dripping for me. The rhythm of her hips falters under my touch, and my tongue slides up the salty trail between her breasts.

Pressure builds in my lower back, rising to a crescendo. Not yet. Not yet.

I close my teeth on her left nipple at the same time I press down with my thumb, and she ignites. "Eyes on me when you're coming." I command her.

Her lashes drag up until I'm staring into those liquid pools of chocolate. Their rich depths are hazy with need and pleasure.

"Cole," she screams, and the sound of my name on her lips is enough to send me hurtling over the edge as she sucks me in deeper, coming apart around me.

I swell and release inside her, head falling back as the wave crests crashing over us both.

My hips rock in gentle thrusts as I ride out the pleasure.

"Fuck, that was incredible."

She collapses forward onto my chest, head falling to my shoulder, and I stroke the smooth length of her hair down her back.

"Thank you," her lips brush my chest as she speaks and I twitch, still buried deep inside her.

After our sweat covered skin starts to cool, I lift her gently off me, tucking her under my arm, and rolling down the condom.

I scoop an arm under her thighs, carrying her to her bed. She's awake, but barely, blinking sleepily at me.

After laying her down on her bright pink comforter, I head to the bathroom to clean up, bringing a damp cloth back to look after her.

I tuck her under the covers, sliding underneath beside her.

She curls into my side, and for the first time in a long time, everything is right. I'm not afraid of tomorrow.

CHAPTER TWENTY-SEVEN

BIG FAN OF YOU

JAZZ

I was reluctant to leave the house after waking Cole up with my mouth on his cock. He was more than appreciative, returning the favor, and then fucking me so hard I can feel him down there as his car rumbles down the small residential streets.

I didn't know how I'd feel when I woke up. Scared? Ready to turn tail? There is a hint of nerves fluttering away, but it's a low hum. Manageable. There's some uncertainty in me about what comes next. Now, next week, after graduation. There are so many unknowns. But I'm not scared of him, or what he's going to do. Instead of fear, there's a whole lot of happiness mixed in with the lust and post sex contentment.

He said he had a surprise for me, and now here we are in Glen Valley. The small town is an hour's drive from

Lakeview, but I've never been here. It's adorable. Little shops line the main street and there are those black lanterns on every street corner that make it feel like Stars Hollow.

"First stop coming up. Close your eyes."

I shake my head at him.

"Are you looking to get spanked later, Coffee Girl?"

My eyebrow arches as I study him. "Maybe."

A low whistle slips between his lips. "Trip canceled. Heading home right now."

I laugh. "Fine by me."

He groans. "No, no. I drove all the way here. You're not conning me into canceling my plans. No matter how badly you deserve the palm of my hand on that luscious ass of yours."

My nipples ache at his dirty promise. I'm looking forward to that.

When I finally close my eyes, I hear the creak of Mabel's rusty door, followed by a slam. I'm about to open my side when it gives way under my arm. His hand closes on my elbow to prevent me from tumbling out, and he helps me up.

"How am I going anywhere with my eyes closed?" I ask him.

"I'll be your guide." He loops my arm through his elbow, pulling me in close to his side. Usually, I'd be nervous walking around blind, but I trust him more than I thought I could trust a guy again.

There's the jingle of a little bell, and then he says. "Watch out, there's a little bump in the doorway."

I pick up my foot in an exaggerated lift to get over whatever obstacle is in my way and step through the door. A wave of my favorite aroma engulfs me. Maybe my second favorite now. I turn my head to bury my nose in his shoulder to drag in a noseful of his cinnamony goodness.

I know exactly where I am before he tells me to open my eyes.

The hissing of an espresso machine and the delicious scent of perfectly roasted beans gives it away.

"What's this place called?" I ask, drinking in the place eagerly. There's a scattering of cozy looking rounded black bucket chairs in one corner by a fireplace. The rest of the place is all small round wooden tables with matching chairs and tiny vases with a single cheerful carnation resting in the center of each table. A long wooden counter stretches across the back where a smiling barista is serving customers. Her hair is pulled into a high knot of tightly coiled curls on top of her head.

"This is Better Beans. Our first stop of the day. I know you said you love checking out independent coffee shops to see what fun stuff they've got going on, so I mapped out a little tour of three for you."

"This is amazing, but when did you plan this?" We only agreed to date for real last night. Did he stay up all night planning a day out? Judging from the steady rhythm of his breathing any time I woke up in the middle of the night, I highly doubt he was googling coffee shops at two am.

He rubs a hand down the back of his neck, eyes falling to study his worn sneakers. "I've been thinking about this for a while. I've been thinking about it and researching all the nearby coffee shops since you told me how much you like to do this. I wasn't sure if I would ever get a chance to actually take you to them, but I was hoping. Is that weird?"

"Weird? No. It's the sweetest thing anyone has ever done for me. Planning a day just for me when you weren't even sure if we were going to get together officially. I could barely get Darryl to come to All Capps to meet me after work. He said he didn't like the smell of coffee. Always made me take a shower after I got home from work." If I thought my heart was full before, it's on the verge of bursting now. No one has ever done something this sweet just for me.

Cole buries his nose in my head. "Let's not talk about that asshole. Coffee is my new favorite smell. Now what should I get?"

"What do you like?"

He shrugs. "I never buy myself fancy coffees. Just drink whatever we're brewing at home or in the cafeteria."

I wrinkle my nose. "Do you like sweet things?"

There's a wicked gleam in his eyes as he reaches out to brush a strand of hair behind my ear. "I like you."

"Come on." Now he's got me blushing as I brush his hand away. "You know what I mean."

"Yes, lots of sugar. Enough to rot my teeth."

I laugh. "We can work on that, but for now. Let's see what they've got here."

The large chalkboard hanging behind the barista has their standard offerings written out in colorful chalk ac-

companied by little doodles. But there's a smaller chalkboard on the counter with a couple of specials on it.

"Pumpkin?" I turn to him.

"Not the nickname I would have chosen for myself,
but I guess." His dark eyes are twinkling under the soft
lighting from the multicolored glass chandeliers.

I smack him on the arm. "Not what I meant, but maybe.
Do you like the taste of pumpkin?"

"I like pumpkin pie."

"Okay then."

Cole snags my hand as I step up to the counter. "One
pumpkin spice latte, and one cappuccino please. And a
pumpkin scone with two forks."

"Whipped cream on the pumpkin?" she asks.

He nods when I turn to find him staring at me with a
soft smile curving up his lips. "Definitely."

She hands us a number to put on our table. It's another little chalkboard with the number seven on it and a
drawing of an elephant.

"I love this place."

We settle into the last two unoccupied comfy chairs,
hands still linked as I look around, taking in every single
detail.

"Getting ideas?"

"Yes. Obviously, I want to make my coffee shop unique,
put my own theme on it, but I love getting ideas from
other places. Like these table numbers. Adorable. And
they've got some events listed on their community board
over there." I wave at the far wall. "They've got live music
on Fridays and games night on Tuesdays. It's those sorts

of things that really make a place part of the community. A place that will last because people will go there to spend time and come back every day for their morning fix."

"I'd totally come here to hang out in the evening. Only if you were there with me, though. So, what are you thinking about doing at your place?" The genuine interest he's shown in my plans is disarming. I'm so used to people telling me I can't do it.

"I've always loved the pairing of books and coffee. They're just a perfect match, and I'd love to have a coffee shop bookstore combo with Jordan, but lately. Lately I've been thinking of maybe throwing in a bit of a hockey theme."

His eyes crinkle at the corners. "Really? Big fan?"

"Turns out it's my favorite sport."

"Really? And how would you mesh that into the coffee mix?"

"A hockey/coffee themed logo to start. Then maybe hockey themed drink names. The decor could go along with the theme, but I haven't come up with a name yet."

"You seem to have put a lot of thought into this."

I nod. I have. Hockey has been on my brain a surprising amount lately.

"Maybe I could even make the aprons look like jerseys and all the staff could have numbers. I guess I better hire some hockey fans."

He leans forward, hands clasped in front of him on the table as if he's super invested in my idea. "They'd have to be in the colors of the local team, though. Where are you planning on setting up this shop?"

"Undecided. But I've been doing my research in Detroit. Close to home, still has some growing areas with decent rent, and endless potential. I've been applying for business grants and some of them are intended for local Detroit businesses, but nothing is set in stone for me yet. I could potentially go anywhere."

"It's definitely a hockey town, so that would work. The Wheelers have a solid track record and they're doing well right now."

I nod. I've been keeping up with hockey lately, and even before I met Cole, Jordan had me watching Aspen's games with her. It's actually a pretty addictive sport. Once you get started, it's easy to get sucked into the action. But watching someone you know play is next level. Someone you care about, even if it's taken a while to admit it to yourself.

I hesitate, nibbling on my fingernails. "How about you? Any idea where you're going to end up?" I know this is a bit of a loaded question, but now that I've gotten past my fear of letting him in, it's an important one. This thing between us is new, but it feels serious. Like I could end up with him, but his future is uncertain. The draft is unpredictable.

The same barista stops by to replace the number on our table with our drinks. The red mug looks small in his large hands as he lifts it up to take a sniff. "Smells like fall." He moans as at his first sip. "That is really fucking good."

"Almost as good as an orgasm?" I ask.

"Fuck no." He shifts in his seat. "But good."

I figure he doesn't want to answer my question, so I leave it be, inhaling my cappuccino. It's smooth and light, the espresso balances out the sweet milk and the foam is chef's kiss. Dense and creamy, no big air bubbles. Yum.

"I was drafted by Colorado after my freshman year, and I thought I'd snag a contract by the end of second or third year. Honestly, I wasn't even planning on finishing college. But they released me after the incident, and I moved here to finish up and prove myself. Ultimately, I'm glad I did. The Lightning have helped me become a better player, but now I'll graduate without a contract, so my career is up in the air."

"That's tough." My dream is tough, too. Starting a business is never easy, but at least a lot of it feels more in my control than his. He can play his best, try his hardest, and still not get drafted by an NHL team. "Why did they release you?" From what I've seen, he's a fantastic player. Seems weird that they wouldn't retain the rights to his contract.

He shrinks back, nibbling on his lower lip. "I guess they didn't consider me a good prospect anymore after I left Tampa. Anyway, the team is only getting better and better, and even my work with Hail is helping me be a better team player, so I'm hopeful I'll still be drafted."

I'm reminded that I still don't know why he left Tampa. Feels like there's more to the story than trying to get away from his cheating ex. But it doesn't seem like something he's ready to talk about, so I don't want to push him, especially after he planned this day for me.

"You will. You're an incredible player. I heard Beau talking about how you're on track to be the top scorer in the division."

The tension on his face softens. "I'm hovering there in the top three. I'm really hoping for Detroit. The Wheelers are my team, and nothing would be better than to be able to wear their jersey one day."

I nod. He would look amazing in red. I'm nibbling on my fingers again to stop the question from coming out. I really want to know where he thinks this thing between us will go. What if he ends up across the country next year? What does that mean for us?

But our relationship is so new. It's too soon for such a big question. I don't think I'm ready to face that yet, and I'm definitely not ready to bring it up with him. He's got enough to worry about.

"That was my best date ever." My eyes are shining, and my brain is packed with ideas, so I'm scribbling in a glittery pink notebook on my lap on the car ride home.

His hand has been glued to my thigh since he started driving, but he lifts it to flick the pink, feathery topper. "Nice pen."

"Thanks. Inspiration comes in many forms. If a feathery pen and a glittery notebook keep the ideas flowing, then I'm going with it."

"You do that. I prefer something a little more manly, maybe a blue pom pom, but I understand the appeal of the pink."

I'm practically purring when his hand lands back on my thigh, thumb rubbing in small circles.

"It was my best date, too," he admits in a voice so soft I'm not sure he even wants me to hear.

"Really? Big fan of coffee shops?" I tease.

"Big fan of you."

My insides are a puddle of mush. He's got to stop saying things like that or I'll never be able to move on. Our conversation about the future was a stark reminder that this might not last, even if I'm starting to think that I could stay with him forever.

Chapter Twenty-Eight

Game Misconduct

Cole

I drag myself out of bed, not looking forward to the day ahead. I've got my "date" from the bachelor auction today. My stomach feels like a churning cement mixer full of guilt and frustration at the thought of spending a second of alone time with her. There's a sour taste at the back of my throat that leaves me uninterested in breakfast. At least I have practice first. That'll help take my mind off my impending doom.

I've hardly had enough time with Jazz this week either. Seeing her in passing between classes and for brief snatches of food before one of us is rushing off is not enough to get my Coffee Girl fix. I actually ordered a pumpkin spice latte from All Capps the other day, hoping it would make me feel closer to her, but it wasn't the same, and just left me lonelier.

She's been working on finishing up her report for the charity event, as well as other class projects, and I've been balls deep in essays and hockey. I've been running the same drills with Hail so much that I'm passing pucks in my dreams.

"Man, you look exhausted. Better down some fuel before we hit the ice, or coach is going to work you twice as hard." I sigh, scrubbing a hand down my face. He's right. Coach's solution if you show up for practice tired is to double your laps. He always assumes that if you're too tired to show up for him, then you're screwing around, drinking or fucking. Not that maybe you're pulling all nighters to finish an assignment or that you don't sleep as well as usual when you can't have your girl in your bed.

"I'll try to pretend."

"You do that. Now eat up." He slaps me on the back, steering me in the direction of the kitchen.

I grab a ride with Beau and Dev, because I don't think I'm in any condition to drive, and he squeals into a parking spot with little concern for his brakes or tires. He's barely jammed his car into park when I'm leaping out, snagging my bag out of the trunk and slinging it over my shoulder.

I haven't even had time to strip my shirt off when coach walks in, eyes on me. My stomach twists at the serious look on his face.

"Schaeffer, my office, now."

Dread leaves my hands numb and a little shaky, but I head to his office. He's sitting there with Assistant Coach Jones and they've both got deadly serious looks on their faces.

"We've had a complaint about you, Schaeffer, and as per the athletic department's policy, we are required to investigate."

"A complaint?" My mind races through our last few games, looking for something, anything, that could be worthy of a complaint. A check that could have caused injury. A hit that was too hard. Some kind of rule violation. But I come up empty. I've been squeaky clean since I joined the Lightning. I've never been a bruiser, but my old team had a tendency to play a bit on the dirty side sometimes. Skating on the edge of legal, but still a bit dirty. I didn't embrace it. but made the occasional move, as per my coach's request. Not now though. I've been a freaking angel, because I literally can't afford any mistakes.

"Yes, from a Darryl Lawrence. Sound familiar."

Shit, shit, shit. A vivid picture of my fist slamming into that asshole's face comes flooding back to me. "Yes, I did punch him, but I had a very good reason."

"There is no excuse for punching anyone ever. Until you get to the pros. Then you might have to play to the crowd and take the gloves off sometimes. People like to see a little blood on the ice now and again, but until then it's a hard no. Especially for you."

"I brought you onto this team with a level of trust you hadn't earned, but I understand the circumstances surrounding that incident. I've always genuinely thought you weren't in the wrong on that occasion, but now. Now I'm not so sure. Maybe you bear more responsibility than I originally allowed for. And with that past, you've got no leeway."

"He was harassing my girlfriend. He showed up at her house and if I hadn't walked in, who knows what could have happened? She could have been hurt." I'm so agitated I'm tearing at my hair. Thinking of what he could have done to her has my blood pressure rising and my stomach roiling. I can't believe I'm here again. Defending myself. And in the last situation, I take full responsibility. I was angry, and I let my anger get the better of me, but this. He could have hurt her, and I'm not going to lie. I would do it all over again. Figures that ass wipe would tattle on me, though. What a douche bag. Not even man enough to stand up for himself. He has to squeal on me to my coach. Put my entire career on the line. All because he's not man enough to be able to take no for an answer.

My hand is trembling and all I want to do is slam it into his desk, but that move. That would get me nowhere. All it would do is make things worse for me.

"So, what does this mean?"

"You're benched for our next game pending the investigation. If you can prove some sort of wrongdoing on his part, I might be able to get you out of this after that, but let me tell you, it's not looking good for you right now."

It takes everything inside me to keep calm, not blow up on coach. It's not his fault, but why won't he even hear me out? He should stand up for me too, and more importantly, Jazz.

"You can't do this to me. I've had enough setbacks. If I'm not out there proving myself, it could end my career before it starts. I need to be out on the ice. Every game counts." If my career is over, all my dreams of helping my siblings through college are gone. Helping my dad escape the endless grind of multiple jobs that's aging him way too fast. That's gone too.

"I'm sorry, Schaeffer. My hands are tied. The athletics department has a zero-tolerance policy for violence."

"I'll figure this out. I'll fix it. I promise. I can't lose this." Everybody in my life is counting on me. From my family to Beau and my teammates. I can't let that asshole take everything from me. "Can I at least stay for practice? I need the ice time."

He shakes his head. "I'm sorry. You can't be here until this is resolved. Go home, get some rest, and see if you can figure this out. Let me know as soon as you have something for me."

The thump of my head hitting my hands on the desk doesn't even startle me. I don't look up when I hear the shuffling sounds of both my coaches getting up to leave.

"You can stay here until you get yourself together. I can call you a ride. You probably shouldn't be driving like this."

I shake my head. I'll figure that out on my own, like everything else. And since I didn't even drive, so there's no danger of fucking that up. I'm not even allowed to stay here, at the arena that's usually my safe place. I'm not allowed.

"Okay, then. Let me know when you've got anything we can use. I'm rooting for you, Cole. You're one of the best on the team this year. I need you out there as much as you need to be there."

I don't even bother to reply. My mind is spinning out of control, and I still can't see a way out. I can't ask Jazz to vouch for me. Make her face him again. She didn't want me to go to the police, and I never questioned it, but forcing her to drag her story out in front of everyone? No. I can't do that to her. Because I know she would. Besides, I don't even know if they'd believe her if she did. She's my girlfriend. They'll think she's lying for me.

I don't know how much time has passed when I finally haul myself up and out. I don't even look down the hall that leads to the ice, just drag my heels toward the exit and start walking. Our house isn't that far from campus. The brisk chill in the air should help clear my head.

I'm still lying face down on my bed when the guys come thundering into the house.

"Cole!" Beau's shout doesn't stir me. I can't be bothered to get up. Not even to explain myself.

Of course, that will not cut it with him. I hear him stomping up the stairs, and he barges through the door. Fuck me. I was so upset I didn't even lock it.

"Get up," he says.

If I ignore him, maybe he'll go away.

A heavy hand lands on my back with a thump. "Get the fuck up. I want an explanation and a solution."

He shakes me until I finally push myself up onto my elbows.

"What happened and what are we going to do about it?"

"I've been benched."

"No fucking shit, Sherlock. Why? What happened?" There's a surprising lack of accusation in his tone. I was expecting him to ask me what I did wrong. How I fucked up this time, but it's not there.

That's what finally has me spilling the entire sordid story to him. Jazz. How it's become something real. How her ex showed up the night of the Halloween party. I can't believe that was weeks ago. Feels like a year has passed.

"What a fucking weasel. He's dead. What's the plan? What are we going to do?"

I shrug, confused. "I have to prove he did something wrong. It's my word against his. I don't know what to do."

"You're not the only one who was there that night, Cole. Jazz can back you up. I'm sure she's got a spotless record. They might not believe you, but they have to believe her."

"I can't ask her to do that. She didn't want to get the police involved that night. This will open up so many cans of worms. I can't do that to her."

"If you explain to her what's going on, I'm sure she'll step in. She won't want this for you. Just tell her. Let her decide what she wants to do. Don't just give up. If you're not willing to do it for yourself, do it for the team. Not to mention any other girls that asshole harasses in the future."

When he puts it like that... "Okay. I'll talk to her." Whether she still wants to see me after this is another matter. Even if I can't have her, hopefully, I can still have my future. Feels a little hollow if she's not there with me by my side, but at least I'd still be there for everyone else in my life that's relying on me.

My hand's trembling again as I pick up the phone. This feels like an actual phone call type situation, not a text, so I dial her number.

"Hey, Cole, what's up?" The sound of her voice is soothing on my jangled nerves.

"Jazz. I'm glad you picked up." I stand up and start pacing the small room.

"Are you ready for your date? You should head out soon, right? Wait, you're not backing out, are you? Cold feet." There's a teasing tone in her voice.

Fuck. I forgot about the stupid auction date with everything that's happened since I woke up. "Nah. I was just about to head out." I can't let her down. Not her. Not like I'm letting everyone else down. This auction and the charity mean so much to her. What would it look like if I bailed out on my date? And if I know Charlene, she'd make a ton of noise about it.

"Good, good. Where are you taking her? Never mind. Don't tell me. No, I need to know. Where are you going?"

"We're going to Bolt's. I figure it's crowded and noisy enough. She won't get any ideas."

"Good call. Maybe I'll show up there in a couple of hours. Rescue you if you need it."

"Don't do that!" I still need to talk to her, but the noisy sports bar is not the place for it.

"Oh. Okay."

"I mean. I still want to see you, but not there. Are you going to be home later? Can I stop by?"

"Mmm." I can almost hear her nibbling on a strand of hair like she always does when she's deep in thought. "I'm going to meet my group at the library to work on our facilities design project. Tomorrow?"

"Okay. I'll text you. We can figure something out." My schedule is depressingly clear with hockey practice and training off the schedule.

"Later. Have fun, but not too much fun. How tragic would that be if you ran off with the girl who bought you at the auction I was running? No thanks."

"I would never do that to you, Jazz."

My tone must be more serious than was called for because she laughs. "I was kidding. I know you wouldn't do that."

"Yeah, right. Sorry. I'm getting up in my head. L... Later."

"Bye."

Holy shit. Did I almost say the L word to her? Way too soon for that. Even if I'm feeling it. But now would be terrible timing. She deserves a romantic date and flowers and the moon or some shit. Not her desperate boyfriend telling her he loves her while his life is crumbling around him.

I can't go on this farce of a date now. Charlene will have to deal. At least she shoved her number on me before Jazz got between us at the auction.

Chapter Twenty-Nine

Sleight Of Stick

Jazz

N obody should be at the library this late on the weekend, but this project is like forty percent of my facilities design grade, so I can't afford to do less than my best. A lot of the grants I've applied for hinge on keeping my grades at the top level, but at least we're finally finished.

Rob pushes up from the table a step behind Molly, and Trin lifts her head up from where it was resting on her hands, blond curls spilling out over the table.

"Is this thing finally a lock?" she asks. "I never want to look at another blueprint again in my life."

I kind of agree, but the thought being able to understand the design process and read the prints for my own business one day has a certain appeal, but it's still tough for someone with no design experience.

"I think we've got it. Solved that problem with the placement of the bathrooms so we're solid. We can submit it to Petrie on Monday and then we'll be in good shape to pass this class with a high A."

"Thank fuck. You coming, Jazz?" Rob holds out his hand to me.

"Nah, I gotta stay for another half an hour or so. I need to finish up my case study for environmental management."

"I'm finished mine. Want to swap when you're done? We can proofread each other's work. Make sure everything looks good."

A second set of eyes is always helpful, and Rob does good work.

"Sure, that would be great, Rob. Thanks."

"We can meet up tomorrow to trade papers, unless you want me to hang out here until you're finished." He's hovering over me, and I know I'll be too distracted to do my best work if he's waiting for me.

"No. you go on. I'm sure you've got better places to be on a Saturday night. Text me tomorrow and we can figure out a meetup."

His smile brightens up. "You got it. Can't wait to see you.

I'm nibbling on a strand of hair when another shadow looms over me.

"Forget something?" I look up, expecting to see Rob, and instead it's a familiar blonde.

"Nope. This is exactly what I was looking for. I don't think we've formally met. I'm Charlene."

She snaps the gum she's chomping on, pursing the lips that are as shiny as her blonde hair.

"I know who you are." I turn back to the papers I was about to gather up. "Look, I've got to go. I'm finished here and there's nothing you can have to say to me that I'd care to hear."

"Oh, I think you're wrong there. See, I've heard some things about your relationship with my boyfriend." I don't like her at all, but I really don't like the way she's holding her fingers up in the air in air quotes. She can't know. No one knows. The only person I've told is Amira and I think Cole said he told Beau and that was it. I know Beau would never blab out a secret.

"I doubt it, Charlene. I'm tired and I really want to get out of here."

"Here's the thing, Jazmin. I know all about what you and Cole have going on. I know it's not real. You've been faking it with him. I get it. He's a good guy. I'm sure he was helping you out with something, but it's over. He told me about it because he wants me back. And now you're just in the way. So if you can just back off, that would be great."

Cole told her? No way. She's lying. I know she's lying, but at the same time, where would she get this information? How is this girl, this stranger, getting under my skin?

"Whatever you've heard, it's a lie." No way am I telling her it used to be true. She doesn't need to know that. What matters is that it's true now. "You're not getting between us. You cheated on him and hurt him so badly he left his old team. So why don't you run along and find some guy who actually wants you?"

There's a gleam in her eyes that I don't trust. But I guess there's not much I trust about her. "You think he left because I cheated on him? I'm sorry to disappoint you. He got kicked off his last team."

It's like a physical blow to my chest, knocking the wind out of me. I don't want to satisfy her smug expression, but I can't help it. I need to know. "What are you talking about?"

"See, I knew you were lying. You're not as close as you're pretending to be. He beat up one of his teammates. Jeremy was off the ice for like two weeks because of him."

That doesn't sound like the Cole I know. Except when I remember that feverish look in his eyes when he was going after Darryl. I guess it is possible he's capable of something like that, but not without reason.

"What did they do to him?"

"That's not for me to share. But Jeremy was his best friend before that."

There's got to be more to the story, but if so, why didn't he tell me himself. Especially after I shared all my secrets with him. It hurst that he didn't trust me enough to share.

"It doesn't matter." It does, but I'm not giving her the satisfaction of knowing how much she got under my skin. "He's never going back to you. We're together, so leave us alone."

I stand up, satisfied that she backs up a step when I move into her. I would never get physical, but I don't mind using the intimidation tactic just a little to tell her to mind her own business.

She huffs. "You're going to be sorry about this. In fact, you might already be."

What does that mean? I don't know and I don't care. Nothing she says can affect what I've got with Cole. This fragile, growing thing that still needs all our love and attention if it's going to grow. I'll got to him. I'll find out the truth.

"Anyway. I thought you should know the fake dating thing isn't a secret. Cole's laughing at you behind your back when he talks about you."

My fists are clenched at my sides, and I've never wanted to punch anyone more. Now I'm starting to understand why Cole lost in on Darryl. If I saw someone threatening him like Darryl was threatening me, I might lose it, too.

"Get out of here, Charlene. I'm not going to fall for your lies and, like I said, even if I did, he's not coming back to you. Why would you follow him here? That's some next level stalker shit."

"Whatever. Don't say I didn't warn you."

I know there is nothing but lies spilling from her pink painted lips, but I can't help the little seed of doubt from poking up. She knew the truth. So who told her? Five minutes ago I would have said with a hundred percent certainty it wasn't him. But now I'm not so sure.

I collapse on my couch when I get home. I have to work early tomorrow, and I'm beat. My brain is aching from staring at those blueprints and also from my conversation with Charlene. I keep running her words through my head trying to fit the pieces together but nothings seems to match up. Someone told her, and Cole has been keeping secrets from me.

My head is so full of competing thoughts it feels heavy, and it's a struggle to get up to answer the buzzer when it goes off.

It doesn't make sense to collapse back on the couch, so I hover by the door until the knock sounds out. A distortion of Amira's face is visible through the peephole so I let her in.

Soft arms wrap around me, and I relax into them, craving the comfort.

"What's wrong?" she asks.

"It's Cole."

Her arms tighten around me. "What did he do? I'll go find him with a sharpened kitchen knife faster than you can say stabby stabby if he hurt you"

"Nothing. Something. I'm not sure."

She pulls away to shut the door and lock it before slipping an arm around my shoulder to lead me back to the couch.

"He's great. Well I thought he was. But you know how we were doing the fake dating thing. We made it real the night after the auction. He asked me to be his girlfriend." Just the memory of it is enough for a tentative smile to creep up.

"Okay," she says as if she's reserving judgment until she gets the whole story. "Then what did he do?"

"I told you how he had an ex that cheated on him."

She nods.

"She came up to me yesterday and told me something. She said she knew our relationship was fake, and that he was the one who told her. Plus, she told me that he got kicked off his last team for beating up a teammate. He never told me that, and I just don't know if I can trust him anymore."

She pauses, chewing on her lower lip. "Did you talk to him about it?"

"Not yet. I only just found out and I called you. I needed someone to talk to about it."

"I'm glad you did. I'm happy to be here for you, but I don't want to drive you off with my advice if it's unwanted."

"Please tell me. I won't be mad."

"Misunderstandings are what sink relationships. You have to talk to him about it. Ask him straight up. Honesty and communication are the most important things in a relationship."

Right. I know she's right, but... "What if I was wrong about him?"

Her entire body softens, and she pulls me in for another hug. She smells like lavender shampoo, and it's such a soothing aroma I relax into her. "At least you'll know. But don't give up on him without talking to him. Figure this out and see if he's the one for you. Give him a chance, but make sure he's worthy of you. If he doesn't worship the ground you walk on, he's not worth your time."

"Okay. I will. I'll talk to him. Thanks so much for coming over, Amira. I don't deserve you."

There's confusion pursing her lips. "Of course you do. You're an amazing woman, and you've had my back on more than one occasion. Everybody deserves a friend."

Her words fill my heart to the brim, sending pulses of warmth through my body. I do deserve a friend. And Cole. He's at least earned the opportunity to explain himself.

CHAPTER THIRTY

HAILSTORM

COLE

Even though I'm the one who originally asked her to meet up, I'm nervous. I get up and sit down like five times. I'm alternating between checking the time on my phone and glancing at the doorway that leads in from the quad. The can-we-talk text message was way too much for my already shattered nerves.

She asked to meet here in the big impersonal school cafeteria and refused my offer to pick her up. It leaves a dark cloud hanging over my head, and the worst part is wouldn't blame her if she broke up with me.

"Hey, Cole." Her soft voice comes from behind me and I turn around slowly, afraid of what I'm going to find in her eyes. I don't think I could handle an ending before we've gotten through the first chapter of our story.

"Jazz." I stand up, gesturing for her to sit down.

The only good thing is the caf is pretty empty on a Sunday mid morning. Only the occasional students are gathered around chatting or studying. I picked a table as far away from anyone else as I could to give us the semblance of privacy that I'm going to need if she's here to break up with me.

My lips are tingling with the urge to kiss her, but I resist, wanting to see what she's got to say. If it really is over, there's no point in sharing my news with her. I wouldn't ask her to go through that for me if we don't even have that connection.

She's wringing her hands together on the table and I can't resist some small touch. Placing my hands over hers. They're cold under mine.

"I was just at the library, trading papers with Rob. That's why I was already on campus."

I nod at her, not needing the explanation, but it does ease the load on my mind a bit.

"Anyway. Charlene came to see me yesterday."

That almost throws me back in my seat. Not what I was expecting her to say. "What?"

"You didn't know?" Her head tilts to the side, studying me for a minute before she glances over my shoulder.

"No. What kind of shit was she stirring up?"

She shallows. "She knows."

Knows what? That I've been suspended? About Darryl? She must sense the confusion in my eyes.

"About us. The fake dating thing."

"What?!" My fingers flex over hers and I almost push up off the table, looking for someone to fight. But that's not the answer.

"How?" I swipe a hand through my hair.

"She told me you were the one who told her, but I never really believed that. She said you wanted her back, and I was in the way."

"Fucking lies. Nothing but lies come out of that girl's mouth. I've been doing everything in my power to avoid talking to her. You know that."

She looks a little relieved, but there's still tension bracketing her eyes. "That's what I thought. I mean, at first I had a few doubts, but it didn't make sense. But if you didn't tell her, who did Cole?"

"Good fucking question."

"I thought we were keeping it to ourselves. I told Amira, you told Beau, and that was it. Have you been telling other people?" She nibbles on her lip. "Have you been laughing at me behind my back?"

"What? No. Never. I love you, Jazz. I would never do that to you." Her eyes widen and I rear back. Holy hell. After everything I was thinking earlier, I just let that slip. In the worst way. But I guess I couldn't keep it in any longer. The feeling is too big to contain. Too much for me.

"You..." Her hair swishes from shoulder to shoulder as she shakes her head, and she goes to pull her hands away, but I close my fingers around hers, not letting her escape.

"I do. I love you, Coffee Girl. This is not the way I would have chosen to tell you, but it's true. I don't know when it started, but it's been growing on me every day. With every smile and every touch and I can't keep it in any longer. And I don't want to."

"Okay. But if that's true, why didn't you tell me the real reason you left Tampa?"

My heart sinks. There may have been lies dripping from Charlene's tongue, but it looks like she revealed some secrets too. Although why she'd tell Jazz that one is beyond me. The truth doesn't look much better on her than it does on me.

"What did she tell you?"

"That you beat up a teammate. Your best friend. That can't be true. You wouldn't do that." There's a pleading tone to her voice. She's begging me to deny it.

"I would if he was the one who cheated with Charlene." It's a relief to tell her. I'm almost light headed, and I kicking myself for not telling her before. She was honest with me, but I kept this from her. It doesn't look good on me.

"I guess I can understand why she didn't tell me that part, but why didn't you tell me Cole? I thought we were being honest with each other, only to find out you were keeping this huge thing from me." Now she's disappointed and I hate hearing that. Knowing I caused her pain.

"I'm sorry. I should have told you, but I was embarrassed. That it could happen to me. That they both betrayed me. I've hardly told anyone. But I should have told you."

She nods, but doesn't make any move toward me. There's no way to tell what she's really thinking about me.

"I hope you can forgive me. What Jeremy and Charlene did hurt me so bad I didn't think I'd be able to trust anyone again. And then I met you. Not only do I trust you, but I also love you. It's not the right time, or the right place." I glance around the mostly empty cafeteria. "But I can't hold it in any longer."

I shut my eyes and take a deep breath. I sprung that on her. It's not fair to expect her to respond. I get it, but it still slices through my gut.

"Okay. I think I can understand why you kept that from me. I still need some time to figure it out, but I think I can move past it. In the meantime, we need to figure out how she found out about the other thing."

"You're right. We need to figure out who told her..." I trail off, remembering the day I was talking to Beau in the locker room and Hail walked out. He must have overheard us. He must have told her. Damnit. I thought I was getting through to him. I though t things were going well. Hell, I even thought maybe he liked me. Apparently not. You wouldn't betray a teammate's confidence like that if you had a sense of loyalty.

"I think I know who it was, and I'll deal with it."

This time she's the one who doesn't let me go when I try to stand up. "Wait, Cole."

"Yes."

"Didn't you want to talk to me about something? You said yesterday."

Yesterday feels like two years ago, but yes. I should tell her this. I told her I love her for fuck's sake. She should know the kind of mess her boyfriend is in. Then she can decide if she wants to stay with the hot mess who was keeping things from her.

"I'm suspended from the team."

"What? What for? What happened?"

"It was Darryl. He ratted me out for what I did to him in your apartment."

She's shaking her head again. "But that's not fair. He was... he had his hands on me." Her hands go a little shaky under mine.

"I know, and I told my coach, but he couldn't do anything about it. There's a zero-tolerance policy and without proof, he couldn't do anything. I'm off practice and one game, and if I can't prove that I was in the right, I'll be off the team."

"No." She pulls back. "No, they can't do that to you."

"They can and they did. Look, I'll understand if you want nothing to do with me. I'm cursed. I get it. Fucking bad news."

"I've gotta go."

She pushes up to her feet, walking off without a backwards glance, and I'm confused. I know I told her she could go, but that was. She just took off. I watch her rushing off through the glass door, too stunned to stop her.

My head falls to my hands. Hail. Mother fucker. Look what I get for trusting a team mate again. Bit me in the ass in the worst possible way. Without hockey, without Jazz, I've got nothing. Nothing to lose. A burning rage builds, giving me the push I need to get out of here. At least accomplish one thing.

Maybe I can't solve anything with Jazz, but at least I can deal with this. I'm not allowed in the arena right now, so I'm hanging out in the parking lot like a chump. Waiting. Every fiber in my being wishes I was in there with them. On the ice. Where I belong.

I blow on my numb fingers to warm up. Can't afford to be idling my engine to blast the heat. Mabel only has so many miles left in her engine, and I've only got so many dollars in my bank account.

A few of the rookies are the first ones out, but there's no sign of Hail.

My fingers drum on the steering wheel while I imagine what I'm going to do to Hail. Everything is all fucked anyway. What difference will one more bloody nose make? NO. I can't think like this. It could still get resolved. Yeah, if there's some miracle out there waiting for me. My life hasn't exactly been full of them, so probably not. But I shouldn't go in there hot. That only ends badly.

There he is. His tall form steps out the front door. He's walking with McAllistair. All casual and carefree, as if he didn't try to fuck me over. Sneaky asshole. Joke's on him. I can fuck myself over better than anyone else.

I take a deep breath to slow the pounding of my heartbeat. Count backward from five and get out of the car.

He looks up, startled, as I storm toward him. And the rage on my face must look as palpable as it feels because he throws up his gloved hands, taking a step back.

"Why, Hail? That's all I want to know. Why did you choose to fuck me over? I thought we were getting along. As teammates, at least. If not friends. But teammates don't do that to you." At least they shouldn't. Apparently, I've learned nothing from my past experience.

"I don't know what you think I did, Schaeffer, but I had nothing to do with getting you suspended."

My laugh is bitter. "I wasn't thinking that, but thanks for putting that idea in my head. I mean Charlene."

"Who the fuck is that? Your girlfriend? I thought you were dating, Jazz."

I take a step closer, satisfied when he backs up until he's pressed against the concrete wall beside the back door.

"Really? You're going to deny it? Let me jog your memory. Blonde hair likes to wear shiny pink lip gloss while she's riding your best friend's dick. Ring any bells?"

He swallows and understanding dawns on his face. "Is that your ex?" And then something else happens. There's awareness, but he's surprised by it. Shock. "No. No. I didn't know. I'm sorry. I never meant."

He's still holding his hands up to hold me off like he can sense the dark need in me to take out my anger out on his face.

"So you admit it? You told her?"

"What the fuck, Schaeffer. You're not even supposed to be here. Back off of Hail. He didn't do anything to you."

I ignore my captain for the first time. Laser focused on Hail.

He swallows again. "I didn't know. I didn't know it was your ex. I was an idiot. A drunk idiot. She came on to me. Said her name was Char. I never even knew."

"I don't believe you. When she first showed up on campus, Beau told everyone to keep her away."

"Yes, but I didn't know it was her. You have to believe me, man. I would never. I've been screwed over before by a teammate, and I would never do that to anyone else."

I loosen my hold on his shirt, taking a step back and swiping an arm across my face. Beau's hand is hovering near my shoulder, but he doesn't touch me. As if he trusts me to keep my shit under control.

"Well then, explain. What the fuck happened? I know you know abut Jazz and I. That it wasn't real. At least not at first, but then it was. I really like her. Fuck that. I love her, and now she doesn't know if she can trust me and my hockey career is fucked and I can't..." Heat wells behind my eyes, but I clench my jaw and keep it in.

"I did. I heard you and Beau that day, but I swear I would never tell anyone. But I was at a bar. I'd been drinking and this hot chick started coming on to me. She bought me some drinks and took me home. I slept with her." He flinches back as if he's expecting me to lay one on him for that. But I don't give a shit.

"Anyway. She was talking about doing it again. Dating, and I laughed. I told her she could be my fake girlfriend because I don't do real relationships. And I may have mentioned that one of my teammates was doing it and it was working for him. She asked who and my head was blurry and I was all sex-high, and I told her."

"So you admit it."

"Yes, but I didn't do it intentionally. I didn't know who she was. Hell, I figured she'd forget about the entire thing in the morning. If not, I would have told you I swear."

I turn to Beau, looking for assistance, but he shakes his head at me.

"That was a dumb fuck thing to do, Hail. You don't spill your teammates' secrets. I don't care how drunk you are. Alcohol is no excuse." He turns back to me. "That being said. It sounds like it was a mistake. He's an idiot, but not a traitor. And let's face it, we've all been idiots over some girl or another at some point in our lives."

He's not wrong. I was an idiot for years.

Hail finally takes a step away from me as the dangerous vibes dissipate. "Is there anything I can do? Want me to talk to Jazz. I can tell her what happened. Let her know it was my fault. You had nothing to do with it. Whatever you need, man."

"No, it's fine. It'll be fine. I'm sorry I went on the attack, but it's not the first time I've been fucked over by a teammate. I didn't want to let myself be the fool again."

"You're not a fool. This is all on her. She's bad fucking news, and Hail is a grade A moron for sticking his dick in her.

"Come on. Let me give you a ride home." Beau slaps me on the back as the adrenaline seeps from my body, leaving me with a slight headache and trembling hands.

"I've got my car here." The protest is weak.

"You shouldn't be driving in that condition. Don't be a dumb ass. I'll give you a ride home and we can play some Mario Kart or something."

"Fine." I relent. That's one problem solved, but it doesn't do anything to get me back on the ice, which is now the most pressing issue.

CHAPTER THIRTY-ONE

DEFENSIVE LINE

JAZZ

I haven't seen Cole since Sunday. I wanted to get a few things in line before I saw him again. Fill him in on my plan. I figure we've got four hours together on our Walk Safe shift, so it'll be the perfect time to catch up. I really hope he doesn't think I've abandoned him.

The stairs disappear two at a time as I fly up to the office to check in and grab my safety vest. It's only been three days, but I miss him. I love him. It's been creeping up on me so slowly that I didn't until he said it. That warm glow that's always simmering in my chest now only bubbles up when he's around. When I see him or talk to him on the phone. When I get a random text from him during the day. That's love. I'm sure of it, and I want to tell him, but not until the time is right. Not until I've sorted things out. Fixed what I broke.

"Cole!" I call out, rushing into the small storage room, but my heart sinks when the guy that turns to face me isn't him. It's Kenneth. The coordinator for the team. I've seen him around, and he's usually the one who signs me in and out for my shifts. Grabs the phone out of the locked cabinet for us, but I don't know him that well. I try to hide my disappointment under a warm smile, but all the radiance has drained away. All the expectation of speaking with Cole again.

"Hey, Jazz. I'm on his shift tonight. He's not allowed to volunteer here until everything's resolved with him."

They heard, and they've pulled him from this job too. He's losing everything, and it's all my fault. I wish I had never met Darryl. Fallen for his lies. And all for what? I was never in love with him. Not like this. I've never felt like this before in my life.

"You don't think he was in the wrong, though, do you? You know what really happened?"

"I just heard he punched some guy. We can't have anyone escorting vulnerable people around campus with that kind of thing hanging over their heads."

He doesn't know. This could be helpful. "Here's how it went down." Kenneth is a hundred percent on board once I explain the situation to him. Perfect. This is what it's all about. I've learned a few things from my big, crazy family, after all. It's all about teamwork.

I'm eager to finish this shift. To gather the troops and get my plan under way, so of course the night drags on. And I'm sure sleep will be a just a hope and a dream at this point, since everything is set for tomorrow.

I'm fiddling with the thin gold bracelet on my wrist while I wait. Of course he's late. All I want is to get this over with.

"Jazz. I'm surprised you called me. Have you reconsidered?" Darryl sits down across from me, and I pull back in disgust when his knee grazes me. I had my reasons for picking this neutral cafe downtown, but I didn't think through the implications of sitting across from him at such a small table.

"No, Darryl. I have not reconsidered, but I think it's about time that you reconsidered."

He scoffs, a derisive smirk twisting his lips. "And what exactly do I need to reconsider?"

I place my palms on the table, leaning in closer even though his mere presence pains me.

"You need to recant your accusations. You need to go to his team. The athletics department. Whoever you squealed to in the first place and admit that you were wrong."

"What are you talking about, Jazz? I didn't do anything. You saw him. He broke my nose."

"He did not break your nose. He merely pulled you off me. I asked you to leave. I asked you not to touch me and you ignored me. Your advances were unwelcome, as was your presence in my house."

His smirk deepens, and he folds his arms across his chest. "Sure, fine. You asked me to leave. What of it? You can't prove anything, Jazz. No one is going to believe you. Hysterical girlfriend trying to make sure she doesn't lose her meal ticket when her boyfriend gets kicked off the team. Nobody is going to believe you."

I can't believe I ever let this guy into my life. He's disgusting. Too bad he hides it so well at first.

"See, that's where you're wrong." I pull my phone out of my pocket, laying it on the table in front of me so he can see that I've been recording our conversation. "Take everything back and I won't call the police to get a restraining order on you. Or press charges. You violated my home. You touched me when I told you not to, and I've got the proof." I pat the phone in front of me. My insurance. "I don't think Daddy's going to be able to get you out of this one. At the very least, you'll probably get kicked out of school. And that would be a shame after three years of working toward your degree."

I had no idea his reflexes were so fast. He snatches my phone like a snake snatching its prey.

"You've got nothing, bitch." His breath is sour as he hisses in my face, but the triumph falters when I don't even ask for the phone back. I just mirror his former posture, leaning back in my seat and smiling at him.

His face blanches. "What do you look so happy about?"

"You didn't think I was so naïve that I wouldn't bring along an insurance policy, do you?"

He looks around just as the four guys at the booth behind him slip out of their booth to circle our table. Beau, Dev, and Hail all look intimidating with their height and biceps bulging out of their t-shirts. Kenneth a little less so, but I thought it would be a good idea to have an unbiased observer in on the action. Otherwise he might be able to call foul.

Darryl hits the screen on my phone, then throws his hands up in the air. "Fine, I'm leaving, but you still don't have the proof. It's gone. I deleted that, and if you try to use these guys as witnesses, I'll just say they were threatening me. Obviously, I can't fight all four of them, and they're on Cole's side."

I shake my head at him. "Do you really think I'm that stupid? That I'd let you delete my evidence without a fight. There are four phones recording this conversation right now. All of it. Including that last threat. You've got nothing. I've got all the power here and I know you hate that. You prefer your women to be obedient and beaten down. But that's not me. It never was. I may have fallen for your charms for a little while, but I got out, and now I'm in charge. Fix what you broke. If Cole's not back on the team by tomorrow, I'm going to the police."

Dev crosses his arms over his chest, tilting his head. And I can't think of too many people who wouldn't be intimidated by that glare attached to those arms.

"Okay. I'll go. I promise."

"Today?"

"Today."

"Now? Want me to get the guys to escort you?"

He shakes his head. The fear is finally in his eyes. Now that he knows, I've got him. "No, no. I'm fine. I got this. I'll go."

"Perfect. Excellent doing business with you. I can't say it's been a pleasure, but I feel a lot better than I did when I got here, so thanks for that."

"Whatever. Just stay the fuck away from me, Jazz. And keep your guard dogs away, too."

"Hey. I never want to see you again. And if all goes well and you do your job, I won't have to. Bye, Darryl."

Holy crap. I lean back in my seat. I got through it with almost steady hands, but now that it's over, my vision is going a little fuzzy around the edges and I'm really glad I'm sitting down, because I don't think my legs would hold me up right now.

CHAPTER THIRTY-TWO

HERE FOR YOU

COLE

"**G**et your sorry ass up and come with us."

A few sharp raps on my door accompany the command as JJ's obnoxious voice cuts through my wallowing. I'm lying on my bed, reading a book. If you can call it that. I think I just read the same page ten times or so. Not a single word soaked in through the muddy haze of despair. The guys let me wallow on Monday, but they dragged me out of bed to go to class yesterday, but that's it. I guess if I don't have my future as a hockey player, I'm going to have to study extra hard so I can pursue my back up career.

"I mean it. If you don't get your ass up, I'm coming in."

"It's locked, asshole," I tell him, smugly.

"Then I'll break the door down, and I'm pretty sure Beau will be pissed if you break your door."

I heave out a sigh, swinging my legs over the side of the bed. I wouldn't put anything past JJ.

Beau will no doubt blame me.

He pounds on the door again, increasing both the frequency and strength until it's rattling under his fist.

"Fuck. I'm coming. Ease up." Maniac.

He's all smiles, stumbling through the door right into my arms when I open it. I shove him off.

"I didn't need a hug. Get the fuck off me."

"Awww, I think you need a hug, Coco. Coco's sad, Gigi. Come, give him a hug."

"Nah. We're going to be late, and Beau will make us do suicides if we don't show up on time."

Well, at least that's not something I have to worry about.

"Right." JJ jumps to attention, saluting Grant. "Come on, Coco. Time to go."

"Go where exactly? I don't have class right now."

"I dunno. The captain didn't trust us with the information, but he told me where to take you, or else."

Grant slaps his friend on the shoulder. "He didn't trust you. I know where we're going and why, but I'm not allowed to tell. It's a surprise."

JJ's lower lip pushes out in a pout. "Come on. I'm the only one who doesn't get to know? Not fair. Whisper it to me. I won't tell, I promise." He slings an arm around Grant's neck, bringing his mouth down to his ear.

Grant shoves at him. "Fuck off. Everyone knows you can't keep a secret. And if we're late, I'm telling Beau it's all your fault."

"Fine." JJ huffs, stomping toward the stairs. He turns around to look at me. "You coming?"

"Um no. I don't have any part in this. You two go on ahead."

Grant's hand lands on my shoulder when I go to turn around and disappear back into my misery. "No, you don't. You're coming with us if we have to tie you up and carry you out to the car."

"You're not going to tie me up." They wouldn't, would they? JJ's eyes are shining with delight at the idea. "Fine, fine. I'll come. Let me just go grab my bag."

"Nope. Now."

"Will you at least tell me where we're going?"

"Retro Diner," Grant says, not turning his attention from the road. He made me sit in the passenger seat, claiming I was a flight risk and he needed to keep an eye on me. JJ protested, but as usual, was overruled.

My eyes narrow at the sight of Beau's SUV parked out in front of the diner, and Grant slides his little sedan in behind the larger vehicle.

I'm still sitting in my seat, arms crossed, when Grant comes around to my side, opening my door. "Get out. What do you need an engraved invitation?"

"Maybe a hint of what we're doing here. I'm not up for a social gathering. In case you didn't notice, my life is kind of a hot mess right now."

"You need this. Trust me."

Trust. The thing I've been working on this year. The thing I thought I had started to get down when it all blew up around me. And even after that, I kind of do still trust these assholes, so I step out of the car, ignoring the hand JJ is holding out as if I'm his date. That's pushing it.

The music fits the vibe as we walk through the door. Elvis or some shit. Framed vinyl records hang from the wall, and the servers are wearing light pink dresses with full skirts, paired with white aprons.

I'm looking around for Beau irritably when I spot her. It's only the back of her head, but I'd recognize it in a crowded club. Long, sleek black hair held back by a bright yellow polka dot hair band. I take a step back.

"I can't go over there. If this is some sort of setup and we're surprising her, I'm not into it. She doesn't want me here."

Grant shoves me. "She's expecting you dick head. The only one being set up is you."

What? She wants me here. I'm still cautious, walking forward slowly, as if I might startle her off if I move too fast. She tilts her head up to look at me as I walk past her. There's a smile on her face, but it's a little tentative. A little wobbly.

"Cole."

"Jazz." I'm not sure if I have the right to use her nickname anymore.

"Sit down." I slide into the seat across from her. I'd do anything she asked me to.

"It's over, Cole."

What the fuck. I feel like I've been shot. Pain rips through my heart, and I reach up to grab my chest. Did they bring me here for this?

Her eyes go wide, and she throws up her hands. "Shit. Sorry. I'm so sorry. I didn't mean us. I didn't think that through."

My heart's still pounding triple time in my chest, and I'm wary.

"No, you I love, I mean I love you. I'm not breaking up with you. I promise."

She's cute when she's flustered. Flapping her hands around in the air while she stumbles over her words. And then it hits me. She said it. She loves me. All the fear is gone, and my heart is racing for a different reason now. I don't even care why she brought me here. She loves me. Unless there's a but.

"But?"

"But nothing. I love you. I'm yours. I never stopped being yours. I just needed to sort a few things out before I saw you again. I was hoping to see you at Walk Safe last night, but you weren't there. Anyway, like I said, it's all good. It's over."

Her babbling may be cute, but I'm no less confused than I was when JJ and Grant kidnapped me.

"I love you, but what are you talking about, Coffee Girl?" The word flows with ease now, like the dam's been lifted now that she said it back.

"Right. I'm sorry."

I drop my hands over hers. "Stop apologizing and just tell me what's up. Put me out of my misery. Please."

"You're back on the team. Or you will be very soon. I'm sure you'll get a call from your coach by the end of the day or tomorrow. I don't know how these things work, but you're back."

"What? How?"

"I talked to Darryl, and I told him I'd go to the police if he didn't clear your name."

"You talked to him. Are you okay? Did he touch you? If he did. I swear to every god out there, Jazz."

"No. I had a little help." She curls her fingers in a come here gesture and guys start emerging from every crack and cranny in the diner.

Beau and Dev come over first, and I swear there's almost a smile on Dev's face. I haven't seen him around as much as usual. No idea what he's up to, but maybe I'll be able to catch up with him if things ease up. Grant and JJ, of course, are smiling like fools. Even Hail is here. He showed up for me. After I jumped all over him the other day, he still came out to help. I feel like shit for jumping straight to accusations. And even Kenneth.

"Kenneth?" I ask. The stringy math whiz from Walk Safe doesn't exactly fit in with the rest of the guys, but here is.

"Yeah. Jazz told me what was going on during our shift the other night. She explained everything, so when she asked me to come out and be an unbiased observer, I was all in. You're a good guy, Cole. I never doubted that, but I had some reservations until I heard Jazz's side. That guy was a real piece of work. The things he said."

"Kenneth," Jazz hisses at him and my eyes narrow to slits. It's probably better if I don't know what her ex said to her. I'd probably get myself right back into the boiling pot if I did.

"Tell me everything. How did it go down?" I turn back to Jazz.

She explains the story to me with an occasional interjection from one of the guys. I love everything about how she took him down. My only regret is that I wasn't there to see it, but even I know why that would have been a terrible idea.

"You should have seen her. She was incredible. Hopefully, he learns his lesson, but I have my doubts," Beau says. "Listen, we're going to leave you two alone to catch up. I'll grab a ride with Grant. You can borrow my car."

I snag the keys he tosses at me. I've never driven his car before. He claps me on the back, and then I get a fist bump from all of them. It's incredible. I feel like I'm in a dream. Not quite believing that they stepped up for me after my rough start with the team last year, but it feels really good. Like I've got a new family for the year. And probably for the rest of my life. We may end up on opposing teams, but I have a feeling we'll still stay in touch. You can't go through shit like this and not stay tight. But it's good to see the backs of their heads. Now I have Jazz all to myself.

"Where were we?" I ask my girl.

"Right here," she says, leaning in for a kiss.

CHAPTER THIRTY-THREE

HAT TRICK

JAZZ

I've got a death grip on Jordan's arm. I squealed and dropped my phone when I found out she was going to make it out. It's an important one, and I needed the moral support of a fellow hockey girlfriend. Some of the other Lakeview girlfriends are nice, but Jordan is my OG bestie.

I don't even know why I'm so tense. The Lightning are shooting ahead with a three to one lead. Two of those goals scored by my love, no less. But I know how much it would mean to him to get a hat trick tonight. He wants to prove once and for all that any pro team would be lucky to have him on their roster. And he's not wrong.

The action on the ice is intense. Back and forth. The puck flying faster than I can track it. Cole swoops in, snags it from their center and makes a hard drive down the ice. He's so fast. I know Jackson was always considered the fastest player, but I don't think I'm being biased when I say Cole has gotten even faster. His legs are almost a blur as his he zigzags around the opposing team.

I think he's got it this time, and I'm halfway to my feet when I gasp rips from my chest as one of their D-men swoops in from behind him. These are the hard parts to watch. I'm wincing in sympathy as he slams into the boards with a rattling crash that I can feel all the way to my skull. I can only imagine what it feels like for him.

I'm so focused on my man that I miss him flipping the puck to Hail, who slams it under the goalie's glove. Cole shakes himself off, skating over to congratulate his teammate with a glove bump. His line gets sent off for a break, and the game can't hold my attention anymore. My eyes are on him. He ripped his helmet off as soon as he hit the bench, and now he's sitting there, knee bouncing incessantly, eyes glued to the play. I know he's just waiting for his turn to get back out there.

Jordan's eyes are focused on the game. Her man may have moved on, but she's still friends with a lot of guys on the Lightning, and she's been a hockey fan since she was a kid.

"This never gets any easier?"

She turns to me with a smile, running a hand through her fiery curls. "Nope. Sorry to disappoint."

Cole flies onto the ice as soon as his line is called and he's back out there, searching for his opening. The other team is getting dirtier the farther behind they get, and he's on constant alert to avoid another hit.

Beau and Dev are defending their goal when Grant and Hail start tossing the puck back and forth, weaving around the opposing team with a grace and agility I'll never possess. But even though I'm invested in the game, I can't help my eyes from tracking back to number thirty-two. He's well positioned near Penns net, leaving himself open as his teammates fight their way closer.

The strategy pays off when Hail returns the earlier favor, sending the puck his way. The D-man that slammed him into the boards gets up in his face again and he loses his open shot, but Hail nods at him and he goes for it, anyway. He sends it high and to the left. Cole is never predictable. He practices shots from every angle, every spot. His accuracy is unmatched. The goalie is a fraction of a second behind the puck, but it's enough to light up the lamps and send the crowd to their feet.

I was hovering over my seat, too excited to stay sitting, before he even made the shot, and now I'm screaming so hard I'm sure my voice will be hoarse later. I smirk. Cole won't mind. He likes it when my voice is all husky from cheering him on. I can only imagine the things he's going to do to me when we get home.

He skates right up to the glass below our seats, banging and pointing his stick at me.

It was for me. He says it's always for me. Every goal now is for us. For our future together. A future I'm still worried about.

I can hardly sit still for the rest of the game. They finish it seven nil, but after Cole's hat trick, I know they're going to drag him off to do some media.

It's fine. I can wait. I've waited long enough to find him. My perfect man.

"You can go on home, Jordan. I know you're heading back to Chicago tonight. I'll get a lift from Cole." Aspen was at a series of away games, but he'll be back home tomorrow, and I know Jordan's planning on surprising him.

"Are you sure you don't want me to stay? Maybe we can go out for a late dinner? Coffee?" She blinks those big green eyes at me, all innocent concern. But I'm familiar with the mischievous sparkle in her eyes.

"Not unless you've been lonely with Aspen away." I smack her shoulder.

"Don't worry. I know you're going to jump his bones as soon as he gets out here. I don't need to see that. You going to tell him tonight?"

I nod. "Sure am." An entire flock of Starlys is flapping around my stomach.

"Okay. Well, let me know if you need anything. Sex tips, best positions when your man is tired after a tough game, favorite toys."

"Stop it."

"Fine. I know when I'm not wanted. I'm out of here." She wraps me up in a warm hug before she flounces off.

"Bye, Jordan."

She swings around. "Bye."

Only three quarters of the team have walked past me by the time he emerges. He's all smiles and damp hair looking smoking hot in his simple gray post game suit. As if these guys aren't hot enough in their gear, they have to dress them up in suits that strain to contain all those well-honed muscles.

I'm so busy admiring those delightful arms he wraps me up in them before I've even registered how close he was. My feet lift off the ground as he swings me up.

"Every fucking time I walk down that tunnel to see you standing here in my jersey, it hits me the same."

My legs twine around his waist and I can feel exactly where it hits him. His steely hot length is pressed right up against my softest place.

I grab his face, pulling him to me, greedy for a taste.

"Your place or mine," he mumbles against my lips.

"I'd say mine, because I have a feeling you're going to make me scream tonight, but you're the man of the hour. Which would you prefer?"

"Oh, I'm going to make you scream. I was going to say three times. One for every goal I scored tonight, but why stop there? Let's double it, Coffee Girl."

"Oh, feeling ambitious. Going for a record?"

"I want to break all the records with you."

I lean into his ear as he walks, not even bothering to put me down. "You know the most goals scored in a game by a single player is seven."

"Malone, I know. You want to go for that? Was that a challenge?" I've been taking some time to learn more about hockey, and in return he knows way more than he ever thought he would about coffee. There are few things as sexy as my tough hockey boyfriend talking different roasts with me.

"Maybe."

"I think I can handle it."

As we're about to push through the back door, some-one calls Cole's name. The high-pitched voice cuts through the mood, and I narrow my eyes, giving the blonde to our left a vicious side eye. How dare she inter-rupt us?

He sighs, letting me slide down his body, but keeping a tight hold on my waist. "What do you want, Charlene? Haven't you caused enough shit between us?"

Something about her looks different. She's still all bright and shiny, with smooth hair and carefully applied makeup. What is it? Fuzzy pink sweater... That's it. She's not wearing my man's jersey. That's a relief. I think I might have ripped it off her if I saw her in it again.

She nibbles on her shiny pink lower lip, eyes dropping to her toes. "I just wanted to apologize. To you Cole, and to you Jazz. I'm sorry."

My eyes widen to the size of hockey pucks, and my mouth falls open. That's a new tactic.

Cole sighs, rubbing his hands up and down my waist in a steady rhythm that's probably meant to soothe him just as much as me.

"I mean it. I came here looking for something I'd lost, and I thought it was you. I thought you would be the one to make me whole again. But I was wrong. I was all messed up, and I took it out on you both. But I'm figuring things out now and I wanted to let you know I am sorry. I know it doesn't make up for what I did, but it's all I've got." She's wringing her hands together and it seems sincere.

"What are you expecting from me?" Cole asks.

"Nothing. I don't expect an apology or your friendship, but we had a lot of good years together, and I owed you that. I'm going home to Florida after the school year is over, so this is goodbye. Congratulations on your win. It was amazing, and I'll be rooting for your team wherever you end up."

With that, she gives a tentative smile, turns around and walks away.

"That was unexpected," Cole says as we stare at each other.

"Completely. I'm not one to wish someone ill, so I hope she figures herself out."

His brow lowers, and it looks like a million thoughts are passing through his head. "Me too. I'll never be her friend again, but I've got you and that's all that matters when it comes down to it."

When you're as happy as I am, you can't begrudge someone else their own happy ending, even if they're not your favorite person in the world.

He scoops me back up, nuzzling into my neck. "But I'm not letting her ruin the mood for me. Where were we?"

A mild breeze picks up my hair, swirling it around his face as he passes out the back door to get to his car.

Apparently, he's eager to get back to business. His hand slips up between my legs, stroking a slow and steady rhythm that's enough to have me squirming in my seat on the ride home, but not enough to take me all the way.

"Cole, stop teasing."

"Hey, I've got to focus on the road. Precious cargo, you know. I can't make you scream yet. That would be too much of a distraction."

"Ass." My hips are pressing forward into his hand, trying to speed up his rhythm. Get him to take me to the place we both want to go.

"Naughty girl." He yanks his hand away. "I didn't say you could come yet."

"Fuck." I throw my head back in frustration. He's left me all tingly and wet. My nipples are already tight and aching when he pulls into the parking lot of my building.

"Okay, now where were we?" His hand slips down the front of my leggings and I hear the click of his seatbelt. He slides between my lips, teasing a finger at my entrance. "Is this what you were looking for?"

"Yes, yes, please." His teasing on the way home left me on the verge, so it doesn't take much to send me over the edge. His finger plunges in deep as his thumb circles my clit and I'm shaking in my seat. I let loose, making some noise for my man like I promised.

He leans in, capturing my lower lip between his teeth, pulling back with a wicked grin on his face. "That was one."

His finger is slick with my honey as he slides it between his lips. "You taste so fucking good, Coffee Girl."

My pussy clenches again at the sight of him tasting me.

"Now, let's get you upstairs so I can finish the job."

Job right. I had news. I was waiting until after the game so we could have a double celebration, but he distracted me with those skilled fingers and the dirty words.

He tucks me under his shoulder as we hustle inside.

"I had something to share with you."

He turns to me. "What's up?"

"I got that grant. The one for a Detroit based business."

He scoops me back into his arms, spinning me around until I'm dizzy. "You did. That's incredible? We're going to have to scout locations for you."

"What if you don't end up there?" I nibble on my bottom lip, not wanting to spoil the moment, but knowing this is something we need to talk about.

"It's looking good. The Wheelers have been sniffing around, but if doesn't happen, we will still make this work. No matter what. I'm not leaving you. You're mine now and I'm not letting you go. Ever. Your dreams are just as important as mine."

I nod, trusting every word that comes out of his mouth. This is it. We're end game. If I turn down this grant, I'll find another. He's my forever.

Chapter Thirty-Four

Epilogue

Cole

M y girl looks so hot, smoothing her apron down over her lush hips. Underneath it, she's wearing a simple black dress with yellow daisies. Perfect. Easy access for later. Or for now.

I step into her, slipping a hand up her smooth thigh. She slaps it away.

"Stop it. My staff is going to be here any minute."

"My girl has staff. That's so hot. You can be the boss of me any day."

"Not right now. Back off."

I sigh but can't resist wrapping an arm around her waist and pulling her against my body. I need to feel her soft curves.

"Are you hard again? Don't you ever get tired?"

"Not of you, that's for sure. It's really your fault. You're too damn sexy. I can't keep my hands to myself or my dick down when you're around. And that dress. It would be so easy. I could just press you up against that counter, slide inside. I bet you're wet for me. I'd be quick, I promise."

"How did you know every girl's dream?"

I trace a line up her arm. "Don't try to lie to me. I know you like it quick, dirty, and hard just as often as you like it slow and sweet."

"But not right now. On the opening day of my cafe, when my staff is about to arrive. Keep your hands to yourself." She giggles when I kiss her neck, so I know she's not actually angry with me. She couldn't possibly be.

"Fine. I guess I'll have to wait until the boss lady gets home."

She grabs my arm, twisting around to look at me, and there's panic in her eyes. "You're not leaving, are you?"

"Of course not. I told you I'd be here." I went to practice this morning, but I've got the rest of the day off. She worked her ass off to get her new cafe ready to open before the hockey season kicked off so I could be here with her. I wouldn't dream of letting her down.

There's a rap on the door, and I catch someone peering through the window. Autumn. I've met all of her employees while we worked away, setting everything up to her specifications. I even got some of my new teammates to pitch in. It's been a great bonding experience.

The petite woman has her mass of curly blonde hair piled on top of her head and she's wearing all black for opening day. Jazz wanted to really show off the jersey aprons on her first day open, so she asked the staff to wear all black.

I can't keep my hand from rubbing circles on her back as I follow her to the door to let Autumn in. Kyle sneaks in behind her.

"Welcome to our first day. I've got the espresso bar all warmed up. Coffee is brewing, and the iced tea and coffee are ready to go. Doors open in half an hour. Normally, this would be time to get all the opening tasks done, but I got here pretty early today, so I already got everything set up."

"No complaints here," Autumn says.

"Shots?" Jazz asks.

Her staff nod enthusiastically, but the bitter bite of straight espresso is still too much for me, so I shake my head.

"And a pumpkin spice latte for you?" she asks me.

"You read my mind."

She swishes off, and I'm content to stand back and watch her. She looks so at home behind the espresso bar and so happy to have a place all her own. Exactly what she always wanted.

I've been meshing with my team. It's been an adjustment. I miss all the guys from the Lightning, but we have a group call every week to stay in touch. Maybe I'll even swing by to catch the odd Lightning game. See how Hail is doing. But I'm sure I'll be busy enough with the Wheelers.

There's a lineup outside even before she flips the sign over from closed to open. She adds a little flourish to the simple action, twirling her hand around, and then bouncing up and down on her toes. As if I didn't already want to drag her to the back room for a taste of her sweetness, now I don't think I'll survive until close.

"That's all for you," she whispers to me.

It sure doesn't hurt having an NHL player on site for your opening day, but this place is perfection. She'd be successful no matter what. I'm just here for a little boost. Get some extra bodies in the door. Once they've tried her amazing drinks and the scones that I would literally kill for, they'll be as addicted to her as I am. Fine by me as long as they keep their hands on their drinks and away from what's mine.

The place was packed all day, and everyone is exhausted when she flips the sign back to closed. It was more exhausting than a day at training camp.

"That was incredible," she says, eyes shining.

"You were incredible." I dip my head down, meeting her lips in a lingering kiss that leaves me tingling all over.

She breaks it, a guilty look on her face, hustling to the back room.

A moment later, Kyle and Autumn are heading out the front door. They were amazing too. The customers loved them. They might not look like typical hockey fans, but they were pretty excited to meet me. And I walked in on more than one conversation throughout the day about the Wheeler's prospects this season.

Coffee and hockey. Who knew it would make such a great combination? But then again, Jazz and I are perfect for each other, so why wouldn't our jobs mesh just as well?

I've got my hands on her hips, and I'm kissing a trail up the back of her neck as we're walking down the gray carpeted hall to our condo unit. I found one nice and close to her cafe. It's not that far from the arena, but proximity to her place was the most important factor.

"Cole, stop it!"

Her words are more serious than teasing, and I pull back. "But I've been waiting for this all day." I'm not above begging. I usually make her do the begging, but I'm pretty desperate to feel her underneath me right now.

"Well, you're going to have to wait a little while longer."

"Why?"

She swings the door open.

"Dad?" I see him first. He looks better than I've ever seen him. I wanted him to move to Detroit, but he wasn't having it. Said his home is in Florida and always will be, so I used my signing bonus as a down payment to buy him his own house there. Now he's only working one job and his skin is brighter, no dark circles under his eyes from working long nights and days. I'm so happy I'm able to do that for him. He sacrificed so much for me and my sisters over the years. He deserves it.

"Hey, son." He pulls me into a rough hug, then I spot my sisters over his shoulder.

"Lissa? Bella?" I untangle myself from my dad, turning to Jazz. "You did this? For me?"

She smiles and nods, and I have to blink a few times to clear away the tears that are burning the back of my eyes. With everything she had going on. All the last-minute details to get her cafe open. The stress she's been under with the city inspection and the hiring and the delay with the espresso machine. In between all of that, she arranged for my dad and sisters to come out for a visit.

"I wanted to get them out yesterday so they could be there for opening day, but the flight times didn't work, but they're here now. They can't stay for your season opener because of the girls' school schedules, but this seemed like the next best option."

I hug each of my sisters in turn and then scoop Jazz back up, spinning her around. "This is the best option. I wouldn't have had any time with them if they'd come during the beginning of the season. This way I can take them for a little sightseeing. We can go out for dinner. And they can visit the number one cafe in the city."

"Yes, Jazz. We can't wait to come to Pucks and Grinds. Cole's been sending us pictures. It looks amazing."

"It is amazing, Liss. Like I said. Best cafe in Detroit." I turn to Jazz. "You couldn't get any of your family out?"

"Oh, don't worry. Gen, Gisele, and Caro are all going to come for your home opener. They're very interested in the hot hockey guys."

"But they're all married or engaged."

"Oh, they're not going to let a little thing like that stop them from checking out all the hockey butts. Their words, not mine."

I lean in to whisper in her ear. "Only one hockey butt for you." Her skin ripples under my hands and she leans back into me.

"Yup. Now stop it. Your family is here."

"Gross. Break it up," Liss says, so I reluctantly pull away.

"Now. I didn't have time to make anything for dinner, what with the opening and all, but we're going to order in. We can get anything you want. It's on Cole." She winks at me.

"Of course. Sky's the limit. You can get McDonald's or Burger King. Whatever. Singles only. No doubles or anything. I'm not some NHLer or something. Oh wait. Yes, I am. Steak and Lobster for all."

"Ew, I don't eat meat," Bella says, nose scrunching up in disgust.

"Since when are you vegetarian?" I ask her.

"Since last week," she replies.

Of course, my fickle sister has a new dietary restriction. We'll see how long this one lasts. "Well then, salad and tofu for you. As much as you want."

There's so much to catch up on that we don't stop talking until the buzzer sounds, letting us know dinner has arrived.

Jazz puts the food on plates and sets the table with cloth napkins while my dad asks her about her first day. My sisters want the dirt on the team, and I just want to sit back and drink it all in.

My beautiful girl and my family all together, eating around my table. This is it. This is what we've been working so hard for, and now that we've got it, I feel so full of love that it's spilling out of me. You couldn't wipe the smile off my face if you tried.

Having my family here is going to be awesome, but I'm glad Jazz got them set up at the Grandview down the street. They're excited to stay at the five-star hotel, and I'm excited to have her to myself again, finally. I kiss the top of her head as she shuts the door, spinning around to look at me.

"Happy?" she asks, wrapping her arms around my waist. I lean into her hug like a needy cat.

"I've never been happier in my entire life. But you know what? I have a prediction."

"What's that?"

I pull back enough to cup her cheeks in my hands, staring into her chocolate eyes. "I predict that every day from now on is going to be my happiest day yet. Because every day I get to spend with you, every time I get to come home to see your beautiful face, every game I see you out in the stands. That's my happiest day."

And I lean in for the kiss I've been longing for all day. All my life, really.

THE PENALTY

NIKKI JEWELL

C raving more steamy hockey romance?

Dev's story is up next in **The Penalty**. If you're curious about his story and you love a grumpy sunshine, brother's best friend romance, preorder The Penalty.

Two Friends. Two Days. One Bed. What could possibly go wrong? - If you haven't read Aspen and Jordan's story yet you can get it for free when you sign up for my newsletter, along with bonus content (maybe some more Cole and Jazz scenes to come), contests, and all my latest writing shenanigans. Author Nikki Jewell

Thank you for reading my book. I hope you enjoyed getting to know Cole. Jazz, and all their friends. I've got lots of plans ahead for these characters and I really look forward to sharing the rest of their stories with you.

If you enjoyed this book, share the love. Reviews are the best way to get a book in the hands of other like-minded readers.

If you'd like to keep up with all the latest steamy shenanigans you can follow me on Instagram, Threads, and TikTok @nikkijewell_books or check out my Facebook Page.

THANK YOU READERS

Thank you so much for choosing to read The Game. Cole's story has been lingering in my brain since I started planning the Lakeview series back in April of 2022, and it was so much fun to finally see him get his happy ever after. With his girl and his team.

Need to chat about the guys of the Lakeview Lightning, share your favorite moments, and keep up with the latest Nikki Jewell news? Join my Facebook reader group Nikki Jewell's Romance Reader's Rink.

Devlin's story is coming up next, and this is another one I'm very excited to write. You can preorder The Penalty on Amazon now if you love a grumpy sunshine, brother's best friend story.

You can also follow me on Threads, Instagram, Facebook, or TikTok to see what craziness is going on in my author life. Visit my website authornikkijewell.com to get these links or sign up for my newsletter. My newsletter subscribers get all the latest news first in addition to bonus scenes, freebies, and giveaways. As a thank you for signing up you'll get to read The Breakout for free. This is Aspen & Jordan's friends to lovers, trapped in a snowstorm, only one bed novella. Newsletter sign up.

Finally, if you loved this book please leave a review on Amazon, Goodreads, or wherever you buy your books. Reviews mean so much to us indie authors.

ALSO BY NIKKI JEWELL

The Lakeview Lightning Series

The Breakout: Book 0.5

Three days. Two best friends. One Bed. What could possibly go wrong? When Aspen drives his best friend Jordan to a romance book convention, he's not expecting the storm of the century to trap them in a bed and breakfast on the way home. But what happens when the chill of the snow can t cool the fiery heat between them? Available free when you sign up for my newsletter.

The Comeback: Book 1

In the game of love and hockey, second chances are rare, but Abby and Sebastian are about to get theirs. From childhood friends to heartbreak, their story is a testament to the power of forgiveness, and the courage to face one's fears. Available in ebook and discreet paperback.

The Red Line: Book 2

The Red Line takes you on a wild ride where hearts and skates collide. Natasha and Jackson's tale is a fiery mix of passion, and ice, challenging the rules of the game and love. Will they be able to keep things hot when their no-strings fling grows into something more? Available in ebook and discreet paperback.

The Game: Book 3

These two college seniors have some serious ex problems. And fake dating is the perfect solution. But when the steam between them gets too hot, they both might end up getting burned. Available in ebook and discreet paperback.

The Penalty: Book 4

Dev's grumpy sunshine, brother's best friend story is coming 2024.

The Opposition: Book 5

Beau's story, coming 2025.

ACKNOWLEDGMENTS

Cole's story has been living rent free in my head since I started planning this series. Time to pay up. Some parts of this one were a little harder to write, and some were very cathartic. I'm looking at you and your evil customer, Jazz. So, as always, thank you to my characters for playing nice most of the time.

I can't hit publish on any book without thanking my husband. He's always there for me when I'm stressed out of my mind that everyone is going to hate my book. Or when I'm on a deadline and I need to stay up all night working. He supports me every step of the way and I couldn't do it without him. To my wonderful, creative, bookworm twins. You inspire me to live my best life and I encourage you to do the same.

To Steph, my best friend and number one fan. I promise I'll write a PWHL book for you one day. It's just there are so many ideas I have to get to.

Thanks to my editor Susan. I've enjoyed working with you on the last two books, and I can't wait to share Dev's story with you. I love that you share my nerdy soul, sarcastic attitude, and of course passion for my book boyfriends. Your insights constantly keep me on my toes and lift my stories up.

My cover designers knocked it out of the park once again. Taylor at Sweet 15 Designs LLC brought it with the hot manchests, and Hope Brown of Nerd Sisters Designs gave me some beautiful discreet covers.

And to Meg, my PA at Literary Inspired. I love being an author, but there are so many tasks that take away from the writing that I love. Meg kicked off my ARC team and brought it to the next level, started up a reader and ARC group for me, and took over some of my social media posting. You've been professional, supportive, and helpful in taking my next step toward living my dream as a full-time author. Thank you.

To my ARC team. You have been amazing. The support I received from this awesome group on the release of The Red Line was so inspiring. I'm afraid I'll miss someone if I list names, but trust me, I see you and I appreciate you so much. The feedback for The Game is already making me squee.

And of course I can't forget about Alby, my conference bestie. This year is our year. We're going to achieve amazing things, and I can't wait to share the journey with you. See you in Vegas '24.

About the Author

Nikki Jewell is the queen of steamy romance and sipping coffee like it's her lifeblood, and she's always up for a new book boyfriend. Whether it's one she wrote or someone else's creation. She has a coffee addiction so legendary that she's even convinced her coffee beans to write her a thank-you note.

When she's not mainlining caffeine, Nikki is busy crafting tales of passion, love, and swoon-worthy heroes. She's especially fond of athletes, celebrities, and rock stars, so you'll find lots of those in her books. Her steamy romance books have been known to raise temperatures, set hearts aflutter, and make readers swoon in public.

When she's not writing, she escapes the confines of her writing cave to wander the great outdoors, communing with trees, birds, and squirrels that judge her for drinking coffee in the wilderness.

Nikki's secret identity as a romance writer is so well-guarded that her twin children don't know about her double life. But let's face it, what kid wants to read about their mom's romantic escapades? Probably none. Her husband is in on the secret and he's the real-life hero who keeps the inspiration flowing, even when her characters refuse to cooperate.

So, if you're in need of a fictional escape filled with passion, laughter, and maybe a few coffee stains, Nikki Jewell is your go-to romance guru. Just be sure to have a fresh brew on hand and monitor your heart rate—her stories have a tendency to make it race!

The Game is the third book in the five book Lakeview Lightning College Hockey Romance series. You can follow Nikki on Instagram, Threads, and TikTok @nikkijewell_books to keep up with her latest shenanigans. She's got a new Facebook page that she doesn't know what to do with as well.

instagram.com/nikkijewell_books

tiktok.com/@nikkijewell_books

Made in the USA
Coppell, TX
11 April 2025

48173108R00215